The Samurai Cowboys: Book Three

WAY OF THE RONIN

NATE WAGNER

Publishing Services provided by Paper Raven Books LLC
Printed in the United States of America
First Printing, 2024

Paperback = 979-8-9872592-6-9

For all of the fans of this story – thank you.

Crossroads

Cade Wilson has been hiding out at Moira's cabin during the cold months of winter, and he has been training Joanna Carter in the Way of the Samurai.

In this quiet corner of the country, Cade has been unaware of any stories about him since the train explosion in Colorado. Rumors of his death provided the time he needed to heal and regain his strength, but he remains haunted by the curse of stolen gold and a deadly bounty hunter from his past who believes he's still alive.

To be free of his Benefactor, Cade knows he will need to defeat Toshi, the samurai warrior who trained him, and the private bodyguard of Joseph Whitmore II. As the surviving member of the three samurai cowboys, he also knows that Whitmore wants him dead and any approach to the fort will be defended by a private army of shadow riders.

As a samurai without a master, Cade is now a ronin with a desire to be free. He must choose his own path when his loyalty to a principle has come in conflict with loyalty to a person—as he no longer wants to be honor bound to fight or spill innocent blood for another man's ambitions.

The final battle will decide his fate, as the fight for those he loves, and for his very soul hangs in the balance.

"Once you know what you want, you must be prepared to sacrifice everything to get it."

Oishi Yoshio

Forty-Seven Ronin

CHAPTER 1

Footsteps

In a small clearing surrounded by trees, Cade knelt quietly on the soft ground to listen to the world around him. As he closed his eyes, the cry of a hawk carried across the foothills on a cold wind that cut to the bone.

It was early March, but frozen patches of February snow still lingered in the shadows that surrounded this patch of dry earth. That's why he chose this spot for this morning's exercise, as the crunch of the icy crust behind him was soon followed by the quickened pace of footsteps.

Cade remained low to the ground as he turned to block Joanna's attack with his wooden training sword. The running charge carried her a few steps past him, but he anticipated that she would be quick to recover and come again. As she charged to attack, he jumped up and lunged toward her from his crouched position and aggressively closed the gap between them. She was so focused on her attack that she wasn't able to defend his, and in two moves he forced her wooden sword down and then snapped his to a stop at her neck.

Joanna lowered her wooden sword and bowed her head as Cade withdrew. The frustrated look on her face said much, but he didn't just want to teach her how to fight—she needed to learn how to be ready for anything. It also happened that these training sessions were an opportunity for him to test a new attack and fighting style.

"That was very sneaky of you trying to attack me from behind," Cade said with a thin smile and bowed to his student. "Next time, be mindful of your surroundings and the sounds that can give away your position. You also shouldn't assume that a crouched opponent can't still be deadly. Those are your lessons for today."

Joanna shrugged. "You're too good for me. Even after months of training, the only chance I have to beat you is to catch you by surprise."

"Not true. As a samurai, you must consistently hone your skills to master your fears and doubts. And regardless of the skill set of your opponent, there is always a way to win. You must believe that, here," he said, and pointed at her heart.

"Yes, Viper," she replied, and Cade nodded his approval. He struggled with the idea of being called master or sensei, because he didn't believe he was qualified to be either. But referring to his samurai name created some separation between his friendship with Joanna and the big brother role that he had adopted over the past couple of months. This distinction also helped him be the taskmaster while doing his best to share some of the knowledge he had gleaned from Toshi—and as many fundamental fighting skills she was able to learn.

"As your teacher, I'm trying to pass on my experience and show you how to harness your fighting skills. But you must also be yourself. Only you can fight like you. Trust your instincts and try not to get discouraged," he said earnestly as he tried to provide some perspective. "You've already learned so much and you're better with a sword than I was at your age."

The compliment was enough to elicit a smile, and he hoped it would be the boost of encouragement she needed to continue with the exercise. "You must learn how to approach your opponent without being predictable in your attack. Now come at me again, but this time, do not overextend your thrust to the extent that you leave yourself off balance and vulnerable."

Joanna raised the wooden sword and resumed a fighting stance. He waited patiently as it took her a moment to recover from the defeat and think through her attack, but then Cade saw the fire in her eyes return and she came at him with full force.

As Cade defended the high strike to his face, he noticed that her power had increased significantly since he introduced strength exercises. Joanna was learning how to use her core strength and extend her arms with each thrust. She also had natural instincts and a good sense of balance as a fighter; traits that would've been harder to teach in such a short time.

But she commonly underestimated the speed of her opponent, and those lessons had to be learned the hard way. When Joanna tried to spin low and slash at his leg, Cade easily blocked her attack and countered with a spin of his own and a slash across her back.

"Argh!" she groaned, and again Cade could hear pain and frustration in her voice. Teaching Joanna had to be different than sparing with Scorpion or Falcon. She was very intelligent and motivated through encouragement and the philosophy of fighting techniques—and less through the aches, blood, and bruises. But if she really wanted to learn how to fight like a samurai, she had to accept pain as part of the process.

"I know what I did wrong. Please don't remind me," she said defiantly and stepped back into her attack stance. "You are faster than me, and better than me. I have to accept that," she continued. "But I will never give up."

Joanna pressed her attack and Cade again defended her strike. The thrust was a predictable move he had taught her, but it was the tenacity of her attack that made her second attempt at a low spin successful—because she blocked his counter strike over her shoulder and followed with a slash to Cade's abdomen.

The slash would leave a new bruise on his left side this evening, and he deserved it. She struck him fair, and she did so by changing her attack and focusing her energy on cutting down her enemy. He was both proud of her accomplishment and feeling the sting of his pride.

Cade wondered if this was how Toshi responded to his attacks, as if his teacher knew exactly what he was going to do when they fought—and still challenged him to do better. If so, then Joanna taught him a lesson today, too. And she reminded him that he needs to continue to evolve his fighting style to be less predictable and more aggressive when he faces Toshi again.

"I finally got you!" she said, and then composed herself and stopped to bow.

"Yes, you did," he replied with a bow, and held his left hand over the new bruise. "How were you able to channel that level of ferocity?"

"I wasn't angry at you," Joanna replied. "But I was angry about losing and getting hit. I focused that energy on seeing past you and not repeating the same mistake."

"Interesting. What do you mean by 'seeing past you'?" he asked.

Joanna hesitated, and he sensed she was trying not to hurt his feelings. "To fight you, it's better if I don't think of you at all. The fight has nothing to do with you as a person… it's about beating you, and not getting hurt in the process."

Cade was intrigued by the wisdom of her youth when the sound of a familiar bell chimed in the distance. It was the old woman who held traditions and familiar rituals close to her heart, and she signaled that it was time for afternoon tea.

• • •

Tea Time

Cade's cheeks became flush the moment he stepped inside. It was easy to appreciate how Moira's cabin was so warm and welcoming compared to the bitter windy conditions outside, and the glow of the crackling fire blended with the rays of afternoon sunlight coming in through the west kitchen window.

The only table in the room was already set with three teacups, and Cade and Joanna took their respective seats while the old woman fetched the kettle from the coals in the fireplace. And even though they had been guests in her home for almost six months, Moira always seemed to act as if it was the first day they arrived.

"Hello you two. It's always a pleasure to have company for tea," the old woman said as she brought the kettle to the table and began to pour.

"Thank you," Joanna said with a chuckle, as if trying to humor Moira's quirky musings. Then she took her cup and held it with both hands. "This is my favorite time of day, and not just because it's so cold outside," she continued before she took a sip and stretched back in her chair. "But you know it's just us. Why do you always say it's a pleasure to have company?"

"Because each day is special in its own way, and we should appreciate the moments we share," the old woman replied. "So tell me, how was your training today?"

Cade looked at Joanna with curiosity. He was always interested in hearing her perspective on the lessons of the day and what she may have learned. Once a student of the Way himself, he often compared her new experiences to his past—even if his method of teaching was much different from Toshi's over the years.

"It wasn't too bad today. Whatever new pains and bruises I've added to my collection of 'lessons learned' won't hurt as bad knowing that I finally scored a strike against my teacher," Joanna said with an enthusiastic grin.

"Indeed," Cade said and acknowledged his student with a tip of his hat. "You did well today. And now I will need to suffer the painful reminder of not wearing my chest armor."

"So, she finally got to you? That's great news!" Moira said with a big smile and reached over to give Joanna a pat on the arm. "It also means that you're making progress and getting better. You wouldn't have been able to say that a month ago."

"Yes, but I'm still not good enough to take Cade in a real fight," Joanna replied. "I don't know if I will ever be that good. But I certainly feel stronger… and I'm a better fighter than I was when we arrived in October."

Moira nodded and took a sip of tea before Cade felt her gaze turn toward him. "What about you? What did you learn today?"

He wondered why she asked, as it was rare that she took an interest in what he was learning. But they had spent so much time together over the winter that he felt he could be completely honest, and that she might even understand.

"I've been practicing a new fighting technique. I call it the viper strike," he said with a side glance at Joanna. "Vipers coil and then spring to strike. From a crouched position, I can both defend and counterattack in a way that takes advantage of my speed and reach with the element of surprise.

"Today, I timed the viper strike perfectly when I sensed Joanna was so focused on her attack that she wasn't prepared to defend mine," he explained. "It's also a move I've never used before, so it might also be something my next opponent has never seen."

Both Moira and Joanna gave him a look of approval, and Cade assumed they all knew the next opponent he was referring to. But the only reason he didn't talk about this new fighting technique was because there would only be one true measure of success, and that would be if it worked against his former master.

"That's good," Moira said. "You should remain as open-minded as possible and continue pushing yourself to try new things. Heaven knows I'm still learning new things," she added with her signature cackled laugh, and then raised her teacup to take another sip.

Cade adored the old woman, and he appreciated her warmth and generosity. But he couldn't help but think she was oversimplifying the obstacles in front of him. "If only everything in life was that easy," he said skeptically. "The more time I spend away from the fort and try new things, the more I wonder how things might have turned out if I'd made some different choices along the way."

"Oh child, everything happens for a reason," Moira said with a soothing, motherly tone. "The path to who you are today was never going to change, but you can change who you want to be tomorrow."

Cade laughed at himself and admired Moira's wisdom. Sometimes there were noticeable similarities between her and Toshi, and especially in the way they could pull his thoughts out of the air like threads and weave them into knowledge that could only come with experience over time.

"The same goes for you, too," she said to Joanna. "Whoever you were before we met matters less than who you'll be when it's time to go."

The last part of what she said seemed to linger for a moment as the three of them sipped their tea. Cade knew the days were growing longer, and it would soon be time for them to leave. They couldn't hide here forever, and both of them still had challenges ahead. But just as she had given a gentle reminder of this eventual day, the old woman was always good at changing the subject and ending on a positive note.

"But today is not that day. Now how about you two wrap up the afternoon chores before supper," Moira said with a smile.

...

Balance

Splitting firewood was a tedious chore, but one that gave Joanna an opportunity to swing an axe at something that wouldn't hit back. There was also something satisfying about the sound of the cleave as it split the rounds into smaller pieces—and with each stroke she tried to focus on her balance and strength to split the wood in one clean strike.

She took the samurai training quite seriously, and the bruises on her legs, arms, and hands were painful reminders that learning how to fight came with consequences. But she embraced every exercise whole heartedly, and the respect she had for her teacher and the principles of hand-to-hand and weapon combat were something she could feel beyond the physical. It was spiritual, too. As if something inside her was awakening.

After she stacked the pile of split wood by the back door, she went to see if Cade needed help in the barn. She had been training with him in the barn almost every day for the cold months of winter, and as proven this morning, she was getting better and becoming more confident in her abilities. And since they saw each other every day, the bond she formed with him often felt like the relationship she wished she had with her father.

Life on the railroad was demanding, and when her father wasn't working, they would sometimes go hunting or study maps. But most often they found themselves busy doing things that always seemed to be work related or to take care of the Carmichaels. The more she thought about this, she regretted that she never got a chance to know her father as a person before he was killed over a game of cards. What were his hopes and dreams? What were his struggles? Would he be proud of her if he could see her now?

"I heard what you and Moira were talking about. What is something you would have done differently in life?" she asked Cade as they finished cleaning the smell from the stalls to make for a more pleasant evening.

"That's a pretty big question, don't you think?" Cade replied, and she had anticipated that type of response from him. Her thoughts sometimes blurted out of her mouth before she considered the sensitivity of the situation or the question, and he was quick to put up a defense if the subject was too personal.

"You said there were some things you wished you'd done differently. I'm just curious what those things are?" she continued, but not necessarily expecting an answer.

Cade said nothing but instead grabbed the two wooden staffs they crafted for spear fighting—and then took his familiar spot in the training circle they'd drawn in the dirt in the center of the barn. When he took this position in the circle, it meant he expected her to take the place opposite of him and be prepared to listen.

"There are some things I can't share with you, or I choose not to tell you," he said and tossed her a fighting staff. Joanna caught the smooth wooden rod and immediately spun it around her head and waist before she stopped and flexed in a fighting stance. She had been practicing that move for weeks, and she smiled confidently while she set her feet and twitched her shoulders in anticipation. After her sparing strike this morning, she was hopeful and ready to score another this afternoon.

But Cade remained steadfast as he held his staff to the ground—and she relaxed a bit, thinking he had something to say and the sparing session would have to wait.

"I don't think you'd be able to understand, because it's not just one thing I'd do differently. My experiences and my pains are a collection of things, and some of those stories you've already heard. But the decisions I've made are my own, and I can't change that now.

"The lessons I've learned from my mistakes also give me

strength and knowledge I can pass down to you. So maybe there's an opportunity here for you to learn from my experience," he began to explain.

"I was taught that a samurai had to live a life of balance. Your mind and your body had to be as one. Loyalty to my master and my commitment to the code were equally honor bound. Taking a life, and accepting death, was also a balance.

"Life is full of choices, and balance is weighed in choices," he said firmly, as if to make his point. "Do you understand?"

Joanna nodded respectfully.

"Toshi said the Way of the Samurai is found in death, and the most dangerous opponent you will ever face is one that has already accepted death. When you choose to fight, you must be prepared to either kill or die to protect those you love. Both choices honor the code, but defending what you care about most might also require the ultimate sacrifice," he continued. "But life or death is a choice nonetheless, and you must be determined when you advance."

"I understand," she replied. Then she watched Cade's expression change as he looked at the rafters and slowly shook his head.

"Months ago, I made a choice to turn against my Benefactor and protect the innocent, and now it stays with me. Everything about that night and everything that has followed since has been a result of that choice," he said very solemnly. "While I have come to peace with it, I can't understand why my life feels out of balance. It seems like I'm lost somewhere between the life I want and what I've done, and it's hard not to wish things could have been different. But I can't change the past and what's done is done. And I'd rather not imagine the person I would be today if I had stood by and watch innocent people killed. Or even worse… if I'd been the one to use my sword or pull the trigger."

As what he said lingered like the dust filled rays of the late afternoon sun, Joanna sensed there was more to this story than he was willing to tell. But she got an answer to her question, and she opted to console him instead of pressing for more.

"Whatever you did that night, I'm sure it was the right thing," she said, trying to bring him back from wherever his mind had wandered. "You're a good man, Cade Wilson. And I know that in my heart."

"Thank you for saying that," he replied. "I want to believe you, but so much has happened in the wake of that night. And now we're here—"

"Yes. Here we are," she quipped. "And as dangerous and hard as everything has been since I met you, I would rather focus on tomorrow than worry about yesterday."

As his attention seemed to return to the moment, she gave a nod and tapped her staff on the ground to make sure he'd heard her words. She didn't feel the need to reconstruct the conversation to let him know she also understood regret and how one event could change a person's life. And while she was not on the run for the same reasons, she was grateful to know Cade, and was happy to embrace the new life ahead of her.

"Can we train now?" she asked with a smile.

CHAPTER 2

The Bohannon Brothers

The following morning brought cloud filled skies, and Cade loved the sweet smell of the early spring rain.

After some early chores and a light breakfast, Cade and Joanna resumed her training in the barn. The wooden swords he was able to craft weren't as sturdy as the ones he remembered back at the fort, but he was able to use two handles of a plow that looked out of use for years. And for what they had to work with in the humble dojo they had shared with the animals all winter, it was good enough.

Today's lesson was how to attack with a balanced lunge and combination strike, and he was pleased at how well Joanna was picking up the concept and the ability to make multiple moves. "You're getting much faster," he complimented while blocking her last attack. "I would be foolish to take it easy on you."

"You call this taking it easy on me?" she asked with a flustered look and stopped to wipe the sweat from her forehead.

"Well, maybe from your perspective. My training experience was a bit different," he said with a chuckle, and stepped back to get a drink of water. The fire in the iron stove was burning nice and warm, and it was enough to encourage his thirst. But as he rested his training sword against the wall and raised the canteen to his lips, he heard something out of the ordinary.

"Why is the dog barking?" Joanna asked, and Cade was equally curious. They had been staying with Moira for months, and he rarely heard that dog bark at anything, including him. But now the dog sounded genuinely excited about something, or someone.

As Cade stepped toward the barn doors, one of them was being pushed open from the outside. The blast of cool air was accompanied by a strange man who entered with his right hand on his pistol and left index finger over his lips. A moment later, a larger fella followed in behind the first while the dog excitedly danced around his legs.

"Who are you?" the first one asked quietly while he gave Cade a look, and then Joanna, and then around the barn, as if to see if anyone else was with them. He wasn't very tall, but he looked lean and strong for a man of his stature, and the way he asked the question sounded like someone who belonged here more than the two of them.

"Who's asking?" Cade replied with a question of his own. He was just as curious about them and why they just walked into the barn uninvited. It was also the first time they'd seen anyone else around Moira's place in months, so their presence was intriguing and concerning at the same time.

"You hear that, Finn?" the larger, second man said to his companion as he tipped back his derby hat and walked over to stand in front of Joanna. "He wants to know who we are," he continued with a chuckle.

"Of course he does, Mick. Because I think he's equally surprised to see us, yes?" the smaller man replied while keeping his right hand on his holstered pistol. "Sound about right?" he asked rhetorically, and his brown eyes peered out from under his tweed flap cap.

Cade could feel Joanna looking at him, and he just shook his head. He didn't want her to move or say anything to start a fight, because he still didn't know what to make of these men. But he thought it was safe to assume they weren't bounty hunters, or they'd have pulled their guns already.

"We're guests of the old woman that lives here," Cade said to acknowledge the smaller man's question. "In exchange for room and board, we do some work around the place. I can't speak for her, and I don't know what you're looking for, but we don't have much to offer you," he continued.

"The old woman," the large fella said with a laugh. From the tone of his voice and the expression on his face, he sounded as if he knew her well. "I'm guessing she didn't see us coming because we decided to surprise her and come for a visit. We also figured she'd need some grain and flour after the winter."

Moira's keen perception was something only a friend might understand, and Cade felt a little less concerned these men were a threat. "Do you know—?"

"Indeed, we do. I'm Finn, and this is my brother, Mick," the smaller one said while handling the introductions. "Moira is our aunt. Our mother's sister."

"We've heard all about you," Joanna said, and her sudden outburst caught Cade a little off guard. She also appeared to surprise herself as the color of her cheeks began to blush. "Sorry. I meant to say that Moira has told us about you."

Cade sensed this was the moment to interject and exchange introductions. "This is Joanna, and my name is Cade. And yes, Moira told us about you and how you helped build this place," he said, with a glance at the surroundings of the barn. "We've appreciated her generosity and letting us stay the winter. It's nice to finally meet you."

"So, you're Cade Wilson, the man with swords. But we heard you were dead," Finn said and tilted his head back to get a better look. "Then you must be Joanna Carter. We've heard about you, too."

Mick opened the buttons of his coat and hooked his thumbs under the suspenders that held up his pants. "Pleasure to meet you," he said as he turned his attention to the training circle drawn in the dirt and the wooden sword in Joanna's hand. "So, what are you doing out here?"

Joanna again looked at Cade, but this time he gave a nod. Since they had all exchanged pleasantries, he didn't see the harm in her answering the question. "We were training… well, practicing, really. It's something we've been doing out here in the barn," she replied.

"What type of training?" Finn asked, sounding a little puzzled.

"Samurai training," Joanna replied, and Cade appreciated hearing the confidence in her voice. "He's been teaching me how to fight like a samurai warrior."

Mick let out a billowing laugh that echoed throughout the barn. Cade estimated that he stood about the same height, but the man was at least twenty pounds heavier. He was a barrel-chested fella with strong arms and broad shoulders. The auburn colored hair under his derby hat matched the sideburns that framed his face, and the bushy mustache under his nose. "Teaching a girl how to fight, you say? Why on earth would you do that… and what's a samurai?"

Cade could see by her expression that Joanna didn't take well to that comment. She didn't like being underestimated, and whatever excitement she might have been feeling about at the arrival of Moira's nephews had quickly soured to disappointment.

"I can fight. You'd be surprised," she replied, and Cade just quietly stood back and listened. "And I'm tired of men thinking that they're better than me. Because I'm not scared of them, and I'm not afraid of you."

"Oh, lass," Mick said with another laugh. "That's quite a mouthful. But you might want to know your business before you start picking fights."

"My brother is a bare-knuckle boxer, missy," Finn interjected. "He's beaten over a dozen men from Pittsburgh to Cheyenne. And I don't think you'd appreciate what you'd be getting into if you try and go a round with him."

Joanna tossed her training sword to the ground, and Cade knew what she wanted to ask before she even said it.

They exchanged a quick glance, and he gave her a nod as she smiled back and turned to face her next opponent.

Cade figured that he and Joanna probably didn't look like much of a threat. Moira was very handy with a needle and thread, and she made both of them some work coats from the two gray dusters of the shadow riders he'd left here months ago. But what Mick didn't know was that Joanna had been learning a combat style that blended bushido with karate—and she looked anxious for someone new to practice on.

Mick appeared somewhat insulted that Joanna didn't heed the warning, and he was no longer laughing when Joanna took a fighting stance. But he also didn't look ready to back down either. "Now, now, lass… I'm not about to fight a girl," he said as he stepped forward and reached out to pat her shoulder.

Faster than he could react, Joanna reached over with her left hand to grab his arm. After bending his wrist and twisting his forearm, she spun around and used his momentum to pull him off balance and flip him onto his back.

Finn laughed as his brother landed on the ground with a thud. The surprised look in Mick's eyes was as dramatic as his brother's reaction to what just happened. But then Mick was suddenly more focused on what he could see while lying on his back.

"Whose things are in my loft?" he asked as he got up and dusted himself off.

"That's where I sleep," Joanna replied with a smile.

Mick peeled off his coat and tossed it aside. He looked even bigger now that he'd been embarrassed and was no longer amused. "No lass, that's my spot," he said as he cracked his knuckles and raised his fists toward Joanna. "Just remember… you asked for it," he said as he lurched forward and poked out a left jab.

Joanna was quick to avoid the punch and ducked to the right of the jab—and then countered with a karate punch to his ribs. And when he swung his backhand to return the favor, she ducked again and then jumped in the air and kicked him in the chest with her right foot.

Mick staggered back with the wind knocked out of him, and he fell into his brother, who was still laughing. They would have both fallen down if they weren't able to back into a post and collect themselves. Now the fighter's eyes looked full of frustration and rage, and after he shook off the kick and took a deep breath, he charged at Joanna.

She waited to take the full brunt of his advance before she jumped. As she put her feet in his midsection, she used her hands to grip his suspenders and leaned all the way back to use the boxer's momentum against him.

Cade watched Joanna do as he'd taught her, and she skillfully went to the ground on her back and flipped Mick over her. As he landed on the ground with another dusty thud, he yelled out in anger so loudly that it seemed to shake the barn.

"Dammit, Mick," Finn snapped at his brother. "Are you going to let her keep beating you, or do we have to shoot her?"

As he watched the fighter pick himself off the ground a third time, Cade sensed that this little game was about to come to an end. He was proud of how Joanna handled herself against a much stronger opponent. But when Mick squared off in a fighting stance, Cade noticed he changed his tactic and held back instead of attacking. If he really was a bare-knuckle boxer, his pride was on the line and he wasn't going to fall for the same stunt again.

"Be careful," Cade said quietly and tried to warn Joanna. But he watched her confidence give way to carelessness as she became the aggressor and tried to step into a roundhouse kick. But being physically larger, the fighter blocked and absorbed the kick with his left arm and shoulder—and now that he was in range, he snapped a right punch to her gut.

The blow was powerful enough to knock Joanna to the ground and leave her doubled over in the dirt. And while she struggled to catch her breath, Cade shifted slightly closer to her, but did not come to her aid. This was her fight, and he wasn't looking to get involved, but he would be ready if things got out of hand.

"Michael Bohannon!" Moira's voice called out from the open barn door. "That is not how we treat a lady, or our guests."

Cade hadn't noticed the old woman come to the door, and neither had anyone else. But there she was, and she started giving her nephews an earful.

"And you, young Finnegan… are you just going to stand there, or are you going to help that young lady up?" Moira asked in a scolding tone that could only come from someone that raised a man from childhood.

"Sorry, *aintin*," Finn replied and walked over to help lift Joanna to her feet.

"I'm sorry, too," Mick replied to his aunt. "But she started it, and I warned her."

"It's true," Joanna said with a cough. "I was looking for a

test of my skills on someone besides you," she continued and turned to Cade. "I'm sorry, Viper."

Cade just smiled back at her. "Well, I hope you learned the lesson for today. Underestimating your opponent can be your undoing," he said to her, and acknowledged the two brothers to amend the situation.

"Now enough with these shenanigans," Moira said in a way that snapped everyone's attention back on her. "Let's come inside and get better acquainted."

• • •

New Acquaintances

Lunch rolled into teatime as the Bohannon brothers told their stories and listened to Cade and Joanna's as well—and it was no small coincidence that the brothers had previously worked for the railroad company laying track through Colorado.

Cade was surprised to hear the brothers talk about the train explosion north of Colorado Springs, and he was intently interested in hearing their perspective. They spoke of coming to help with the cleanup and getting the train running again. When they learned all of that work was because of him, it seemed to establish a new understanding between them. It also piqued their curiosity to hear more about the samurai cowboy who was so rumored about.

"So, what were you doing up north, Mr. Wilson?" Finn

asked as he leaned back in his chair. "I can't imagine you were on your way to Denver to destroy a train."

"I was trying to confront the man I once worked for, but things didn't go as planned," Cade replied. "And while I can only imagine what stories are floating around out there about us, we weren't the ones responsible for blowing up that train."

As Cade went on, he could tell the brothers seemed to care less about the personal details and more about being entertained by the fight with his Benefactor. They shared what they heard while working for the railroad, but thought the stories were too fantastic to be true. Their work and experience also said a lot about them. Mick was a strongman that laid steel and hammered the spikes. Finn was more of a survey and demolition expert, and it seemed possible that he may have worked with Joanna's father.

"We've been out of work for over a month now," Finn said. "The cold winter and a fire at the iron factory in Pueblo slowed down the production of rail lines. So, the company sent everyone home that wasn't an immigrant with nowhere else to go."

Cade exchanged a look with Joanna, but didn't offer up the story about Marshal Blackburn and the fire in Pueblo. She winced a little and just subtly nodded back. For today, there was enough out there about why they were all sitting around the table in Moira's cabin.

"Now what?" Mick asked very bluntly. "Are we all going to be here for a while?"

"Not too much longer," Cade replied. "Moira was nice enough to let us stay for the winter. The fight on that train took a lot out of me. Out of both of us," he explained and referenced Joanna. "I'm waiting for a friend of mine to return, as we have some business to attend to east of here."

"We all have some business to attend to," Joanna said. "I'm better off seeing this through with you than being off on my own. Besides, I'm not ready to leave my teacher just yet."

Cade could appreciate Joanna's enthusiasm, but he would have to think of a way to protect her from herself. "You're a better fighter than you think. And as a ronin, you don't have the burden of serving a master," he said.

"Besides, I'm a ronin now, too. Toshi, my teacher, told me that's what they call a samurai without a master," he explained. "I may be free to fight for whoever needs me, but I know that my former Benefactor would never stop looking for me if he found out that I'm still alive. And right now, if he thinks I'm dead, then that element of surprise is on my side."

"The element of surprise to do what?" Finn asked with a chuckle.

It was a good question, and Cade knew he didn't really have the answer as he took the last sip of his tea. He would need more than the element of surprise to approach the fort. But there was a thought creeping through his mind that meeting the Bohannon brothers was going to be the push he needed to start plotting his next course.

...

Dark Shadows

Supper was a little leaner than what Cade had become accustomed to, as the brothers arrived with an appetite that demanded their share. But the big sack of flour and other supplies they brought with their wagon helped restock the pantry, and it was nice having some new energy around the cabin. More hands also made light work of the cleanup.

The cold night sky was full of stars as everyone but Moira had finished their evening tea and made their way to the barn. It had been an eventful day, and the only remaining chore was to negotiate sleeping arrangements. Finn set up where Red Sky had been sleeping, and Mick conceded the loft to Joanna without any further argument or contest of strength. As the bigger man, he took the best spot of ground away from the drafty front door.

After building a fire in the potbelly stove, Finn broke out a harmonica and was doing his best with something he called "a fine Irish tune" while Mick sipped on a small bottle of whiskey and tried to sing along. They weren't the finest of musicians, but Cade could tell they did this often by the way they effortlessly performed their song together.

"Good night, everyone," Joanna said from above, and that seemed to put everyone at rest for the evening. But even though Cade had closed his eyes long before she offered her salutation to the darkness, he was having a difficult time getting comfortable.

There had been many nights when thoughts and memories danced through his mind and made for a restless sleep. One of the recurring memories was images of Lucy and being at the Johnson Ranch. The bunkhouse in the Johnson barn was very similar to his current accommodations, but without the rooster crowing on the opposite side of the single planked wall. And even though he appreciated Moira's hospitality, it was hard not to dream about where he'd rather be.

He started thinking about the day when he first met Lucy at the turn in to the ranch. It didn't seem like much when he helped her and Eli fix their wagon wheel, but his small act of kindness proved to be the start of something much bigger. He would never forget the way the sun highlighted her hair as it fell about her shoulders, and how her hardened exterior softened enough to invite him to the house for supper.

Now he felt part of the Johnson family, and he longed to return to Rocky Creek. These feelings and memories began to blur into a dream, and he imagined the long walk up the well-worn trail the led from the arched sign to the house.

As he drew closer to the property, he could see Lucy and Eli standing on the front porch as if they were waiting for him. She wore a soft yellow dress, and Eli had his arms wrapped around his mother's waist.

"Hello!" he called out, but they didn't answer, and they weren't looking at him. They were looking beyond him as if distracted by something. Cade waved his hand to get their attention and continued to approach the steps to the porch, but they still wouldn't answer. Suddenly, the sky darkened as if the sun had become blanketed by storm clouds, and the dream that began as a pleasant memory became cold and dark.

"Lucy, what's the matter?" he asked as he climbed the stairs.

"They're coming," Lucy replied, and pointed at something over his shoulder as she issued her warning. When he turned to look, all he could make out against the darkened landscape were three shadows on horseback coming toward the house as she issued her warning. "They're coming for us all."

CHAPTER 3

The Message

It felt like an unusually long day, and Lucy knew there was still work to be done. Enough chores that she had to make two trips into town and decided to pick up Eli on the way home.

"Don't forget that we still need to clean out the barn when we get home," Lucy reminded her son as she drove their wagon down the south road. "And I don't want to hear any complaining about it either. It's well past the time we usually do the spring cleaning."

Eli looked discouraged, but resigned to the truth in his mother's words. But then he pointed to something on the horizon and Lucy had to squint to focus on what had drawn his attention. "Looks like riders coming this way," he said.

There wasn't anything out of the ordinary about the three men on horseback, as the road through town also led north through the mountain pass into Colorado. She was always mindful of strangers, and usually did her best to avoid them if possible. But at their current pace, Lucy estimated that they might cross paths with the riders around the spot they turn to the ranch.

As they were almost to the trail home, Lucy was able to get a better look at the three men who had stopped at the arched sign—and by their appearances, her level of concern about their intentions began to rise. One rider was dressed all in black, and the other two looked like the shadow riders who had attacked their home last year and held the family hostage in the barn. But being the only other people on the road, and just before their turn, there wasn't anything else she could do to try and awkwardly avoid them.

"Whoa there," one of the shadow riders said with a hand in the air, and Lucy pulled the wagon to a stop. "Is this the place?" the rider asked aloud.

"Indeed, it is," the man in black replied, and took a long drink from his canteen. "The last time I rode by this sign, my old partner was still alive."

"Well, let's get on with it and head into town," the rider said as he stuffed his cheek full of chaw and spit.

"Is this your place, young lady?" the man in black asked Lucy while he dismounted his horse and stretched his legs. The left side of his face was horribly scarred, and she did her best not to stare at it while the man walked over to the side of the wagon where Eli was sitting.

"It is… and it's private property," Lucy replied. "What's your business?"

"Oh, we're just here to deliver a message," he answered as he turned to Eli. "What's your name, son?"

Lucy put her hand on Eli's arm to hold him there and keep him quiet. But as the man in black waited for an answer, he pulled a knife from his belt and a folded piece of parchment from the inside pocket of his coat.

"Answer the man," the other shadow rider said, and sounded a bit impatient.

"Eli," he replied, and his mother could hear the shaky uncertainty in his voice. But then he responded in kind, and Lucy was proud of his courage. "What's yours?"

"My name is Bill Swift, but most people know me by another name. And those that don't are probably dead," he said and took another step toward Eli.

"What do you want?" Lucy asked again, and more bluntly than before. Her heart began to race as her fears about this man continued to grow—and she didn't like that he was so focused on her son with a knife in his hand.

"How about you let us ask the questions," Swift replied in a callous tone. "But I like it when people get straight to the point, so I'll extend you the same courtesy."

After clearing his throat, Swift stuck the knife through the middle of the folded parchment. "Do you know a man named Cade Wilson, otherwise known as Viper?" he asked.

"Yes," Eli replied, and Lucy gripped his arm even tighter to silence him. Her concerns about their intent were confirmed, but why were they here looking for Cade?

Swift turned to his two companions but spoke loud enough for everyone to hear, "How fortunate. This brave young man could go far in the world, if he can answer one last question."

Eli shifted in his seat a little and Swift snapped his fingers to get his attention. "Now listen closely, and don't try to be clever.

"When was the last time you saw Cade Wilson?"

Lucy released her grip on Eli's arm and carefully watched the man in black as he brandished the knife and slowly waved it back and forth in her son's face as if he were keeping time.

"Cade is dead," Eli replied. "He left last year to return to some fort and see his Benefactor. We haven't seen him since," he continued, and then paused to take a breath. "Is that his knife?"

"Oh, do you recognize it?" Swift asked and held it out for the boy to see. "It was found up in Colorado, and it was the only thing found. But I think Cade Wilson is still alive. He's out there somewhere," he said and looked around to survey the landscape.

"I also think he's going to come back this way, and I want you to make sure he gets this message when he does," Swift said before he flipped the blade in his hand and threw it at one of the wooden posts of the Johnson Ranch sign.

The point of the blade stuck perfectly in the dry wood along with the folded parchment pinned to it—and then the man in black gave the knife a long look before he turned back to Lucy. "You tell him that Bullseye is looking for him… and I'll be back in about a month to settle things between us."

•••

The Offer

Jon Cobb sat at his desk as the afternoon sun poured in through the second-story window of his office. He had a map of the valley rolled out in front of him, and he was mulling over the two different paths to lay railroad track through Rocky Creek.

Since hearing the news back in October of last year, the possibility of the railroad coming through the valley had become more than a daydream of being in the right place at the right time. There would be formalized plans being drawn up right here in early June, and he would have a place at the table with representatives from the United States government and some of the most powerful men in the railroad business.

The more he studied the map, the more he knew that the best two options would come through the west side of town and head south along the creek through his land. But the rails would also need to pass through part of the Johnson family ranch. If he could own that land, or marry Lucy and join their land, he would be able to expand his ranching territory and become one of the richest men in the New Mexico Territory.

As he took a sip of his whiskey and leaned back in his chair, he looked out onto the street to casually imagine how much this town would change when the railroad came through. But instead of feeling pleased with himself, there were three riders coming in from the south road that caught his attention. Two of them looked like he remembered Whitmore's men in their gray coats, but with them was a man in black he had never seen before—and he didn't like the looks of him.

"Hicks!" he yelled out to his right-hand man and then listened to hear his footsteps coming up the stairs. As his foreman entered his office, Cobb stood and invited him over to the window.

"Did you see those fellas who just rode in?" he asked and pointed at the riders approaching. "Two of them look like the 'shadow riders' that Whitmore sent after Cade Wilson. Do you agree?" he asked, seeking confirmation.

"Yessir, Mr. Cobb," Hicks replied. "They sure do."

"Who's the man in black?" Cobb asked. Hicks was the man he counted on to manage his affairs and operations, but he was also more likely to have met some of the strangers and bounty hunters tracking through town. And if this fella was a bounty hunter, then why was he riding with Whitmore's men?

"There's something familiar about him, but I can't place it," Hicks replied as he pulled his hat and scratched his head. "I don't get a good feeling about them, that's for sure. They must be passing through town for a reason."

Hicks was a good man, but Cobb would often remind him to know his place and let his boss manage the business side of things. Yet there was something that rang true in his foreman's observation as he watched the riders pass through the crossroads at the center of town and pull up in front of the new sign he put up for the Rocky Creek Landholdings Company. "I guess we're about to find out," he muttered under his breath.

Riders like that would usually stop first at the Five Point

Saloon. But now it seemed they were most likely sent here by Whitmore—and he could only wonder why. Without another word between them, both men gathered themselves and put on their coats. Cobb finished his whiskey and placed the empty glass on his desk while Hicks put his right hand on the butt of his pistol as if to confirm it was there. "Let's go talk to them and find out," Cobb said and tried to sound confident as he made his way to the door.

As the two men descended the stairs, Cobb could see the riders dismount and tie up their horses. Instead of being caught off guard in the parlor like last time Whitmore's men came to town, he decided to meet them outside in public view. He thought it was less likely there would be trouble out on the street, and he could decide whether or not to invite them in after he learned why they were here. And when he stepped out and got a closer look at the scarred face of the man in black, he already decided that man wasn't taking one step inside his business.

"Hello," Cobb said to the riders, and cleared his throat. Their horses had kicked up a little dust, and he waved his hand in front of his face to clear it away. Then he turned up the charm to be polite and get to the point. "Welcome to Rocky Creek. I couldn't help but notice you tie up in front of my business here, and I'm wondering what I can do for you today?"

He watched as the man in black moved slowly behind the horses and then proceeded to walk up the steps to the planked platform. The two shadow riders stood back and followed the lead of the man in black who was now front and center—and he reached into his coat to produce an envelope.

"Are you Jon Cobb?" he asked.

"Yes sir, and how did you assume that?" Cobb replied.

"I have a business proposition for you from Joseph Whitmore II," he said while he handed over the envelope and looked as if he needed some form of confirmation.

Cobb took the envelope and tried not to look at the man's face. Not because it was rude to stare. But because there was something about the scar that made the man seem so sinister. "Thank you, mister—"

"Mr. Swift will do just fine," he said and glanced at Hicks. "We're here on behalf of Mr. Whitmore. He wanted you to receive this message personally, as it's just between the two of you… if you know what I mean?" he explained, but the tone of his voice implied there was still more to be said.

"Yes, I understand," Cobb replied. He already didn't like this guy, and the less he had to talk to him the better. But because he was sent by Whitmore, he figured the best thing to do was play along.

"Good. My friends and I are going to wander over to the saloon and get a drink. We've been on the trail for a good couple of days and might stay the night if we're so inclined," Swift said with a glance at the hotel. "And it would be of great benefit if we could have your answer before we leave."

"My answer for what?" Cobb asked.

"Mr. Whitmore's offer," Swift replied. "I'm sure it's all explained in the letter you're holding. He's a very meticulous man and knows how to say and get what he wants. So how about you read it while we step across the street," he concluded with a tip of his hat.

Cobb struggled with his feelings about all of this as he tore the envelope open and its delivery boy walked away. He wasn't expecting a message from Whitmore, or an offer, for that matter. And he certainly didn't appreciate being put on the spot as he unfolded the enclosed parchment and read it to himself.

MR. COBB
THE RAILROAD WILL BE COMING SOUTH
THROUGH MOUNTAIN PASS FROM COLORADO
AND THROUGH THE TOWN OF ROCKY CREEK.
I'M OFFERING $20 AN ACRE TO ALL RESIDENTS
WHO OWN LAND MARKED FOR DEVELOPMENT.
AS THE LANDHOLDINGS COMPANY, I'LL GIVE
YOU THE OPPORTUNITY TO MANAGE THESE
DEALS AND PROFIT FROM THEM.
PLEASE SHARE YOUR ANSWER AS SOON AS
POSSIBLE. I WILL BE COMING
IN ONE MONTH TO CONCLUDE OUR BUSINESS.
J. WHITMORE II

"Who does this man think he is?" Cobb asked rhetorically. Hicks had not seen the contents of the letter, but he responded with an answer Cobb wasn't expecting at all.

"Now I remember that fella. He's a bounty hunter," Hicks said quietly. "He came through here months ago with that Marshal I told you about. But he didn't have the scar on his face then," he explained and seemed pleased but leery to remember the interaction.

"I wonder if our friend Mr. Wilson gave him that scar?" Cobb asked curiously while he folded the paper back up and stuffed it back into the envelope. "But what really matters is why Whitmore sent that man to deliver this offer to buy land that will be worth ten times more when it's time to lay track on it."

Feeling a little miffed about the intimidation factor, Cobb snapped his fingers for Hicks to follow him as he stepped into the street after the man in black. In an attempt to catch him before he entered the saloon, Cobb called out to get his attention.

"Excuse me, Mr. Swift," Cobb said loud enough to make the man stop and face him. As he continued to make his way across the street, he lowered the volume of his voice but still spoke loud enough to make his intentions clear.

"You can have my answer now, if you like," Cobb began to say once he knew the man was listening. "Tell your boss that I appreciate him sending this message personally, and that I look forward to doing business with him. But he'll need to make a better offer than this," he said while holding up the envelope. Then he suddenly regretted his decision to react impulsively when the man in black pulled his pistol.

"I'll make sure to tell him that," Swift replied, and slowly shook his head. "But just so we understand each other, I'll need you to remember this conversation… and know that Mr. Whitmore won't be coming here to negotiate."

Cobb was looking down the barrel of a gun, and he cringed at the sound of the gunshot. The bullet went through the envelope he was holding and into the middle of the first

'O' in the Rocky Creek Landholdings Company sign—the new sign Cobb had just put up to impress all the important people who would be coming to town in June.

Then the man in black holstered his pistol and smiled as if he'd proven his point.

"Bullseye," he said.

...

News from the East

The journey seemed longer than he remembered, but Red Sky was also being mindful of tracing his way through the prairie without being seen or followed. Once he recognized the familiar surroundings and Moira's cabin was in sight, he felt glad to be back.

He was also happy to arrive before the sun dipped below the mountains. The bitterness of winter had passed, but nights out on the trail were cold and he could still feel the bullet in his shoulder when he slept on the hard ground. It would be good to see his friends again, and hopefully enjoy a nice warm meal and other comforts he'd appreciated not so long ago.

As he approached the cabin, the first thing he noticed was the strange wagon parked out front. It had not been there before he left, but somehow it looked like it belonged. There were no signs of trouble as he advanced, but paused when he heard a strange voice call out.

"Hello there… are you lost?" the voice boomed from

a man who emerged from behind a tree—and Red Sky did not recognize the man on his horse with a hand on his pistol.

Red Sky was about to answer when Cade rode up behind the stranger with a deer on the back of his horse.

"It's okay, Mick," Cade announced, loud enough for all to hear. "That's Red Sky, the man we've been waiting for," he continued with a big smile. "Welcome back, old friend."

Coming up behind the two of them were Joanna and another stranger on horseback. "Red Sky!" she said and rode up to greet him. "It's so good to see you again."

"It's good to see you, too," Red Sky replied. Whatever unease he initially felt when he first saw the wagon and the stranger quickly subsided as Joanna made introductions.

"This is Finn," she said with a twist of her head, and then pointed to the man over her shoulder, "and that's Mick. They're Moira's nephews, and we just got back from a hunt. I took down my first deer with a bow!" she continued and sounded very excited about her accomplishment.

"Well now," Red Sky said with a smile. "It's nice to see you're learning the way of the bow."

"Pleasure to meet you," Finn said while he continued on to the cabin. "Now about this deer. How about we get it skinned and dressed before dark?"

While everyone made their way to the barn, Cade was first to appreciate the spear Red Sky was carrying. "I see you were able to restore that samurai spear to its former glory," he said.

Red Sky nodded and held it out for Cade and Joanna to see. "Yes. It took some time to find the best piece of wood, but it feels strong and balanced." He was able to fix the spearhead to a sturdy shaft that was long and smooth—and used some twine to fashion a grip for a handle in the middle. The weapon was formidable again, and he was proud of the craftsmanship.

"Are your people safe? How was the journey back?" Cade asked, and Red Sky could tell his friend was curious to hear any news he had to share.

"The winter was hard, and we had to travel south to the big river bend. But there is more I need to tell you," Red Sky said while he tied up his horse. "Let's go inside. I'd like to see the old woman, too."

Cade gave a nod and the two of them made their way inside the warmth of the cabin as Joanna and the nephews took care of the deer. Red Sky thought this might be best, as it would be good to talk with his friend and the old woman alone. And after Moira gave him his welcome hug, he began to tell them both what he'd seen.

"I was careful to avoid being seen as I rode past the great house," Red Sky said to Cade, as a reminder of their first encounter. "But I watched for two days as many riders have been coming and going. I've seen many wagons and shadow riders arriving from the east. It looks like they are preparing for something."

"What makes you think that?" Cade asked.

"The wagons I saw are the same ones the blue coats used to bring guns and supplies for war. This is what they did after they promised peace, but it was a lie. The peace talks gave them time to advance their army and push us out," he replied.

"Will your people be safe?" Moira asked, and sounded very concerned while she poured them all a cup of tea.

"I don't know if we'll ever be safe," Red Sky replied. "The blue coats only bring death and destruction. But the elders are leading our people through the canyons to the north and the high ground now that the snow has melted, and blossoms have returned to the trees. The canyons and the high ground offer us our best defense.

"And now I have returned because our fight is not over," he continued. "The men at the great house that also bring death are still a threat to my people, and I'm prepared to join my ancestors in the spirit world to protect my tribe and avenge my family."

"Agreed," Cade said solemnly as he sipped his tea. "We need a plan. I've been thinking about this for some time. And now that you've returned, we should be prepared for the worst if what you've seen is true."

"Yes. But for now, I could use some rest and something to eat," Red Sky said with a smile.

CHAPTER 4

Time to Leave

Red Sky's return was a sign, and while everyone made the best of the crowded conditions for the first night, Cade knew it couldn't last. But he also didn't have a clear vision of what leaving Moira's cabin might look like, so after the morning chores, he continued to work with Joanna while they were still here.

It was a beautiful sunny day with a gentle breeze coming out of the west, and the doors to the barn were wide open as Cade trained Joanna with the wooden swords. This wouldn't have been anything out of the ordinary, but now they had an audience.

"Your counter strike can be as deadly as a slash or cut, and it's a critical fighting technique to practice," Cade instructed as they circled each other in the barn. "By anticipating your opponent's moves, and weaknesses, you can let them over-extend themselves… and then catch them off guard."

To prove his point, he made an obvious thrust at Joanna that was easy to defend—and then she ducked and quickly spun around to catch Cade across his right thigh.

Red Sky and the brothers had been quietly watching as Cade taught Joanna this counter strike technique, but now they erupted with a roar of approval as she executed it. "That's a clean hit, lass," Finn said with a whistle, and it made Joanna smile.

As they stood and faced each other, Cade gave a bow. "He's right. That was a nice move, and it was an important part of your lesson today," he said. And while he was being sincere with his compliment, his mind was somewhere else.

"Thank you, Viper. But I think you let me have that one," she said with a look of concern. "Are you feeling okay?"

"Yes, of course," he replied instinctively. It was just a little lie, because he felt healthier than ever. But he couldn't get the images of Lucy out of his mind, and he'd been troubled by the dream that started as a pleasant memory of Johnson Ranch and gave way to a vision of riders shrouded in darkness.

"I may have telegraphed my attack to make my point, but the rest was all you and the application of your speed and skills. You're getting better every day," he said. It was the easiest way to close the conversation as they all made their way to the cabin for lunch. But that was also true, as he was proud of how much Joanna had learned in such a short period of time. It could also be because they did nothing but practice almost every day all winter long.

Once inside, the angle of the warm spring sun illuminated the potted herbs on the windowsill. But Cade was still lost in thought as everyone but him seemed to be good spirits as they sat around the table—and Moira was quick to ask while she put a loaf of bread on the table. "You can fool yourself, child, but you can't fool me. Tell me, what's clouding your mind?"

Cade couldn't fool Moira, or distract or disguise himself like he did with Joanna. He also didn't feel like talking about his concerns in front of everyone, but he knew the old woman was persistent.

"I've been having recurring visions of Rocky Creek in my dreams, and they've increased since Mick and Finn arrived. But recently I've seen the dark figures like shadow riders descending on the Johnson Ranch," he explained to Moira. "What does it mean?"

"Is there a rider in black with a scar on his face?" Moira asked, sounding very concerned.

"I don't know. I can only see the shadows of three riders on horseback. But the family I knew at the Johnson Ranch are afraid, and they are trying to warn me that these men are 'coming for us all,'" he replied.

The old woman sat down and got comfortable before she looked Cade in the eye. If he couldn't hide anything from her, then she seemed willing to do the same—but her voice cracked as if she shared a sense of danger in his visions. "It means it's time for you to leave," she said. "You need to return to Rocky Creek."

...

Scorpion's Sword

The mood around the cabin was a bit somber after lunch, and Joanna was feeling a little uncomfortable since the conversation about leaving. But now it was supper time, and she didn't know what to talk about, as everyone else seemed content to eat quietly and avoid talking about visions and bad dreams.

Beyond the lack of conversation, it was the silence that made her feel uncomfortable. At times, the only thing she could hear over Mick chewing his food was the crackle of the fire. There seemed like a cloud of uncertainty hovered over the cabin. And the more she thought about it—she thought that if Cade and Red Sky were planning to head out for Rocky Creek, then she was going with them.

"When are we leaving?" Joanna asked Cade and Red Sky, but everyone at the table looked at her. "Because there is no way I'm letting you go to Rocky Creek without me."

Cade finished his stew and dropped his spoon in the empty bowl. His furrowed brow gave the impression that he hadn't planned that far in advance. "I was thinking about leaving tomorrow after the morning chores. I need to get back to the Johnson family as soon as possible, and protect them from whatever dangers are coming," he replied.

Joanna smiled as if to assure him that he had trained her well and she was ready. "Sounds good to me."

"But Joanna, I can't keep dragging you into danger, too,"

he said very sincerely. "I don't know why I'm being pulled back to Rocky Creek, but it's easy to imagine the worst, given the thoughts I've been having. Maybe you should stay here and head west to California when the mountain snow melts."

Joanna could appreciate that Cade was always trying to protect her, but what he said didn't make much sense to her either. "I would love to go to California, but I'm not traveling alone, and neither should you," she said matter-of-factly.

"Besides, you know I can take care of myself… and I'm going with you. Nothing you can say is going to change that," she said confidently, and then smiled, feeling a little amused and proud of herself. "And since I've never been south of Colorado, I figure it's something to see for myself."

When Cade smiled, she knew they'd all be leaving together tomorrow morning. "Tell you what," he said. "I'll pay you for seeing me safely to Rocky Creek. It will be your first mission as a samurai, and you can save up your money for California."

"What about us?" Mick asked from his usual spot at the corner of the table. At first, Joanna laughed because he sounded so wounded, but then she realized it was rude that they had not been included in the conversation.

"Yeah," Finn chimed in while also sounding overlooked. "Don't know if you've noticed, but we've been out of work for a bit. If there's some money to be made traveling to Rocky Creek, then you can count us in, too."

As Cade started laughing, Joanna could feel the entire mood in the cabin lighten up. "Sure," he said. "Why not. What's your going rate for escorting me to Rocky Creek?"

Finn sat back quietly while Mick put one finger to his

temple as the rest curled in to cover his mouth. They both looked like men trying not to be swindled, but Joanna was anxious to hear whatever the brothers had to say next. "How about three dollars a day… for each of us?" Mick asked and pointed his thumb at Finn.

Cade didn't seem to flinch, so Finn must have felt compelled to go for more. "No. Five dollars a day," he said and looked back at his brother. "For each of us," he continued, and Mick sat back as if to defer to his older brother.

"How about five dollars a day for all of you," Cade said, as if the deal had been struck, and Joanna was happy to nod in agreement. She had never made five dollars a day doing anything before, and the idea of taking this journey just got much more interesting.

The brothers also seemed pleased with the negotiation, as they nodded and shook hands with each other.

"Done!" Cade said, and he stood up to walk over to the hutch along the wall. Joanna watched as he went to the corner where he had put some things; his saddle bags and the Katana sword that had belonged to Scorpion. After digging into his bag, he returned with the sword in hand and something else in the other.

"Consider this a payment for the first two days," Cade said while flipping a gold coin to Finn. As he caught it, Joanna could see the excitement in his eyes while he rubbed the coin between his fingers. Then he handed it over to his brother and the two began to argue over who should keep it.

Cade chuckled as he turned to Joanna. "And this is for you," he said with another gold coin in his hand. She remembered the weight of the coin as she reached out to take it from him. It was beautiful, and the glint of light from the fire made it shine in her hand. But it was not as beautiful as what was in Cade's other hand. "You'll need this, too," he continued and presented the sword for her to take.

Joanna gasped at what he just said and put the coin in her coat pocket. He was gifting Scorpion's sword to her—and it was something she had coveted since she began her training. The scabbard was sleek and black, with ornate designs and an elegantly adorned handle. She reached out to touch it, but then paused as her outstretched fingers hovered over the sword.

"Are you sure?" she asked as the moment seemed so surreal.

"Yes," Cade replied, and pushed it closer and invited her to take it from him. "This is a samurai warrior's weapon, and you have proven yourself. It is time for you to take the next step."

Joanna grasped the scabbard with her left hand and took the sword from him. As she wrapped the fingers of her right hand around the handle of the sword, she also stepped back to have more room as she slowly withdrew the blade. The weight and balance of it surprised her—and she was completely mesmerized by the glimmering light reflected by the steel as she practiced a slashing strike.

The sound it made while cutting through the air was both dazzling and deadly—and like nothing she'd ever heard as she pointed the blade out in front of her. The feel of it was much different than the blunt weight of her knife, and she only stopped staring at the blade to take a closer look at the symbols decorating the scabbard.

"Do you know what this means?" Joanna asked as she held it out for Cade to see.

"I think it's the sign of the dragon," he replied.

• • •

Dignity

The glass of whiskey in his hand looked a little blurry, but it wasn't going to stop Sinclair from raising it to his lips to finish the last drink.

There were no answers to life's questions to be found in the empty bottle, or in the relatively quiet and dimly lit saloon where he occupied a familiar seat. He had spent two cold months just trying to walk without pain, and another two months learning how to shoot with his left hand. The doctor did his best to remove the buckshot from his ankle and reset his broken right arm, but he never felt the same again. And as he looked at his reflection in the dusty mirror behind the bar, he felt ashamed of himself. He knew the whiskey was more about nursing his wounded pride than soothing the injuries he suffered at the train station in Colorado Springs.

"Hey Sinclair… there's someone here asking about you," he heard the bartender say. Hearing his name was enough to get his attention, but not shake him from his daze. Still, he was curious enough to look over his shoulder to see—because he didn't know who would be looking for him in a place like this.

"I'm surprised to find you here," he heard a familiar voice

say as two men made their way toward him at the end of the bar. When one of the men came into focus, Sinclair also recognized him by sight. It was Victor Carmichael, and this was the first time they had crossed paths since that fateful day.

"I thought you would have gotten away from Denver and headed back east. And if you don't mind me saying so, you barely resemble the man I met last year," Victor continued. "Are you still in the business?"

Sinclair stood up and leaned into the bar for stability. He may have stopped shaving a while back, and he wasn't exactly dressed like he used to—but he was still a young man and felt a little insulted by Victor's comment and the look he was getting from the fella behind him. "Still in the business of what?" he asked.

"This guy's a drunk, boss," the man behind Victor whispered into his ear. "We can do better than this."

"Calm down, Alan," Victor said, and corrected his man. "You were in the business of finding people. That was your 'vocation' as you used to say, yes?" he asked.

Sinclair tried to muster up some spit in his mouth, but his tongue was as dry as the air as he licked his lips. Now that he knew why Victor was looking for him, maybe there was some money to be made—and he wasn't exactly living the good life anymore.

"I haven't been doing any hunting since last October, but I would suppose it's time to get back to work," he replied and felt the need to compose himself before he addressed a potential employer. "Who do you want found?"

"Joanna Carter. The girl that cold cocked you at the train

station," Victor replied. "You're the only one of your kind that really knows what she looks like, or looked like. Because she hasn't been seen or heard from since. It's like she just up and disappeared without a trace. And trust me, I've been looking.

"So, my offer is this. I'll pay you two hundred dollars now to hunt her down and tell me where to find her," Victor said firmly, before he cleared his throat. "And two thousand dollars more if you bring her back to me alive."

"Why do you want her alive?" Sinclair asked.

"That's my business, and I don't want her death to come at anyone else's hands but my own," Victor replied.

Sinclair could sense that Victor was being completely serious as he tried to remember what Joanna looked like. He could picture her dark hair pulled back into a ponytail, the paisley blue dress that she wore, and the rope belt with the knife around her waist. Her face was a little less clear, as the bump on his head wasn't the only thing that clouded his mind and the details of that morning. And Victor just confirmed the one thing he couldn't recall before he woke up on the floor of the train station—Joanna Carter was the one responsible for his headache that day.

He usually didn't care to know why someone was being hunted; only what they were worth. But something about the look on Victor's face said this was personal, and he heard that Victor's son Spencer was dead. "Did she kill your boy?"

Victor didn't answer the question, but instead reached into his coat pocket and pulled out a folded stack of paper currency. "Two hundred dollars to find her, and two thousand more if you bring her back alive," he said as he held out the money.

Sinclair staggered back a bit, as the limp in his right foot reminded him that he was a little off balance. But then he propped himself up against the bar and stood tall to address this man as honestly as possible. "That's an interesting offer," he said without having any idea where to start looking. "But that was also some time ago. The girl could be anywhere."

"Well, that's why you're being hired, jackass. You're supposed to be a big game hunter. But from the looks of it, you're just a bum who would spend the money on whiskey," Alan said with a chuckle. "And what kind of hunter carries a bull whip?"

Sinclair followed Alan's pointed finger to the coiled whip on his right hip. He didn't appreciate this man's tone or his comments, but he did feel obliged to answer the man's question.

"This whip is a painful reminder of Marshal Blackburn, the man who broke my arm and shot me in the foot," he said aloud, but looked only at Victor. "When I came to at the train station, there was a sheriff and his deputies standing around the bodies of the dead. Stories circled between them that Cade Wilson had removed the head of the man who shot me, so I appreciated that.

"The first thing I could remember was this whip lying next to me, and I used it to make a splint for my wrist," Sinclair said while flexing his right hand. "Since then, I've lost some of the feeling in this hand and had to start shooting with my left. But I've also discovered that there is something special about this whip. Would you like to see?" he asked, but did not wait for an answer.

Victor's man was likely surprised by the speed at which Sinclair pulled the whip with his right hand, cracked it back once, and then cast it forward to wrap it around Alan's neck. Then after he gave the whip a clockwise turn, he watched as Alan dropped to his knees—trying to pull at the whip with his hands as he was being strangled.

"There's one word scratched into the handle, as it would appear this whip has a name," Sinclair continued. "Its name is Widowmaker, and I think you'd agree that it could end your life with another flick of my wrist."

"Enough!" Victor said. "You've made your point. Now stop this nonsense."

Sinclair twisted the whip counterclockwise and released it from Alan's neck. "Fair enough. But where I come from, we have manners, and this fellow you brought with you needs to learn some."

As Alan got up cursing and spitting, Victor put out his hand to calm his man before he resumed the conversation. "Have you heard anything about Cade Wilson or his whereabouts?"

"Not a word," Sinclair replied and shook his head while he coiled his whip. "I was stuck in Colorado Springs for a couple weeks, but not just because I was on the mend. The damage caused by the train explosion and the reports of his demise are almost legendary around these parts. And unfortunately, by the time I was able to make it back to Denver, Whitmore was gone and so were my personal belongings.

"So, I've been holding up here for the winter… drinking whiskey to stay warm and rehabbing my skills," Sinclair continued. "But I would like to get my belongings back, and that means I still have some unfinished business with Whitmore.

As for Cade Wilson, the Viper, the bounty was pulled and so have my interests in finding him."

"But the ten thousand in gold has never been recovered, and some say Cade Wilson is still alive. I'm starting to believe that he didn't die in the blast on that train," Victor said with a curious tone. "Joanna Carter was last seen traveling with Wilson and a Comanche Indian, and no trace of any of them has been found since. Some say he and the girl have been hiding somewhere in No-man's-land or the Indian Nation.

"I also have some unfinished business with Whitmore, and I haven't forgiven him for what happened that day," Victor continued. "But I've sent him a message to keep an eye out in his corner of the New Mexico Territory."

The conversation challenged Sinclair to think hard and try to recall events from months past. "I remember the Comanche," he said while he stepped forward to take the money from Victor's hand. "And the girl, too. So, I'll take the job and see where I think their trail leads."

"Where would that be?" Victor asked.

"I heard about a town where Cade Wilson was hiding last summer," Sinclair replied, and he was intrigued by the thought of ten thousand dollars in gold that had to be somewhere. "Maybe I'll start there."

Victor chuckled. "Are you talking about Rocky Creek? That's on the other side of the mountain pass at the south border. Why start there?"

"Well, Mr. Carmichael," Sinclair replied. "If Cade Wilson is alive, he would likely seek shelter somewhere familiar. And like you've said… you have already looked everywhere else."

...

The Messenger Returns

In the fading glow of twilight, Joseph Whitmore II stood on the front porch of his home and waited for his message party to approach.

The three riders coming up the hill were dispatched to Rocky Creek almost two weeks ago, and he hoped to hear some good news. At the very least, he wanted to know that in the absence of his samurai cowboys, his new hired gun had delivered his offer to Jon Cobb. And he figured that "Bullseye" Bill Swift was just the kind of man to deliver that kind of ultimatum.

"How was your trip?" he asked Swift, when the three riders stopped their horses in front of the house. "You must be tired from your journey."

Swift tipped back his hat. "Yes, boss. And the trip turned out like you thought it might," he replied as he dismounted.

"Oh, did Cobb accept the offer?" Whitmore asked.

"Not quite," Swift replied. "But he will. He definitely got the message that we expect nothing less."

Whitmore grimaced and shook his head. The last thing he wanted was more trouble, but he wasn't going to lose out on being part of the most important thing to happen in the New Mexico Territory—whatever the cost.

He also didn't appreciate the word he'd received from Victor Carmichael before he sent his men to Rocky Creek.

That nowhere town was about to become the center of a plan to connect the railroad through Santa Fe and beyond—and there was a big meeting scheduled to happen in June, with government and business leaders gathering to formalize everything.

Unfortunately, the events in Colorado and the fallout he'd had with Carmichael meant he would need control of that valley before that meeting and any plans to lay track were finalized. And the message he had delivered gave Jon Cobb one month to start making deals with the townsfolk who would need to be bought out.

"Well, that's good enough for now," he said, while thinking through what might need to happen in the months ahead. "They'll have to accept our offer, or—"

"There's one more thing," Swift said, to finish reporting the details of their trip. "I also delivered a personal message to the Johnson family who own some valuable land just south of the town. It's intended for the man we both want dead. And if Cade Wilson is still alive out there, I believe that message will find him somehow."

Whitmore wasn't proud of his hired gun's approach, but deadly men with a moral code who could be influenced by money were helpful during times like this—and they both had their reasons for dealing with the Johnson family. "Are you sure that threatening that family is going to make the ghost of Cade Wilson appear?"

"As sure as you are about Cobb and the good people of Rocky Creek accepting your offer," Swift replied. "If Wilson doesn't care about the money or coming out of hiding, then maybe he will when we come for the family."

CHAPTER 5

Fond Farewell

The morning arrived without celebration as the five travelers left Moira's cabin just after breakfast. It was harder for Cade to say goodbye than he thought, and he had plenty of time with his thoughts after an hour of walking their horses due west.

The old woman had been more than kind to him, and he felt he could never repay her generosity or for the way she made him feel in her presence. It was a sense of calm and focus he hadn't been able to enjoy for a long time. Then there was also the nagging, but realistic thought that he would never see her or be back this way again—which made the farewell tug at his heartstrings in a way he hadn't felt since he buried his mother and left his home in Missouri.

"Goodbye, Moira," he managed to say while trying to hold back the feelings of loss. "I can't thank you enough for what you've done for me. You're the second family I've had since leaving the fort, and I can't imagine where I would have found some peace if not here."

"You're welcome," she replied with the same kindness in her voice that had soothed his pain and helped him heal. "But now it's time for you to go."

"God willing, I'll be sure to stop by this way again someday," he said in hopes it was true. And he looked for a clue in her eyes that might suggest she had a vision or suspected he would, but she didn't answer and only nodded with a smile. That was her way.

"I hope that someday you will find peace, Cade Wilson," was the last thing she said to him as she kissed his forehead and gave him one last hug. He was at a loss for words in that moment, and he wished he could have offered her something more than one of the horses. But she didn't need gold, or want it, and they were too far gone to turn back.

He had noticed that Joanna took the reality of leaving pretty hard, too. The tears rolling down her cheeks told their own story. That Moira was more than a friend to both of them—she was the loving matriarch that they both needed at a time they felt lost.

Red Sky was much more stoic. He didn't spend the winter at the cabin, so it was probably a little easier for him to say goodbye. And the brothers seemed to treat the moment like they had said farewell to their aunt many times before, and that they'd be back to visit with more supplies again soon.

But now it was time to stretch their legs for the road ahead. The mountain pass ahead of them appeared as clear as the blue sky overhead, and he tried to remember the shortcut through the pass and over the Colorado border that Moira had told him about.

"I think our horses have been walked enough. Are you ready to pick up the pace?" Cade asked Red Sky at his side. Then he looked around to Joanna and the brothers—who had left the wagon behind for two of the four horses he and Red Sky had trailed to Moira's months ago. "I'm guessing we could be in Rocky Creek in a couple days if we can quicken our pace a bit," he said with a finger pointed in the general direction.

"Show us the way," Finn replied, and Red Sky smiled as he took the lead.

•••

Reunion

"Dammit all," Lucy cursed herself while trying to chase down their only goat. It was getting late in the day and the goat had chewed through her rope again. "Why are you so stubborn?" she asked the animal after she caught it and walked it back to the stake in the ground. "Or do you just hate being tied down in one place?" she said with a chuckle.

She wasn't above laughing at herself for expecting the goat to answer, or the irony of her questions. She had long accepted her stubborn streak, and she loved the ranch. But there were times she felt like she was missing out on something, and this was one of those days. Sometimes she liked to look out at the mountains and dream about a different life on the other side and being far away from here instead of chasing animals and the never-ending list of chores.

But her daydream was interrupted when Eli's new dog started barking. "What is it, Rolly?" she asked, as if the dog could answer. Then she followed his gaze and squinted her eyes to catch the sight of five riders on the horizon.

They were too far out to distinguish them or speculate why they looked headed in her direction—except one. As she dropped the rope and slowly stepped forward, she barely noticed that the goat had wandered away again. But she didn't care because her heart swelled as she was confident that one of the riders was Cade.

"Everyone, come quick!" she said and ran to the front of the house. The riders were now inside the gate and closing as she bounded onto the front porch and yelled into the open window for her father and son. "Come outside! Cade is here… and he's not alone."

She turned back to face the man she had anxiously hoped would return, and Cade was smiling back at her under all his unkept facial hair. But the closer he came into view, the beard wasn't the only thing she noticed was different about him. Based on his overall appearance, he looked like he had been to hell and back.

"Hi Lucy, it's good to see you again," Cade said once the riders closed on the front porch. "I didn't know I'd be back so soon, and I hope you and Pa don't mind that I brought some friends—"

"Well, I'll be damned," Pa said as he emerged from the house onto the front porch. "You have to be the luckiest man alive, or the stories everyone's telling about you must be crazy. Welcome back, Mr. Wilson."

Cade dismounted his horse and barely had both feet on the ground when Eli ran out from behind his grandfather and dove from the porch right into him. The force of his weight crashing into Cade was a joy to watch, and it would have been funnier if they both fell to the ground. But one of the strongest men Lucy knew just caught her son in his arms with a big hug.

Unable to stop smiling and feeling that it was her turn, Lucy walked deliberately down the steps and allowed room for Eli to be set down and move aside. Then she stepped in and paused only for a moment to study the face of the man she could not forget. His eyes looked happy and rested, but different somehow. Then she slowly raised a hand to gently trace the scar across his cheek, and she wondered without asking what must have caused that.

"It's a scar of disloyalty. Toshi gave it to me as a reminder that I turned against our Benefactor," he said. "How it happened is a long story."

"I'm sure it is," she said before stopping her index finger across his lips. "We've all missed you so much," she continued, and then fell forward to fit herself in the embrace of his arms. The feeling of his worn leather coat against her cheek brought back a flood of memories, and she fought off the tears welling in her eyes as she felt the weight of his arms around her again. "We heard you were dead, but I never believed it."

She realized this moment couldn't last about the same time she remembered she was in the presence of strangers. As

Lucy stepped back to smooth her hands over her dress and regain her composure, she heard her father's voice behind them. "Would you like to introduce us to your friends?" Pa said in the tone he always used to make people sound welcome.

Cade pulled away and began introductions, as if slightly embarrassed. "My apologies. Lucy, Eli, and Pa Johnson… this is Joanna Carter," he said and then paused for the young lady to say something.

"Hello everyone, it's a pleasure to meet you. We've heard so much about you and the ranch that it's nice to finally be here," Joanna said. "It looks just like Cade described."

The girl seemed well-mannered and polite, and Lucy noticed from the softness of her cheeks that she was much younger than her and naturally pretty. But why was she wearing the crimson red coat, and why did she have a samurai sword strapped across her back? It reminded her of that fateful day at the ranch and the man named Falcon that held them hostage.

"This is Red Sky," Cade said while continuing the introductions, but his Comanche friend simply raised a hand to acknowledge himself. "And these two are Finn and Michael Bohannon," he continued and pointed them both out. "We all met… well, that's another long story."

"My friends call me Mick, and we're here to fulfill the first part of our contract, which was getting this man here safely," he said while he tipped back his derby and all the newcomers laughed as if they were all in on the joke.

Lucy didn't know why that was so funny, but she smiled along. "What's the second part of the contract?" she asked.

"That's what we're hoping to find out," Finn replied. "I

think there's more to this man than we know, and I suspect that you're not the only ones who would be surprised to find out he's still alive."

"Indeed," Cade said to his friend. "Could we please rest here for the night and I can tell you all about it?"

Looking to Pa for the nod of approval, Lucy was sure the answer was yes—but wondered what he meant by "for the night" as her curiosity about his return and for how long was quickly getting the best of her.

"Yes, of course," Pa replied and gave an open-handed gesture to Cade and his travel companions. "All of you can set up in the barn, and we'll need to scare up some more food for supper. But we're happy to have you, and for the extra help with the evening chores."

"Can we tell Cade about the man that came looking for him?" Eli asked.

"Not now, it's time you finished what you were doing and help Pa with the supper," she said and turned to usher him along. Lucy had not forgotten about the strange visitor to their property, and that Eli was still in possession of the knife and the note that came with it. But she was already feeling mixed emotions about Cade's return, his companions, and that he wasn't going to stay—so it didn't seem like the proper time or place to talk about the man in black.

"Did the man have a scar on his face?" Cade asked, and to Lucy's surprise, her effort to sidestep the conversation had not worked.

"Yes," Eli replied. "And he looked really mean."

Lucy glanced back at Cade and felt a little shiver on the

back of her neck. The look on his face said enough for her to associate his return with more danger from his past, and now more than ever, she wanted to know why.

•••

Bad Blood

"Can I help you with that?" Cade asked Lucy as he followed her into her room. The warmth and familiar smells of the Johnson house were enough to trigger pleasant memories, including the sight of Lucy's bed and remembering the last time he woke up here. But they were in her room for a purpose, as there were not enough place settings at the dining table that could barely sit six, and they would need her night table and chair for supper.

"Of course," she replied, as Cade moved in to pick up the table, which was heavier than it looked. The soothing sound of her voice was distinctly different from Moira's, but it had a similar calming effect on him.

"I didn't really plan this out very well," he said, feeling a bit awkward for imposing. "But I believed that I had to get back to you and the ranch as soon as possible, and my new friends wouldn't let me travel alone."

Lucy smiled but didn't reply, and Cade figured he'd said enough for now. There was no point in tripping into a conversation that could wait until after they ate. So, he maneuvered the table toward the door and made his way to the open room that served as both kitchen and dining room in hopes he would soon satisfy the grumble in his stomach.

The others in the room were just as busy as Pa and Eli were getting ready to serve supper, and the surprise guests did their best to help set the tables. Then, as everyone had finally found their place, Pa led the blessing before everyone took their seat and passed around the serving dishes.

"Thank you for taking us in," Joanna said to Pa, and lifted the cooking towel to take a biscuit. "I've been riding with Cade for a while now, and he knows good people."

Cade could sense Joanna was trying to be polite and make conversation, but he knew she had skirted the truth. "And some bad ones, too," Cade said with a chuckle.

"Are we some of the good ones?" Mick asked, and his joke got a few smiles and laughs around the table.

"Yes," Cade replied with a wink at Mick. "And some good cooks, too. I think the only rival to your aunt Moira's Irish stew is what Pa Johnson has dished up for us tonight."

As everyone began to plate up and compliment the food, Cade couldn't stop thinking about Lucy and that being here felt nostalgic and surreal at the same time. It was impossible not to exchange glances with her as she sat across the table, and he could only wish he had returned under different circumstances.

What he didn't want to think about was how to explain everything that had happened these past months over the winter—and that he would have to tell her about the unfinished business with his Benefactor. But for the moment, everyone enjoyed the food and made small talk, so Cade just smiled along and embraced the comforts that surrounded him.

After supper was cleaned up, everyone brought their chairs over to sit around the fireplace. But before anyone else offered up a topic of discussion, Eli was first to break the silence.

"What happened to you?" he asked with the unrestrained curiosity of a child that Cade would expect from him. "Were you really blown up on a train?"

"Yes, he was," Joanna replied with a chuckle. "We didn't see it. But we heard it, and then we found him lying on the ground—"

"Before we start there, maybe we should tell them everything that happened leading up to the train," Cade said without trying too hard to correct his young friend. "You need to hear about Red Sky, and Moira, the old woman who helped us," he continued, before giving Joanna a nod. "And how we met you, too."

Cade noticed he had everyone's attention as he sat opposite of the fireplace, the soft glow of the flames illuminating the room. As he told the story in a timeline of events, he did his best to avoid any unnecessary details. He believed the Johnson family needed to know why he traveled north to intercept his Benefactor in Denver—and ultimately how he, Red Sky, and Joanna formed a bond in their fight, and in defeat. But the reasons they had for taking the risk were personal to each of them.

When he eventually shared the story about the fight on the train and the explosive conclusion, he paused to let Joanna and Red Sky chime in from their perspective before their decision to return to Moira's cabin to heal and hide out for the winter. And as he looked into the faces of the Johnson family, he could only wonder what they were all thinking.

"You should tell the part about your mother, if you would like to," Cade said to Joanna when the time seemed right to change the subject and hand off the conversation. "We all left Colorado Springs a little disappointed, and that's your story to tell."

As he listened to Joanna share her story with everyone, Cade noticed that she too had opted to leave out some of the details regarding her personal feud with Spencer Carmichael. But she was very forthcoming about the bounty on her head, hiding out at Moira's, and her samurai training over the winter. It was a lot for the Johnsons to take in, but they listened intently, and he could sense that his second family could understand why she traveled north with him; why she carried Scorpion's sword and wore Falcon's crimson battle coat; and why she remained.

"But why have you returned?" Pa asked. "It's a pleasant surprise to see you again, and we're glad you're alive… but why did you come back now?"

"I fear your family is still in danger," Cade replied bluntly. He could see the immediate effect of his words on their faces, but they also didn't look surprised. "We've been holed up in a barn all winter and had no news from the outside world until Mick and Finn arrived. And if you've all heard that I'm dead, then that must be what folks are saying from here to Denver. But there's something wrong, and I can't explain it any other way besides a bad feeling I get about visions of my past coming back to hurt you."

"The man in black," Eli said, and it drew everyone's attention. "He was riding with two shadow riders in gray coats. They're still looking for you," he continued and reached over to tap his grandfather on the knee. "Can I get the knife and show Cade the note?" he asked.

Pa nodded and the young man bound from his chair to go retrieve the items from his room. Then he took a sip of his whiskey and grimaced as some wrinkles of concern seemed to spread across his face. "The arrival of the man in black tells me that people haven't forgotten about you," he said with a stern look in his eye.

"Here it is," Eli chimed in as he returned to the room. Cade smiled as he presented the blade and folded parchment. "The man said this message was for you, and that he would be back in a month. That was over a week ago."

As Cade took back the tanto knife, he appreciated feeling its weight in his hand again. The blade had no equal in his eyes, and it was still sharp enough to pierce leather armor. It was also the weapon he had sacrificed to advance on Toshi during their fight on the train. But what was lost had found its way back to him. "Thank you," he said to Eli, and sheathed the blade in his right boot.

"His face was scarred on one side, and it sounded like he knew you," Eli tried to explain.

Cade glanced curiously at Joanna and Red Sky. The thought of a bounty hunter finding the knife and bringing it to the Johnson ranch was unsettling. And why was he traveling with two shadow riders? There was something more to this man in black, and his concern for the family's safety felt confirmed.

"What does the note say?" Cade asked, as he took the parchment from the boy's hand.

"It's some sort of riddle, but I don't know what it means," Eli replied.

Cade cocked his head to one side and snickered. "Well, let's see," he said as he unfolded it and took notice of where the blade had pierced through the paper. Then he held it up to the candlelight and softly read the message aloud.

THE LEGEND GROWS, OR SO I'VE BEEN TOLD,
OF A MAN WITH SWORDS AND STOLEN GOLD.
BUT WHAT WOULD HE TRADE FOR A LIFE,
THE OWNER OF THIS SAMURAI KNIFE?

Cade slowly read the message again to himself before he lightly folded it back up and rubbed the parchment between his thumb and fingers. If he was the man of legend, then *what would he trade for a life?* Was it a trade for his life, or the life of another? And what would he trade?

"They want their gold back," Finn said matter-of-factly. "Whoever wrote that believes that you're still alive, and they followed your trail back to here."

"But the gold isn't here," Cade said and looked at Pa. "Do you still have the map?" he asked.

Pa nodded and reached into his shirt pocket. "I've held onto this since the day you left it for me, but we spent the coins on repairs and a new kitchen window," he said and leaned forward to hand it over. "I kept it safe in a book, but got it out when you arrived."

Cade took the folded piece of rawhide cloth and smiled. "I left this for you in case someone came looking or I didn't return. Either way, I figured it could be valuable," he said while he held it up for everyone to see.

"What does the map say?" Mick asked.

"It's a map," Finn corrected with a chuckle. "It doesn't say anything."

"You're both right. But it will show you what I already know," Cade said. Then he handed it to Finn and watched as he opened it with his brother. "And it says that I need you two to hold on to this map and stay here to protect the Johnsons while I make the trip to the Mission de la Rosa."

"What about us?" Joanna asked while gesturing to herself and Red Sky.

"Oh, you're both coming with me. We'll continue your training on the trail, and we'll need Red Sky for direction," he replied. "And we're leaving tomorrow, because we don't have much time."

...

Gone Again

Lucy followed Cade as he stepped out into the cool night and down the back-door kitchen stairs. She pulled the wool lap blanket around her shoulders as they stood and faced each other—and the sight of their breath in the soft glow of the lantern filled the air between them.

Pa and Eli had turned in for the night, and his four companions made their way to the bunk room in the barn. She was finally alone with the man she prayed was alive, and now he was here and about to leave again. It made sense that he should retrieve the gold, but she was tired of the talk of it and the curse it had over Cade.

"Why did you leave the map with your friends? Are you sure that's a good idea if the man in black returns?" she asked. "Maybe it's better the less anyone knows of its whereabouts."

"Agreed. It's a lot of money. Blood money," he replied. "And a lot of good men have died because of it. But I have to leave this secret with someone in case I don't return. Those two are strong enough to make the journey, and hopefully smart enough to trade it for their lives if necessary."

"You're probably right," she said before she paused and looked away. "Pa's health hasn't been doing too well. It was a hard winter, and I'm worried about him… and you."

The look in his eyes said he understood without saying a word, even if it wouldn't change a thing between them or stop him from leaving tomorrow.

"But you just got back," she said and stepped in closer. "I want to feel your arms around me again."

He moved in to hold her and she welcomed the warmth and weight of his embrace. Then she rested her head against his chest and could hear his heartbeat as he took a deep breath. "I don't want to leave either, but I have to," he whispered into her ear. "It's only a matter of time before the man in black returns, and he won't be alone. This isn't just about me anymore. If we don't have the gold to bargain with, we have nothing," he continued as he brought his hand up to caress her head and stroke her hair.

"I'm thinking that church is three or four days of hard riding from here. So, the sooner we get going, the better," he said as he combed his fingers into her hair to pull her face to his. "But this isn't goodbye. And I promise that I'll come back and make this right—"

"No," she said and raised a finger to his lips. "Don't promise me anything until you return, and we can put this all behind us," she continued, and then slowly removed her finger so her lips could touch his.

CHAPTER 6

South by East

White puffy clouds stretched across the morning sky as Cade and his companions set out for the Mission de la Rosa. The valley was in early spring bloom and a soft, gentle breeze carried the scent of green wheatgrass and sagebrush.

The farewell was more businesslike compared to leaving Moira's cabin, and Cade thought it was better that way. After goodbye hugs with Lucy and Eli, his heart hurt leaving them again. But it had to be done if he was ever to put the burden of servitude and Whitmore's gold behind him and see his sister Sarah again.

He also had a long talk with the Bohannon brothers after breakfast, and Pa seemed happy to oblige them staying on. There was much to do around the ranch, and having two able men around for some protection was a welcome proposition.

Now with four days' rations and a full belly, the three travelers were headed south at a brisk pace while Cade tried to recall the way back to El Rey. That dusty old town was his best landmark back to the mission, even though he laid a day's worth of misdirection tracks due west from where he hid the gold. He also knew they would eventually need to break across the open prairie of New Mexico Territory, and he looked for any other familiar trails that could help point the way.

When they happened along a horse path that seemed less traveled but headed east, Cade pointed it out to Red Sky. It was a good time to get off the south road and walk the horses for a bit.

"Do you know where we're going?" Joanna asked with a chuckle.

"Sure I do. We're headed south by east," he replied, and Cade could appreciate the sarcasm. It had been almost a year since he'd come up this way last summer, and way finding was not his strength. He also felt a twinge of sentiment as he realized how much he really needed Red Sky at times like this.

"I don't like being out in the open," she added. "If anyone was looking for us out here, we would be easy to spot."

Cade gave a nod but just continued to scan the horizon in front of them. For the first time in months, he wasn't being overly mindful of his whereabouts and being out in the open. It would be a long ride to the Mission de la Rosa, and anything could hit them between here and their destination. But he was tired of looking over his shoulder.

He also didn't want to dwell on the comforts of home that they had just left—and the kiss he shared with Lucy last night was just another painful reminder that he wanted to put his past behind him as soon as possible.

"That's been a good walk. Let's pick up the pace," he said to get them moving again and assuage any concerns about their surroundings. It also didn't hurt that moving targets were harder to hit.

Red Sky took the lead for the remainder of the day, and after a few hours of hard riding, he pointed to a small patch of mesquite trees on the open prairie. The clustered bunch of trees had been shaped by the wind over time, and that created a natural canopy of cover. "Let's rest there for the night," he said, and Cade agreed.

Cade and Joanna gathered up some small sticks and dried wood to make a fire, and soon the travelers were nested under their tree shelter and their accommodations on the soft dry ground.

"I can see why you would want to settle down back there, in Rocky Creek," Joanna said to make conversation. "The Johnsons were really nice, and it looked like a nice place to raise a family."

Cade stared at the smoke and flames as he mulled over what was and what could be. "Yes. I think you're right," he agreed.

"Do you love her?" she asked, and her question seemed to abruptly challenge his level of comfortability.

Cade took a deep breath and poked the fire with a stick. "Why do you ask?"

"Because a man only does what he wants to do," she replied. "Most people think you're dead. You have gold and the means to go anywhere and disappear from anyone that might think you're still alive. If you didn't want to return to Rocky Creek… you wouldn't. So, I figure there must be something, or someone, that you care about enough about to risk going back."

There was wisdom in her words, and Cade wondered how a seventeen-year-old girl could be so observant. But then he remembered she grew up on the railroad and probably traveled as many or more miles across this country than he had. That kind of experience can give a person insight beyond their age.

"You're right," he replied. "There is every reason to retrieve the gold and just keep going in whatever direction the wind blows. But I do care about the Johnson family, and all I think about is having a normal life. If I were to choose the other path, there would eventually be trouble. Wherever I go, there's always trouble. And I'm tired of running."

"What do you think will change once you have the gold?" Red Sky asked.

"I don't know. But if the man in black is working for Whitmore, and he wants it back so badly, then giving it back in exchange for leaving the Johnson family alone might be the last thing worth fighting for," he replied. "I can only hope to see my sister again and be free from him. Whether in life, or in death, I will choose who I pledge my loyalty to. That is the way of the ronin… and that's what will change once I have the gold.

"But what about you, Joanna?" Cade asked to turn the tables on his inquisitive friend. "I've been teaching you how to fight like samurai, and you're already a very formidable warrior. What will you do once this is all over?"

"I still want revenge for my father's death. Every day you

train me, the face I see when I attack is that of Remy Chandler," she replied. "Now that Spencer Carmichael is dead, Remy is the last score I need to settle."

"Revenge is a powerful motivator, but be mindful or it can be blinding. And then what? After you've satisfied your desire for vengeance, be careful it doesn't lead down a path of reckless decisions that might come back to haunt you," Cade said to warn his student.

"I remember the first mission our Benefactor sent us on was a matter of revenge," he continued. "Me and my two samurai brothers got caught up in his father's feud. And even though we won the battle and many others, I've learned that vengeance doesn't belong to the victor. It just lingers like an unquenchable thirst with those that feel scorned."

"Please tell that story… the one about your first mission," Joanna said over the dancing flames. "I've always enjoyed hearing about your adventures."

Cade laughed when he realized he opened the door to her curiosity and thought he'd better provide a little context. "It was a long time ago," he began. "I was a different person then."

•••

Cade's Tale: Rio Diablo

Fort Whitmore and the area surrounding it was southwest of Dodge City, on the border of a map our Benefactor called "No-man's-land." I once heard him say that land belongs to those who claim it, and I always thought that explained why he wanted to own as much of it as he possibly could. But equally important to him was his father's land, and the private army he had built to protect it all.

After three of us survived the samurai initiation, we were given swords and our training started to include real weapons. But the more we trained against each other, the more we were itching to test ourselves against someone else. Then one fateful day in late summer, we were all a little surprised when the colonel came to our dojo to fetch us. "Alright men, it's time to put your skills to use," he said. "Gather your gear and load your guns. We're riding south to Texas."

We weren't told exactly where we were going, but there was Toshi and the three of us, our Benefactor, the colonel, and six shadow riders in our company of twelve. And after two days of hard riding, we arrived at a small town on the north side of a shallow river.

As we slow walked our horses through the middle of town, the way people looked at us was something I had never experienced before. I really hadn't been away from the fort in over five years and everything felt so new. I was wearing my battle coat with my Katana sword strapped across my back, and I was full of pride. The way the people stared or moved out of our path reminded me that we were assembled and trained for a reason.

But this was the first time I would really be tested. Battle tested. I looked to my left at both Scorpion and Falcon, and I wondered if they might be feeling a little anxious, too. On my right was the colonel and our Benefactor—and when the colonel stopped all of us in the middle of town, I found out why we were here.

A very well dressed and older looking gentleman stepped out from the largest building at the corner of the main crossroads in town. There were two men coming up behind him, and the closer he got I could see the resemblance with our Benefactor.

"Welcome to Rio Diablo… or what the locals call the devil's river. I was wondering when you were going to get here," the old man said and looked at his pocket watch. "Late as usual, I see."

"Thank you, father," our Benefactor replied with a sarcastic tone. "We made the best time we could with such a large party."

"Who is this with you? Are these the samurai cowboys you've told me about?" the old man asked as he inspected us. "I hope they're as dangerous as they look."

"Yes, they are," our Benefactor replied. "This is Toshi, my personal bodyguard and a samurai warrior from Japan. These three men here are his students, and their code names are Scorpion, Viper, and Falcon," he said with a wave of his hand in our direction. "Between them and my shadow riders over here, we should be more than enough to deal with Captain Diaz."

"Good. Because if they're not, we'll be more than disappointed. We'll be dead," the old man replied.

It was the first time I had seen our Benefactor look so frustrated, but it seemed that we had come all this way to meet his father—and they had a bit of a strained relationship. But here we were, and as the father and son walked off together, the colonel turned to address us.

"Men, this is where we will set our trap," the colonel began to explain. "Our Benefactor wants us to protect this town because his father, Mr. Whitmore Sr., has already staked out much of the surrounding land. The railroad heading west out of Texas will run right through here and along that river," he said pointing at the gulch we had just crossed.

"We're here to settle a score with Fernando Diaz," the colonel explained. "He was once a captain in the Mexican army, but he can't accept that we already fought the war over Texas and Mexico lost. Now he leads a band of ex-soldiers as self-funded mercenaries, and they come north to steal and create chaos because they want nothing more than to stop progress and homesteaders from moving west.

"We've sent some messages that we were coming to survey the land, in hopes that news might get around. And if his band of men think our Benefactor and his father are here, they should be inclined to make a move if there's a chance to get to both of them.

"When they do come, we'll be ready," the colonel continued before he tasked out his orders. "Falcon, I'll want you on the roof of that building there," he said and pointed at the top of the hotel. "You'll be our eyes in the sky."

"Scorpion, I want you and two shadow riders to stay hidden on the road from the south. Assuming they'll come in from that direction," he said and pointed to the expanse of land beyond the town. "I want you to let them pass by and then close off their escape."

Then the colonel pointed at two other spots that would make for good cover, and he instructed the other shadow riders to split up and take positions to the east and west. "Toshi, you and I will remain with the Whitmores in the hotel," he said before he looked at me. "And Viper, I want you to find a spot to remain hidden until you can take out Captain Diaz by surprise."

"How will I know who he is?" I asked. The plan made sense, but I felt so naïve being given a task to take out the leader without a description of Diaz.

"You'll know when you see him," he replied, and offered nothing else.

I just nodded and looked around for a spot I could best ambush my target. There was one good sized tree standing between two buildings and a crooked shed, and it would provide plenty of cover for me to hide and wait.

"Now what?" Falcon asked. "Are we just going to wait around for him to show up?"

"Captain Diaz is hell bent on avenging his brother, who was killed trying to raid the business owned by our Benefactor's father. He holds the Whitmore family responsible, and we want to put an end to his renegade looting," the colonel explained.

"We left a perfect trail leading here. Trust me… he'll come. And he'll likely have twenty or more soldiers with him," he said confidently, and then pointed at a cantina. "Let's get something to eat first, and then we wait."

The colonel wasn't wrong. The following day, the people of the town had already accepted our presence and were going about their business as if we weren't there. But he had tasked a couple of local boys with being a lookout—and by mid-afternoon the trap was sprung when one of them came running to where the colonel was staked out. "They're coming!" was all he said as he pointed to the road in from the south.

"Get to your places!" the colonel commanded. "You know what to do."

I took my place behind the tree, even though it felt a little cowardly to hide. But I was also young and foolish, and too much pride can get a man in trouble. So, I did what I was told and trusted in the colonel's plan.

As the captain and his men first came into view, they rode in a formation that made it hard to count their number. They all wore older looking military coats, but I identified Diaz as the man leading the way—and because he was the only one, like the colonel, with golden tassels on one shoulder. As they approached the town, Diaz raised his hand to slow the riders, and they began to fan out. When they did, I counted at least two dozen men that moved like trained soldiers.

Then Diaz did something I think the colonel had expected. Instead of coming straight into town on the south road, the captain ordered his men to break into three groups—twelve coming straight in from the south and two groups of six or so flanking from the east and west.

If Diaz anticipated a trap, he must have prepared his men in advance. And he waited until his men were spread out and in position before he made his way into town. Once the two other groups arrived on the main street, they stopped their horses and pulled their guns as if waiting for orders.

Everything seemed to be going according to plan, but

Diaz was still holding up. Then I was surprised to see our Benefactor and Toshi emerge from the hotel together. The two men stepped in front of the building and stood their ground on the dirt trodden main road.

"Are you looking for me?" our Benefactor yelled out to Diaz to bait him. "I'm right here, you thieving coward. Come and get me if you dare!"

Whatever discipline a former soldier might have had was being challenged, as he was being openly taunted in front of his men. That was enough for Diaz to pull his gun and scream an order to charge—and the men around him immediately followed with guns blazing.

When the shooting started, it was hard to tell who pulled the trigger first. But as bullets started to fly in every direction, our Benefactor immediately retreated back inside the building. The shadow riders that were staked out along the side roads were firing their rifles on the soldiers coming in from each flank, while the colonel and the old man's bodyguards fired from their covered positions and the windows of the hotel.

Everyone was shooting at everyone. The soldiers attacking from the west flank were initially caught off guard, but now shooting back at the shadow riders. But three or four of them had already been shot off their horses when I saw the first shadow rider take a bullet to the chest. And from my position, I couldn't really see what was happening on the east road, but I could hear the soldiers and shadow riders exchanging gunfire.

But the most remarkable thing I saw was Toshi as he stood his ground while a dozen former soldiers charged straight at him. They were howling and shooting in his direction, but he had not moved since he emerged from the hotel—even as bullets hit the dirt around his feet or seemed to fly right past him and explode into the dry wood of the building behind him.

When the soldiers being led by Diaz were about a hundred feet away and coming in fast, Toshi pulled both of his swords charged. It was the most courageous thing I had ever seen, and it made Diaz rear his horse as his men stopped and circled around to protect him.

It occurred to me how hard it was to take aim from the back of a horse, especially a horse that is startled and caught in a gunfight. That had to be why the soldiers couldn't shoot Toshi as he ducked and weaved his way through the horses and slashed at the soldier's legs and torsos.

From my position, Diaz and his men were now about forty feet in front of me when I pulled my pistol and took aim at the one soldier blocking my view of their captain.

That's when I saw the first arrow stick that same soldier in the chest, as Falcon was also targeting the men who surrounded their captain. Then a second arrow took out another, and the soldiers looked completely confused by the crossfire when Scorpion and the two shadow riders in hiding behind the soldiers began to attack from the south.

As I watched Toshi in the fray, Falcon shooting arrows, and Scorpion's group moving up quickly—I figured it was time to join the fight. But my path to Captain Diaz was cut off by two riders flanking from the west. So, I took aim with my pistol to clear the way.

My first shot caught the soldier in the shoulder, but he remained on his horse. It was my first time shooting at a live target, and I should have focused on my aim. But it did catch him and the rider next to him by surprise, which made them rear their horses and gave me a moment to fix my next shot.

I thumbed my hammer back and got off a second round into the same rider. This time, I caught him in the center of the chest, and he fell out of his saddle. A return shot from the second soldier splintered the tree near my head—but the cover proved its worth. I peeled the hammer back and got off two shots while he was trying to take aim. The fatal bullet caught him in the neck, and now my path was clear. As I trained my attention on Diaz, I holstered my Colt and drew my sword with my right hand, and my shotgun pistol with my left.

As I charged out to confront Diaz, I heard him shouting the order for his men to retreat. The chaos of the battle was still erupting around me, and the thick smell of gunpowder and dust permeated the air.

While the remaining men on horseback had their defensive formation broken, I moved quickly through them while they were confused and firing in all directions—except at me. This allowed me to go straight at Diaz, who had turned his horse and was prepared to flee. If I was going to take out my target, I had to cut off his escape and do it fast.

When I was within range and right in front of Diaz, I took aim with my shotgun pistol. But he saw me, too, and we fired at each other at the same time.

His bullet grazed my neck, while the blast from my shotgun was absorbed by him and his horse. When his horse reared up on its hind legs, Diaz fell off and hit the ground with a thud. My shot wasn't fatal, but before I could advance on him, one of his soldiers again tried to block my path—and I had to fire my second barrel to defend myself.

When I turned back to Diaz, I saw him rise up and take aim at me. But then the hammer clicked empty—and clicked empty again when he tried twice more to shoot me. For what seemed like a calm moment between us in the heat of battle, we both stared each other down as I holstered my shotgun pistol and held my sword with both hands. Then he cast his pistol aside and pulled a soldier's calvary sword from the scabbard that hung around his waist.

There were spots of blood on his right leg and hip from where the shotgun blast had caught him, and I could see that he favored that side when he postured for our duel. Then Diaz pointed the blade at me and muttered something that I couldn't hear, but understood nonetheless. As if he had accepted his fate, he charged me to face his death as a soldier.

He was the first to lunge with a slashing attack, but it was off balance and easily defended. The clash of our swords put me on his left, and I was able to spin quickly as he passed by and I scored a strike across his back. He let out a guttural scream, as if the pain from my blade and the anguish of defeat were both one and the same. But as I would expect from a battle tested warrior, he turned to face me once more and pointed his blade.

The second attack seemed born of desperation, and I could feel the force of whatever strength he had left as the clash of our swords was the only sound I could hear. But again, he succumbed to his lack of balance and left himself open. After I ducked to block his jab with the armor on my left forearm, I was able to drive my sword through his chest for a death strike—and the man I was tasked with killing dropped to his knees.

Diaz coughed up some blood as he looked up at me. "Beware the men you serve. They killed my brother, and they will kill to take whatever they want," he managed to say with his dying breath before he hunched over with my sword still in his chest.

As I stepped back to look around, I saw six retreating soldiers head off to the east without their leader, while the rest lay dead or dying in the sun. There were a few more shots fired in their direction, but the fight was over. Everything that had just happened seemed to signal our victory as our Benefactor and his father approached me from the hotel.

"Gather around, everyone," our Benefactor said as he motioned with his arms. "That was incredible!" he continued as Toshi, Scorpion, Falcon, the colonel, and the two remaining shadow riders slowly made their way to where I stood over the corpse of Captain Diaz.

"My samurai cowboys are everything I billed them to be, yes?" he said to his father.

"They certainly are," his father replied. "Nobody will be able to stand against us."

"Now finish him," our Benefactor said to me and traced a line across his neck with his finger. "I want that man's head on a pole outside of town. We are going to send a message that anyone that tries to stand against us will share the same fate."

After I pulled my sword from the fallen captain's chest, I steadied myself to bring my blade across the back of his neck.

And as the fallen soldier's head was removed from his body, I couldn't help but remember what Diaz had said. *"They will kill to take whatever they want."*

...

The Reckoning

As he looked through the smoke of the fire at his companions, Cade could see they had listened intently to his story. The fabric of his memories was feeling a little worn and faded, and he couldn't tell if that was by choice or just the passing of time.

"The Whitmores sound a lot like the Carmichaels, but even more ruthless," Joanna said as she peered at him through the flames. "I didn't even know that was possible. But given everything that's happened, don't you think that your Benefactor will come at you the same way he did once he finds out that you're still alive?"

Cade winced as he exchanged a curious glance with her, and then with Red Sky—who also seemed to be thinking the same thing. If that was true, then they were both right, and he knew it.

"We should be at the Mission de la Rosa in a couple days, and then we'll return to Rocky Creek with the gold. Whitmore will certainly come for it, and for me," he said while giving the fire a poke and watched as the embers sparked and climbed into the night air. "And I'll have to be ready to face whatever comes with that."

"You didn't call him your Benefactor," Red Sky said while he slowly drew smoke from his pipe. "Did you notice that?"

"No, I didn't. Maybe it's another sign that I'm breaking free from him," Cade mused. "But this time I won't try to reason with him, and I'll fight him to the death if I have to."

CHAPTER 7

El Rey

By mid-afternoon on the second day, Cade and his companions arrived on the outskirts of a familiar little town. It was a welcome sign as he was trying to trace his way back to the Mission de la Rosa, but it also served as a reminder that they still had a long way to go.

"We should go around. I've been through this town before, and it's probably best not to ride through and be seen or recognized," Cade said as they slowed their pace for a bit.

"Where are we?" Joanna asked.

"Welcome to El Rey," he replied and chuckled as he remembered how the old man with the stained white beard had greeted him. "And I figure we are almost halfway to the Mission de la Rosa if we keep riding in this direction. The last time I passed through here, I had been riding aimlessly for over a day to try and throw anyone who might be following me off my trail. By the time I arrived in El Rey, I was in dire need of food and water."

"We are not alone," Red Sky said and pointed to the horizon.

As Cade looked out, he saw a lone rider just outside of town, but he could not make out who he was—or if he would be interested in their party. The rider just sat on his horse and watched as they rode by. "Could be a bounty hunter," he said casually.

"If we were trying to skirt town unnoticed, then we're not doing a very good job," Joanna quipped. "Maybe we should pick up the pace and put El Rey behind us. I've got a bad feeling about this place."

Without a word, Cade agreed and gave his horse a little kick. His friends did the same, and soon the town was a distant speck atop a small hill behind them—and the lone rider followed.

• • •

Ranch Life

Lucy could appreciate that Mick and Finn weren't exactly ranch hands. They mostly remained behind for protection and were doing their best to help out around the place. But she also got the sense that they didn't like being cooped up on the outskirts of town—and she wasn't alone.

"These are grown men, with appetites to match. They

can't just hang around the ranch until Cade returns," Pa said to her while chopping potatoes for supper. "Would you be comfortable taking them with you this afternoon?"

"Into town?" she asked and paced around the kitchen. She knew that's exactly what he meant, but she needed to feel more comfortable with the idea and the potential consequences. "Don't you think that's an awful risk?"

She could see Pa pondering over her question as he continued to chop, but then he put the knife down and responded in the best way he could to try and assuage her concerns. "They're just helping us out for a bit, and they don't pose a threat to anyone. Besides, I'd be more worried about what to do with them if Cade doesn't return," he said with a chuckle and rolled his eyes.

"I don't even want to think about that," she replied. "But you're right, they shouldn't pose a threat to anyone. I will ask them," she concluded and glanced out the kitchen window at their two guests.

As she stepped out from the kitchen door and down the steps, she approached the brothers while they sat resting in the shade.

"Gentlemen, would you like to come into town with me this afternoon?" she asked. "You've done a fine bit of work today, and we appreciate it.

"I need to stop by the General Store, and then pick up Eli and some grain feed for the chickens on our way back. If you're up to it, I thought maybe you'd like to come along and stretch your legs," she explained. "And if you need anything from the store, I'm sure my brother Daniel would be happy to meet you and give you a good deal."

"Sounds good to me," Finn replied as he pulled on his hat. "What do you say, Mick?"

"Me too. I've been wanting to get into town for a sip of whiskey," he replied.

"Great. I'll pull the wagon around," she said and wiped her hands on the apron around her waist. But as she untied the apron and turned to fetch the wagon, she thought it best to add some words of caution. "If anyone asks, you two are just passing through town and hired on with us for the spring. Rocky Creek has its share of curious people, and we don't need to start any stories."

"We're all too familiar with that sort," Finn said with a smile. "But whether or not they'll believe that story is another thing."

Lucy's furrowed brow probably gave away her thoughts as she realized the truth in his words. But she also agreed with Pa. It was the best they could come up with, and it was partly true. Either way, she didn't see the harm in letting them come into town and spend a little money at the store.

About a half hour later, the three of them arrived at the General Store. The brothers laughed and nodded to each other while they tied up their horses in front of the store and next to the Five Point Saloon. Lucy parked the wagon in its familiar spot and did a quick look around to see if Cobb might be snooping out his office window. If they could all go unnoticed this afternoon, it would be all the better.

As the three of them entered the store, the little bell above the door announced their arrival, and Daniel was quick to pull aside the curtain and emerge from the storeroom. "Well hello there," he said in his usual charming voice. "I was wondering when I might be meeting you. Eli mentioned that you two are staying on a bit to help around the ranch."

Lucy smiled. After hearing her brother describe the circumstances surrounding the presence of the Bohannon brothers, it sounded like her son had already sold him the story—and Daniel repeated it perfectly to keep up appearances. Then, after the exchange of introductions, she rolled her eyes, knowing that her brother was always a businessman first.

"Feel free to take a look around. If you can't find something you need, just let me know," Daniel said with a wave of his hand at everything in the store. Lucy knew how proud he was of trying to have something for everyone, as almost every square inch was filled with products and goods for sale. And if he didn't have it, he was true to his word and would find a way to get it.

"Much obliged," Finn replied with a tip of his hat, while Mick was already looking around.

"My brother and I are going to step into the storeroom to do some inventory, if you don't mind. It shouldn't take too long," Lucy said and felt hopeful the two could entertain themselves.

"Not a problem," Finn said with a wink, and then whispered something to his brother.

Lucy nodded and followed her brother as he walked back into the storeroom. Then she took the writing board Daniel handed to her, along with a pencil, to take notes. He always wanted to expand the amount of grocery goods they could offer, and this was the season to plan for it.

"Maybe those two can help you with the planting, and we could double the size of the chicken coop," he said while prattling on about expansion, and all Lucy could imagine was all the work it would take to make these ideas happen. But as she was caught up in a daydream about extra work and how much Eli would have to step up around the ranch, she heard the familiar bell above the front door.

"Just a moment," Daniel said as he excused himself to greet a customer, and Lucy put the writing board and the pencil down. She had just pulled her hair back to reset her ponytail when her brother returned with a puzzled look on his face.

"What's the matter?" she asked and assumed it wasn't anything too important.

"Oh, nothing at all. But the men that arrived with you must have left," he replied.

•••

The Five Point Saloon

Jon Cobb wasn't at all pleased today. He was disappointed to hear that the buyer wouldn't agree to his price on the fifty spring calves he wanted to sell, and he was still having a hard time finding good men to put in a hard day's work.

"Trouble always comes in threes," Cobb muttered to his reflection in the mirror behind the bar at the Five Point. On this rare occasion, he decided to step across the street with Hicks to commiserate in his self-pity over a drink. It's not that he didn't like drinking at the only real saloon in town, it's that he detested mixing company with the common folk while doing so. And today, everything and everyone seemed to add to his irritation.

"Can we get another round over here?" he asked the bartender, and pointed a thumb at himself and his foreman. "I'm here for a reason, and I'd like to forget what that is."

"It's not so bad. Think about all the good things that are happening," Hicks said. "There's a lot to look forward to this year, and I'm sure we're going to be able to work out something with Whitmore before the big railroad meeting in June."

Cobb just shook his head. "Why did you have to bring that up?" he asked with frustrated disappointment. "But you're right, and I've got to find some way to maintain my business with Whitmore without letting him roll all over me. Sending the man in black was also sending a message that he's coming to take what he wants… and with the force he could bring to bear, what will we be able to do to stop him?"

The bartender had just finished pouring the whiskey as Cobb wrapped his fingers around the glass. "We need to offer him something of value to stay on his good side, but what?" he mused and raised the glass to his lips. But before he took a drink, two men entering the saloon caught his attention.

Cobb took a sip and lowered the glass as the two men made their way to the bar. "Who are they?" he asked.

Hicks looked over his shoulder. "I don't know, boss. I've never seen them before."

"Well, they look strong and able-bodied. Maybe they're looking for work?" Cobb asked rhetorically—and pushed the issue when his foreman didn't take the hint. "So why don't you go over there and make their acquaintance. Ask them if they'd like to join us for a drink."

Hicks shrugged and turned to go do what he was told.

"Welcome to Rocky Creek. You fellas look new around these parts," Cobb overheard his foreman say while he approached the men at the bar. "I'm Hicks, and my boss over there would like to buy you two a drink."

"Thank you kindly. My name is Finn," the shorter man said to introduce himself. Then he cocked his head toward his larger companion. "This is my brother, Mick. And since you're offering, we'd be happy to share a drink with you."

"Finn, I'm really starting to like this place," Mick said as all three men made their way down the bar.

"A round of whiskey for these two. They look thirsty," Cobb said to the bartender while he extended his hand. "My name is Jon Cobb, and it's a pleasure to meet you."

"Pleasure is ours," Finn replied while the bartender poured. As he picked up the glass, he raised it to his brother and then turned to Cobb. "What should we drink to?"

"Well, I'm hoping you fellas might be looking for work. And after a few drinks, maybe we can discuss terms," Cobb said with a smile—and a small circle formed around him with raised glasses that clinked as they toasted each other and finished their whiskey.

"We appreciate the offer, and the drink," Mick said as he

put the empty glass on the bar and tipped his hat. "But we're already working for someone."

"Who would that be?" Cobb asked bluntly, and he didn't care if his tone sounded terse. He was not in the mood to be rejected, and he had a belly full of whiskey to fuel his frustration.

Mick and Finn looked at each other as if to confirm their story. "We're doing some work out at the Johnson Ranch. Do you know them?" Finn asked.

Cobb gritted his teeth and was about to reply before Hicks stepped in front of him—and maybe it was for the better. "Of course, he knows Pa Johnson. Mr. Cobb knows everything about this town, and everyone who belongs here," his foreman replied.

"Maybe the better question is, how do you know them?" Cobb asked over his foreman's shoulder.

"Well, we're not at liberty to say exactly. But we're just passing through and doing a little work around the place, so let's just leave it at that," Finn replied with a sarcastic tone.

"Mister, my boss just bought you a drink and asked you a question. It's mighty impolite to not answer," Hicks said as he snapped his fingers. "Hey Kershaw, why don't you come over here and join our conversation?"

Cobb smiled for the first time today. Kershaw had replaced Carl as one of his men who could intimidate people, and he was also the biggest man in town. He was taller and thicker than the largest of the two brothers—and every chair in the saloon shifted at the same time as Kershaw stood up.

As Cobb's big man approached, he noticed that Finn had

turned his hat around and stepped to the side as his brother came forward. "Hey Mick, why do you think he'd call over a man like that?"

"I don't know, Finn," Mick replied with a smile and hooked his thumbs in his suspenders. "He's a mighty big fella. Maybe he's bringing this guy over to do his talking for him."

"Is there a problem over here, boss?" Kershaw asked and looked down at the two brothers.

Cobb stepped around Hicks to assert his authority. He felt his heart begin to race and the flush in his cheeks. Everyone else in the saloon had cleared out of the way, and he heard someone say "go get the sheriff" just before someone out of the corner of his eye left in that direction. But he'd had too much whiskey to care about the sheriff or how far this might go. These strangers not only embarrassed him in front of everyone, hearing they were anywhere near Lucy just fueled his jealousy and rage.

"I'm going to ask you one more time," Cobb said as he sneered at the brothers. And when Kershaw had stepped in front of Mick, he felt confident enough to lean in closer to Finn, thinking the stranger might be intimidated. "How do you know the Johnsons, and why are you here?" he asked, but didn't get the answer he pressed for.

Finn just smiled and head butted him in the face without saying a word. The pain from the blow was excruciating as he maintained his balance, but Cobb knew something wasn't right when his nose felt loose on his face and blood spewed between his fingers.

"He broke my nose," Cobb said to his men, and then stood there and watched as a fight broke out around him.

Mick punched Kershaw in the gut so quick it knocked the air out of him—and then Mick reared back his leg before he put his knee in Kershaw's face and sent the big man flying back into an empty table.

Then Cobb saw Hicks pull his gun, but Finn threw an empty shot glass that hit Hicks in the forehead above his left eye. The weight of the glass was thick enough to stun Hicks and made him pull the trigger and fire a harmless shot into the bar. As Hicks stepped back and tried to shake off the cut above his eye, Finn stepped forward and smacked Hicks in the face with a backhand right—and followed with a roundhouse left to the jaw that dropped Cobb's foreman like a sack of flour.

Kershaw picked himself up and looked like he was trying to rejoin the fight, but Mick was ready for him. When Kershaw came back swinging with a powerful right, Mick ducked the punch and countered with another left to the gut. And as Kershaw doubled over again, it only took a roundhouse right for Mick to put the big man on the floor.

Cobb hadn't anticipated any of this, but he knew better than to press his luck. These two brothers were good in a fight, and much better than he thought. "Enough!" he shouted and held his left hand in the air. As blood continued to gush from his nose, he reached for a handkerchief with his right and held it to his face.

Finn pulled a knife from his belt and pointed the blade at Cobb's neck. "Now, why would you be starting a fight you can't finish? What kind of man does that?"

"I don't know, Finn," Mick replied from over his brother's shoulder. "But I think we may have worn out our welcome. It's a shame, too. Because now I'm thirsty for another drink."

A single gunshot got everyone's attention before a loud voice boomed. "Everyone stop right there, and nobody move. There's enough blood on the floor this afternoon."

"Sheriff Barnes, I want these men arrested!" Cobb screamed through his bloody handkerchief and pointed at Finn. "These men started a fight, and that bastard broke my nose!"

Barnes slowly stepped forward with his gun drawn. "Isn't it funny how you always seem to bring things like this on yourself, Cobb? Now how about we all stop fighting and step outside to discuss. Unless you have a problem with that?" he asked and thumbed back the hammer on his pistol.

"Not at all, sheriff," Finn said and put his knife back in its sheath.

"I'll step outside… but someone needs to help Hicks and Kershaw off the floor," Cobb replied. "Ask them and they will tell you the same thing. Those men threw the first punch. All I did was buy them a drink, and they repaid me by starting a fight."

Then Cobb saw Lucy standing behind the sheriff at the door of the saloon. At first, she had her hand over her mouth with a look of complete surprise, but then her expression turned to disgust and contempt as they made eye contact.

"C'mon, all of you. Let's go," the sheriff said with a wave of his pistol and pointed at the door. Cobb reluctantly made his way out of the saloon and passed Lucy without saying a word. But he did hear one of the brothers apologize to her and say this whole mess was his fault.

Once outside, the sheriff instructed Cobb and the two brothers to stand beside each other shoulder to shoulder. As Hicks and Kershaw were helped out, Barnes held up his left hand to stop them and then motioned for them to sit on the saloon's front step.

Cobb sensed it was time to make his case now that Hicks and Kershaw were present to support his story. "As I was saying, sheriff. These two men—"

"I've decided that I don't want to hear another word from you, Cobb," the sheriff said bluntly. "I'd bet the last dollar in my pocket that you're drunk, and that your men here will say anything to protect your hide," he continued as he holstered his pistol. "So how about the three of you follow me over to the jail and y'all can calm yourselves while I ask around for myself."

"You're putting me in jail with these two?" Cobb asked, feeling absolutely incensed by the idea that he would be jailed for any reason.

"Yes, I am. But don't worry, I have two cells to keep you separated," Barnes replied.

...

Jail Time

It didn't take long for Sheriff Barnes to lock up the men responsible for the fight at the Five Point, and to get introduced to Mick and Finn Bohannon as he locked them in the first cell. But there was a momentary feeling of personal satisfaction as he locked Cobb in the second cell—the man who was a constant pain in his ass.

"Now why don't the three of you take some time to get your stories straight while I go back over to find out what really happened," he said as he closed the heavy door to the cell room.

As he returned to the saloon to interview the bartender and a few bystanders that witnessed the fight, he soon had all the information he needed to resolve the matter. What he didn't know was why the Bohannon brothers were in town, but it sounded like the reason the whole fight started between Cobb and his men. Luckily, Lucy Tucker was waiting outside the jail and she would be the perfect person to ask.

"What's on your mind Ms. Lucy?" he asked and opened the door to let her in. "Because I've heard those two brothers are working for you, and I assume you're here to retrieve them."

"Yes sir, they are working for me," Lucy replied. "But they're just passing through, and I wouldn't expect them to be fighting with Cobb unless he started it."

"Seems like we've crossed this bridge before. Your ranch

hands have a history of crossing paths with Cobb and his men, but at least nobody ended up dead this time," he said sarcastically. "And according to everyone I spoke with, Cobb may have gotten out of line and even threatened them a bit, but your men beat them to the punch. Either way, I'm going to let Cobb out so he can go see the doc about his nose. But you're welcome to stay if there's something else you'd like to share with me in private."

Lucy sat down and looked out the dusty barred window while Barnes made his way into the cell room. "Come on, Cobb, let's go," he said and jingled the keys before he unlocked the door and the iron hinges squeaked as it swung open. "Go on over to Doc Miller's and get your nose looked at."

"What's going to happen to them?" Cobb asked and continued to sound defiant about his time in the cell.

"Don't you worry about them. I'll be letting them go shortly now that everyone has settled down, and they promise to return to the ranch," Barnes replied.

"I can't believe you locked me up with those hooligans. I'm going to press charges and I still want answers. Why are they here?" Cobb asked as he turned to Lucy. "And don't tell me they're a couple of ranch hands, because I don't believe you."

Lucy jumped to her feet and glared at Cobb as if she didn't owe him an answer, but she was going to give him one anyway. "It's none of your business why they're here, Cobb. And trying to control everything and everyone in this town is why you have two black eyes and a broken nose.

"But I'm glad they're here to protect us from people like you and the man in black," she stated as if looking for a reaction, and Barnes was equally curious. "Everyone in town has been talking about the man who came through town a few weeks ago. They may not know what you two talked about, but they saw him shoot a letter out of your hand and you never pressed charges against him. And that same man had stopped by the ranch and threatened me and my son. There's something going on, and you know more than you're putting on."

"I heard about this man in black," Barnes said while rolling a cigar to the corner of his mouth. "What have you got to say about that, Cobb?"

Cobb stepped back. Barnes could tell he put him in a spot, and that he didn't want to answer. But the sheriff wasn't about to back down, and calmly lit his cigar and as he stepped between Cobb and the door.

"That's my business, and nothing more. It was just a misunderstanding," Cobb replied, and he looked antsy and even more desperate to leave.

"That's a lie!" Lucy said and stomped her foot. "The man in black had two of those shadow riders with him. The same men that came after Cade Wilson, and sent by your business associate, Mr. Whitmore. You brought all of that to Rocky Creek, and don't pretend you didn't," she continued. "And my brother heard it from Ron Dearing that you offered to buy his land on behalf of Whitmore for less than half of what it's worth, and that you pressured him when he wouldn't sell."

"Is that true?" Barnes asked. "What's really going on here, Cobb? Things have been pretty peaceful around here before today, and we don't need to be inviting trouble."

"This is all Cade Wilson's fault," Cobb blurted out. "If he hadn't come to town and made a big mess, none of this would be happening. We'd be doing business with Whitmore, and the train would be coming through town to benefit all of us. But now he's dead, and we'll need to be mindful that Whitmore is a very ambitious man. Everything will be alright if you just trust me and let me negotiate with him."

"But I don't trust you," Lucy said defiantly. "And Cade Wilson isn't dead."

CHAPTER 8

Questionable Motives

"That's what I'm telling you," Cobb said, as he became increasingly frustrated that Hicks hadn't yet grasped his explanation of events. "Cade Wilson just passed through town a few days ago, and those Irish brothers out at the ranch arrived with him. So why are they still here?"

Hicks nodded, but Cobb could sense that he still wasn't figuring it out. It was the morning after the fight at the Five Point, and the owner of the Rocky Creek Landholdings Company had tossed and turned all night trying to figure it out himself. But when it all came together in his mind, he couldn't wait to share his plan and put it into action.

"They arrived with him, but then stayed behind. Get it?" he asked his confused foreman. "He left them behind to protect the Johnson family because he's planning on coming back. But coming back from where? And why?"

"He's going to get the gold and then come back here,"

Hicks said with a look of enlightenment in his expression, and it assured Cobb that he was a fairly intelligent man.

"Yes. That's exactly what I'm thinking," Cobb replied with a big smile. "Lucy said the man in black stopped out at the ranch and threatened them, but I couldn't figure out why until last night. Whitmore may have suspected or knows that Cade Wilson is still alive, but he doesn't know where Cade has been hiding and if he has the missing gold.

"Then yesterday in the jail, Lucy confirmed Cade is still alive… and the man in black threatened them because he's betting that would make Cade return to the ranch with the gold," Cobb explained. "And now we know that son of a bitch is still alive, which gives us something of value to offer Whitmore."

Hicks nodded, but then he looked confused again.

Cobb rolled his eyes and shook his head. The level of his frustration began to grow again as he looked in the mirror. He could barely recognize himself with the bandage on his broken nose and two black eyes.

"Never mind. Don't think about this too hard, because I need you to do something for me," he said as he walked behind his desk and took out a piece of parchment and a pencil.

"I want you to send this message to Mr. Whitmore," he said while writing the note. "We're going to tell him that we know Cade Wilson is alive, and that he is returning to Rocky Creek with the gold. Maybe there's still a reward? And when he sees that we have something of value to exchange, I can keep my land and stay in his good graces as business partners."

"I don't know, boss," Hicks replied. "That scar-faced fella

is trouble, and so is Mr. Whitmore. He sent that man here for a reason, and he won't be coming back to negotiate."

"Nonsense," Cobb said as he finished writing and put down the pencil. As he folded the parchment and handed it to his foreman, he felt very confident in what he was about to do. "Information is a valuable asset, and so is loyalty. Mr. Whitmore needs to know we can be trusted to run this town once business is up and running. You just make sure that he gets this message. I'll handle the rest."

•••

Spreading the News

Sheriff Barnes sat outside enjoying a cigar with his coffee. It had the makings of a beautiful day as the church bell just called all the children to school, and the shadows between buildings were being chased away by the morning sun.

This was the kind of day he had become accustomed to lately—and the quiet peace that had settled in after Cade Wilson left town. But he was beginning to suspect he should appreciate today as best he could, because everything that happened yesterday would indicate it was all about to change.

He puffed out a drag from his cigar and took the last sip from his tin cup when something caught his attention. Hicks walked out of Cobb's office and mounted his horse, but instead of heading southwest toward his boss's property just north of the Johnson Ranch, he turned east and then stopped once he got behind the Five Point.

While none of this seemed too out of place, aside from his hat back on his forehead and the white bandage underneath. He did look like he was sneaking around the back of the saloon.

Barnes was up for a little walk, so he stood and put his empty cup on the small wood table next to him. Then he shook his left leg to get it working before taking his first step. Even though the arrow had been removed, he swore he could still feel it in his leg. But putting one foot in front of the other, he was soon at the crossroads where he saw Hicks duck into the alley.

"*What's he up to?*" Barnes wondered. His curiosity demanded he quicken his pace, but he cursed the effort under his breath. Fortunately, he was able to meander across the street without hobbling too much, and then he followed Cobb's man down the alley. About thirty feet later, he saw Hicks on the steps of the General Store and knocking at the back door.

Barnes wasn't trying to snoop, but he was surprised when Hicks turned to acknowledge him. "Good morning, sheriff," he said, as if not startled at all.

The backdoor to the General Store swung open and Daniel Johnson emerged with a concerned look on his face. "What do you want, Hicks? I have a front door, you know," he said while cocking his head in that general direction. "And why did you bring the sheriff with you?"

"I didn't bring the sheriff with me, but I'm glad he's here. You both need to hear what I have to say," Hicks said and then motioned for us to come in closer.

"Mr. Cobb would kill me if he knew I was telling you this, so that's why I came to talk to you in private. Mr. Cobb just asked me to send a message to Mr. Whitmore. The guy that sent his personal army here to kill Cade Wilson," Hicks explained.

"Are you saying that Cobb was trying to have Cade killed the whole time?" Barnes asked. "After all that posturing to force Cade Wilson out of town, it was all true?"

Hicks looked to the ground as Barnes waited for an answer. "That doesn't matter now. What does matter is what's going to happen after I send this message. I think Mr. Cobb might be underestimating this Whitmore fella and what he's capable of."

Barnes had to laugh, and Daniel joined in, too. "So, you're telling us that you're worried about your boss, is that it?" the sheriff asked, trying his best to understand what Hicks was telling them. "Given all that Cobb has done, and what he's sending you to do right now… you're telling us your boss is about to do something else that's both selfish and foolish, and you're worried about him?"

"Yes. But I'm worried about others, too," Hicks replied. "There's something sinister about Whitmore and the people who associate with him, like that man in black. And Cade Wilson used to work for him, too. You know how dangerous he is.

"But there's more. After everything that happened last year, I've heard other stories from strangers and bounty hunters passing through. They all have some half-baked notion of what happened here and up in Colorado, but a few of them also know about Mr. Whitmore and that he's not a man to be crossed," Hicks said with a genuine look of concern on his face.

"What if you don't send the message?" Daniel asked. "It seems pretty obvious to me as we stand back here that you know that's the right thing to do."

Hicks shook his head. "I can't do that. Mr. Cobb could never find out that I didn't send the message. Besides, it's too late anyway. The man in black already said he would return in a month, and the note he gave Mr. Cobb said Whitmore is coming, too. He wants to own all the land planned for track before the big railroad meeting in June."

"Hicks, I appreciate you sharing this information. But there is not a whole lot I can do about it. I'm not here to protect your boss, and I can't stop you from sending this message," Barnes said as he pulled a match from his pocket and relit his cigar. "It's my responsibility to uphold the law for the whole town, and I think you should get a move on before anyone sees us talking back here."

It took him a moment, but Hicks agreed that it was time to go. As he walked away, Barnes could forgive the look of confusion on the man's face, and he could understand that Hicks was just looking out for himself and his employer. But Cobb's foreman was also right about something that was very concerning. Whitmore definitely employed a number of deadly men, and there was every reason to be worried.

"What do we do now?" Daniel asked, as Barnes watched Hicks disappear around the corner.

"I don't know," Barnes replied. "But nothing good is

going to come from this, and I think Cobb owes everyone in town an explanation."

•••

Agua de Vida

Cade began to recognize the landscape the closer he and his friends got to the Mission de la Rosa. He figured they would soon crest over the small rise in front of them that would empty into the expansive basin leading to their destination—and he whistled ahead to Red Sky to slow their horses and give them a rest.

They had been riding hard and fast since putting El Rey behind them, and by late morning the next day, they were at the final stretch. The church wasn't in view yet, but as they slowly walked the horses into the relatively flat and featureless land ahead of them, Cade hoped that it soon would be.

"Do you recognize this land?" Cade asked Red Sky.

Red Sky gave a nod. "I do. There's antelope to hunt, but days between water."

"Agreed. Except for one place, and at our current pace, we should reach the church by the end of the day," Cade said to his companions. "But getting there will be the easy part. Getting inside and retrieving the gold without being seen will not."

"Where did you hide it? Is it in the church?" Joanna asked.

"No. I was on the run… and I deeply apologize, my

friend," he replied with an acknowledgement to Red Sky—and his friend just closed his eyes and gave a nod.

After a moment of silence for Red Sky's tribe, Cade continued. "Everything was such a blur from that night, but two things were top of mind. I couldn't just return to the fort without facing some sort of retribution, and I didn't want to carry all that gold around with me. So, I traced our route back to the church and hid the gold in the only place I could think of.

"I rode all night in the moonlit darkness and arrived at the church in the early morning hours. The glow of the sun was coming up behind me, but it had not broken the horizon, and everyone was still asleep when I snuck past the burnt remains of the front gate.

"I thought it would be best to try and put the sacks into something to protect them, so I retrieved the wooden box from the storage shed where we found the rest of the gold," he said, but then realized that his friends didn't really know the story of how he had come to the church in the first place.

"There's a courtyard with an old well, and I made my way around the front of the church to the courtyard through a small gate. It was hard to see, so I sat down on the small rock wall to let my eyes adjust to the darkness.

"*Agua de Vida* was carved into the wood planks covering the well. After I took two handfuls of coins for my saddlebag, I put both sacks into the wooden box and tied a foursquare knot around it to keep it shut," Cade explained and used his hands to give the box some dimension.

"I took one last look around before I lowered it in. When I felt it hit the bottom, I tied a small loop with the slack and reached around inside the well for something to hook it on. There was crooked root growing through the rock interior that must have been from the only tree in the courtyard, and I thought that would do good enough," he said with a chuckle.

He could sense that Joanna was intrigued, but he didn't know if it was the part about the hidden treasure or where it was that excited her the most. But as he told the story, he felt the weight of the confession fall off his shoulders.

"That's where Whitmore's gold is. It's just sitting in an old well, in a church about a day's ride that way," Cade said and pointed across the southeastern expanse of grassy but featureless horizon. "The gold that's had men chasing me since that night in your camp, Red Sky… and the bounty hunters in Colorado… and the man in black who's still following me with idle threats and riddles."

"If there's a wooden chest of gold a day's ride from here, then I say let's go get it!" Joanna said with a smile and gave her horse a little buck. Red Sky just shook his head as if amused with the girl's sense of impulsive urgency, but he was next to follow after their impatient companion.

"Even if it's cursed?" Cade whispered to himself, as Joanna and Red Sky were already out of earshot.

...

The Legend Grows

Whitmore was having supper with the colonel as Lester entered the house and approached them at the dining table. "Boss, I have a message for you," he said.

Whitmore stopped slicing the beef on his plate and put down his silver utensils. "I trust that the message is important enough to interrupt my meal," he replied with a glance at the colonel sitting to his left. Then he wiped the corners of his mouth with a fine linen napkin and extended his hand.

"The message is from Rocky Creek," his trusted shadow rider replied, and handed over the folded parchment.

Whitmore didn't rise from his chair to accept the note, but his hand fell to the table and the paper almost slipped from his fingers after he read it.

CADE WILSON IS ALIVE AND
RETURNING TO ROCKY CREEK.
IS THERE STILL A REWARD?
J. COBB

"What does it say?" Lester asked.

Whitmore folded the parchment and left it on the table as he pushed his chair back and stood. Then he corrected his vest and fixed the arm cuffs of his sleeves before he walked to the bar and pulled the top from a decanter of his finest whiskey. After he poured two fingers worth into the glass and swallowed it in one gulp, he turned to Lester with a look that forgave him for not being able to read.

"It says Cade Wilson is still alive and returning to Rocky Creek," Whitmore said with heated breath. "The bounty hunter was right this whole time. But how can this be? I saw that train blow up with him on it. You were there, too?"

"I was there, and I remember the explosion. But I didn't see him die," Lester replied, and Whitmore sensed his subordinate was just trying to be honest and didn't want to provoke the situation.

"How can we be so sure?" the colonel asked. "Can we trust this Cobb fella is telling the truth? And if Viper is alive, how are we just hearing about it now?"

Whitmore gazed out the window at everything that was his, and everything he had worked for. It pained him that this loose end and nuisance of a man was allegedly still alive, and that he represented something beyond his control.

"Those are legitimate questions, colonel. But Cobb is a trusting fool, and I don't think he would have sent this message if it weren't true," he said while pouring himself another shot of whiskey. "Maybe the better question is… when is Viper returning to Rocky Creek? Because it would be awfully convenient to take care of all my problems, once and for all.

"Wouldn't you agree, colonel?" Whitmore asked rhetorically and sipped his second drink. "So how long would it take to mobilize three dozen shadow riders and ride to Rocky Creek?"

"That would be our entire calvary of men, with less than ten to stay behind and guard the fort," the colonel replied, and then paused with a sigh. "We'd need a day to prep two supply wagons, and it would be ideal if we could send them out a couple days in advance."

Whitmore nodded. He could tell the colonel understood the scope of his proposal—and since the colonel's experience made him an expert military tactician, he deferred to his old friend's prowess. But the thought burning in his mind was that Viper was still alive, and this mobilization was an opportunity to seize the gateway to Santa Fe and kill the only man standing in his way.

"I know we had planned to let our men get married this spring and move out to colonize our territory. But we need to put that plan on hold," he said with a quick glance.

"I want three dozen men ready to ride in four days," he continued, and then finished his drink before he issued his next order. "And Lester… I want you to find Toshi and Mr. Swift and bring them here. We need to talk."

• • •

An Englishman in Rocky Creek

The violet-colored sky at dusk cast just enough light for Sinclair to navigate the trail toward the soft glow of a town in the distance. He had been traveling south for days, and as the landscape ahead of him began to level out, he smiled, knowing he had made it to the other side of the cold mountain pass.

It had been the same number of days since he had a drink

of whiskey, and as he rode unnoticed into town, it didn't take him long to identify the welcome sight and smell of the local saloon. But a drink and some accommodations weren't the only things on his mind.

As he pushed through the doors and breathed in the familiar smell of booze and cigars, he paused for a moment to survey the room. It occurred to him that any one of these locals could provide some helpful information, and then he casually eyed everyone he passed on his way to the bar.

"A glass of your finest whiskey, if you please," he said to the bartender, who didn't seem at all affected by his presence. "And a little information, if you don't mind," he added as he put three silver dollars on the bar.

The bartender went about his work and pulled a bottle from beneath the bar along with a glass. "This is the finest whiskey we have, and it's not cheap," he said as he pulled the cork and began to pour. "And neither is whatever information I assume you're looking for."

Sinclair smiled and pushed all three silver dollars to the bartender. "I like your confidence. There are probably a dozen other people I could question right now, but none as credible as the only sober person in the room."

The bartender smiled as if he appreciated the compliment. "What do you want to know, Englishman?"

"Oh, you're quick too. I like that. Cheers!" Sinclair said as he picked up the shot glass and raised it for a look. After he finished the drink, he popped the empty glass on the wooden bar. "Much obliged. Now, what can you tell me about Cade Wilson?"

The bartender just laughed and shook his head. "That's a good one. I've lost count of how many men have come in here asking the same thing. The story of Cade Wilson has put Rocky Creek on the map, and especially to every bounty hunter out there looking for him. And as it turns out, you just missed him," he replied.

Sinclair cocked his right eyebrow, as that wasn't at all what he expected to hear. "What do you mean? Are you saying he's dead, or that he was just here in town?"

"Mister, that man cheats death better than a gambler at cards," the bartender replied with a chuckle. "And word has it he just passed through a few days ago. But there's more," he said and paused to wipe the bar with a towel.

Sinclair picked up on the hint and pulled a coin purse from the inside of his coat. After he fingered through it, he put four more dollars on the bar.

The bartender was quick to put his left hand over the coins and pour another shot with his right. "There's talk that he's coming back this way, so you might be in luck. And if you play your cards right, you'll get your chance to dance with the devil himself."

"Was he alone?" Sinclair asked, while putting his hand on the glass. "Because I'm also interested in a young gal that might be riding with him."

"I don't know," the bartender said, sounding a little surprised. "That's the first time anyone has asked about a girl. But if anyone in town did know, I would imagine you could ask Daniel Johnson, the owner of the General Store when he opens tomorrow," he indicated with a cock of his head next store. "Or his sister Lucy, when she comes in from their family ranch each morning."

Sinclair raised the glass and finished the drink. The burn of the alcohol was quick to numb his lips and trigger his appetite as it warmed him from the inside. "Well then, please save me some of that whiskey, because I'll be back after I look into a room and something to eat at the hotel across the way.

"It sounds like I might be enjoying your hospitality for a bit."

CHAPTER 9

Mission de la Rosa

Cade passed the spyglass to Joanna to let her look at the place they'd come so many miles to see. They arrived at the Mission de la Rosa by late afternoon, and for now they would rest and wait in the familiar spot he'd been almost a year ago.

"Who do you think owns those horses?" he asked Red Sky and pointed at the three horses tied up to a post. "They don't look like they belong to any pilgrims or priests."

Red Sky nodded. "Could be trouble."

"I don't really see anything," Joanna said while trying to look through the spyglass. "The only thing I can see is some people inside the church."

"Can you see the little gate on the far-right wall?" Cade asked and guided the spyglass with his hand in that direction. "That's the gate to the courtyard. That's our way in, and hopefully we can avoid the church and being seen all together if we can do this quietly."

"What happens if someone sees us?" Red Sky asked.

Cade took a deep breath and contemplated the worst. It was hard to tell what might happen, and he hoped to avoid a confrontation. "I think we'll need to deal with that if and when it happens. But for now, we should wait another hour or so for it to get dark. Then we go in through the gate and get out before anyone knows we were there.

"And we need a plan," he said as he took the spyglass from Joanna and closed it up.

His friends gathered around and the three sat in a small circle. "I think Red Sky should go first. Once you're at the gate, waive your spear if the way is clear."

"Joanna… once we're in the courtyard, stand guard just inside the gate. And Red Sky, there's a small door leading into the church from the courtyard. Trust me," he said with a grin. "If you can cover that door, I should be able to pull up the chest. Then—"

"Once we have the chest, we leave the same way," Joanna said.

"That's right. But without shooting, if we can help it. It would only bring more trouble and attention," he replied. "Do we all agree?"

Cade wanted some time to meditate. His friends nodded as if they knew what to do, and now it was just a matter of waiting it out. But with no fire and nothing to eat but some jerked beef and the last round of crusty bread, it was as good a time as any to find a spot of ground and focus his senses.

The smells and sounds surrounding him seemed so different from what he'd become accustomed to, and what he appreciated about a place like Rocky Creek. The time between getting here and being here again was easier to measure in days than miles. But here they were, and Cade focused his thoughts on the task at hand.

"Is it time?" Joanna asked and sounded a little impatient.

He didn't really know what time it was, but sensed that his friends were probably just as anxious as he was to get the gold and put this place behind them, even if it was for different reasons. But as he glanced up at the night sky and adjusted his hat, he couldn't help but appreciate the cluster of stars that appeared to descend upon the church.

"I reck'n so," Cade replied and stepped up to see better. Finding a good spot, he motioned for Red Sky and Joanna to come over and take a look. The moonlight would be good enough, and it looked like there were some candles burning on the steps of the church. The brightest light seemed to be coming from a fire pit on the opposite side of the courtyard— and there was very little activity other than some shadows around the light of that fire.

"It's not perfect, but we should be able to get in and put a few miles behind us before we can stop for the night. Or we could wait a little longer. What do you think?" he asked.

"We have the cover of darkness. If we hunt quietly, we should be unnoticed," Red Sky replied and took up his spear.

"I don't see anyone walking around. Let's go," Joanna said and pulled her pistol.

"No shooting, or killing, if we don't have to," Cade reminded her with a smile.

"Right," she whispered back, and holstered her gun.

...

The Well

Joanna tried her best to keep up, but Red Sky and Cade seemed to know their way around in the dark much better than she did. Thankfully, both of them led the way down to the church and the little side gate.

Red Sky was in front, and he held up his hand to stop. Without saying a word, he then motioned with his hand that this was the spot he wanted us to wait. As they watched and listened, she was surprised at how their Comanche friend could walk so quickly and approach the gate without making a sound.

Once at the gate, Red Sky pushed it open and disappeared into the shadows. A moment later, he re-emerged and raised his spear. "Let's go," Cade whispered.

This time she tried to stay close behind Cade as they advanced on the gate, but then she almost bumped into him when he stopped at the wall. He had only paused for a moment to slow their approach. "Quietly," he said softly, but sternly—and now she knew what Red Sky meant about hunting quietly.

Joanna didn't bother to respond or apologize. Silence was the point, and she remembered the times during her training when he told her to be mindful of her steps and lift her feet as she moved—and this would be a good time to follow those teachings as they picked up the pace. Once they arrived at the gate, Red Sky ushered them inside.

The courtyard was dimly lit by two candles at the base of

a small cross, but it was enough to see that everything was just as Cade had described. The garden was very peaceful, and in the center was a formation of rocks covered by planks of wood.

"Joanna, go stand by the gate and keep watch. Use your knife to tap three times on the wall if you see anyone coming," Cade said before he walked to the well and Red Sky moved toward the door from the church into the courtyard.

She found the best position she could in the shadows of the wall, but in a spot she could still see someone coming from the other side of the church. The excitement of this treasure hunt teased like butterflies in her stomach, and for a moment she looked up at the stars and thought of her father. She wondered what he would be thinking if he could see her now.

As Cade did his best to quietly remove the wood covering the well, she watched intently as he reached down into it. But instead of the news she thought she'd hear, he offered up something completely unexpected.

"We have a problem," he said softly but loud enough for her and Red Sky to hear. "Come here."

As Joanna approached where he was kneeling next to the wall, she could sense that Cade was a little embarrassed when he shared the news. "I was feeling around for the rope on the root, but it's not there."

"The rope is gone?" Joanna asked.

"Well, something like that," Cade replied, and shook his head as if to acknowledge his error in hooking it there. "The rope must have slipped off the root, because it's not there," he continued before he stood up and walked over to the shrine.

She looked down into the well with her two companions

as Cade brought over one of the candles from the cross. A damp, earthy smell of water and mud rose from the darkness. The candlelight didn't offer much, but in the flickering shadows, Joanna could see an old wooden ladder about six feet down.

"There's a ladder. If one of us was lowered down to it, I bet it goes down to the bottom of the well," Joanna said confidently, and then noticed that Cade and Red Sky were both looking at her.

"Wait, you want me to go down in there?" she asked and suddenly realized the plan she'd come up with was now dependent on her.

"You weigh the least of the three of us," Cade replied. "I don't know how stable that ladder is, but it would be best not to find out."

"I saw some rope on one of the horses out front. I'll go get it," Red Sky said and put his spear down at the base of the well.

Joanna followed Red Sky back to the gate and watched as he crept toward the horses tied up in front. As he worked to free a coil of rope from the horse closest to them, it riled one of the others just enough to cause a ruckus—and Red Sky paused when one of their owners peeked out to check on them.

"What's gotten into them?" she heard a voice from the other side of the church call out. After the man looked around and seemingly satisfied his curiosity, "Oh, it's nothing," he replied and disappeared to rejoin the others.

Red Sky waited another moment to make sure the coast was clear before making his way back to the gate. "That was a close one," Joanna whispered to him, and he just smiled as they returned to where Cade was still beside the well.

"Joanna, we'll need to tie this around your waist to lower you in," Cade said while handing her the candle and taking the rope from Red Sky. "And you'll need this to see."

Joanna stood firm while they fastened the rope, and then moved to where she could swing her legs over the stone wall. As she sat and looked down into the dark hole, the butterflies in her stomach were back for a different reason.

"It's going to be okay," Cade said, and she could tell he was trying to reassure her, even if there was no way to know that was true. It was easier for her to imagine all the bad things that could be waiting for her down in the darkness—but then she tried to focus on the gold and getting this done as quickly as possible. "Are you ready?" he asked.

Joanna nodded and shifted her weight so that her waist was now on the edge of the wall and her legs dangled into the hole. "Yes, let's do this… and don't let go," she said as she pushed herself off the wall and let her weight begin her descent. The cinch of the rope around her waist was more painful than she anticipated as soon as she was hanging from it, but she was fully committed now.

"We've got you," Cade said softly, as both he and Red Sky had a grip on the rope. "Now we're going to lower you to the ladder."

"Okay," she replied, not knowing what else to say. This was her idea, and she couldn't regret that any more than in this moment. But her companions were doing their best to lower her slowly until she could feel the top rung under the toes of her boots. "I'm at the ladder," she said as she continued her descent, and soon was able to put her feet a few rungs down and grasp the top of the ladder with her open hand.

"I'm climbing down now," she said up to her friends, and began to feel a little more confident in this plan until the candle flickered and some hot wax burned her hand. She froze and held her breath as she waited for the flame to stabilize and restore itself on the curled wick. As she slowly exhaled, she held the candle out and took her first step down the ladder. There was nothing but the damp smell of the earth now, and in the glow of the light she could see bugs crawling on the walls that surrounded her.

She hated bugs, and it was hard not to feel like they were climbing all over her. "Focus," she whispered to herself and tried to shake off the fear and panic trying to seep its way into her thoughts.

After taking a deep breath, she stepped down another rung on the ladder, and then another. It was becoming a little easier now as she kept moving down until the next rung down snapped under her weight. The sudden fall caught her by surprise, and for a moment she flailed until the rope tightened around her waist and caught her.

"Is everything okay?" Cade asked from above, and all she could see when she looked up was the shadowed silhouette of his head peering over the wall. She was further down than she thought, and she grasped the ladder and resettled her feet on the next rung. "Yes," she replied, and she quickly counted her blessings that her friends were holding the rope. "But don't let go. I'm almost at the bottom."

As she held the candle out to look down, she was excited to see a wooden chest and a coiled rope that was tied to it. It was just sitting there in about two feet of water at the bottom of the well, but it was slightly out of reach. And after she stepped down to the last rung where her boots touched the water, she realized that she couldn't get any lower.

She could see the loop Cade had described, but to reach it, she couldn't hold the candle and the ladder at the same time. "Hold that rope… I need to let go of the ladder," she called out, and then slowly leaned back to test that her friends could support her weight. Then she held the candle high and focused on grabbing the loop. She wanted to be quick, and once she felt supported, she let go of the ladder and lunged down as far as she could with her free hand.

"I've got it!" she said as she grasped the loop, and maybe a little too loudly as it echoed up the walls of the well. But she didn't care. The feeling of success overwhelmed her, and with the loop in hand, she leaned forward again and into the ladder. Then, without thinking, she hooked her right arm around the ladder to hold herself up and accidentally dropped the candle.

Panic gripped her as she was suddenly in complete darkness. For a long moment, she just held herself to the ladder with the loop in her left hand. Her breath quickened, and the more she thought about where she was and all the bugs, the more she felt in danger. But then she remembered what Cade had taught her, and she closed her eyes to reset her senses. The dark was the same with her eyes closed, and she could still feel the rope around her waist. She could also feel her right arm hooked around the ladder, both of her feet on the last rung, and the rope tied to the chest of gold in her left hand.

Slowly and deliberately, she pulled the loop of rope up to where she could slip her left hand through it. Once she felt the loop securely around her left wrist, she grasped the ladder with both hands and was ready to begin her ascent.

"You can pull me up now," she said, and even though they did not reply, she could feel the tug of the rope as she ascended. She kept her eyes closed and focused on each step up as she climbed out of the hole. Going up seemed much easier, and she was mindful of the broken rung as she felt her way to the next one. Once she was at the top of the ladder, she finally opened her eyes to see a hand at the top of the wall—and she reached it to pull herself up.

"You won't believe what happened down there," she said as she climbed out of the well, but then found out that not everything had gone as planned.

•••

Fool's Gold

Cade could only watch as one of the gunmen helped Joanna over the side of the well. Two more stood behind him and Red Sky, with pistols drawn.

The three men were able to come up behind them unnoticed because they were busy helping Joanna—and now everything about their plan to get in and out without incident was lost. And as Cade and Red Sky stood with his hands up, he looked at Joanna and encouraged her to do the same.

"What do we have here?" the only one holding a torch asked rhetorically, and Cade sensed that he must be the leader. "An Indian, a bounty hunter, and a girl in a well… now which one of you wants to tell me what's going on?"

Cade wasn't surprised to hear the stranger call him a bounty hunter, and based on his appearance, that seemed like a reasonable assumption. But before he could answer, he was surprised to hear Joanna speak up.

"We were trying to get some water," she said. "But there was no rope or bucket, so I had to climb down and find it."

It was a clever lie, but Cade knew they weren't buying it.

"She's lying, Drake," said the man who helped Joanna out of the well. "There ain't no need to climb down when the pump is right over here," he said, pointing to the pump handle.

"Good point, Halsey. So how about you take her gun and see what's on the other end of that rope," Drake ordered his man. "As for you two," he said and clicked back the hammer of his pistol. "Just keep your hands up where I can see them."

While Halsey pulled Joanna's pistol from its holster and stuck it in his belt, Cade heard the other cowboy come in close behind him and Red Sky. After Halsey loosened the rope around Joanna's waist and let it fall to the ground, she stepped back and held out her left wrist so he could take off the loop.

In the flickering light of the torch, Cade was trying to come up with a plan. They were caught completely off guard, and not in a good position to resist. But these men also didn't seem to understand what was going on or why they were here, so they might make a mistake—and he hoped they could hold out until that moment presented itself.

"Dang, there is something really heavy on the other end of this," Halsey said as he pulled on the rope, and eventually worked at it until the wooden box emerged from the well, all wet and covered in mud.

"What is it?" asked the man standing behind Cade.

"Yeah, friend… what is that?" Drake asked and pointed his pistol at Cade's face.

Cade didn't know how to answer. It was clearly not a bucket of water, so he was caught between spilling the truth or lying. But he liked that the box presented a great distraction, and he was surprised to hear Joanna speak up again.

"It's a treasure chest of gold," she said softly, and gave Cade a wink.

Halsey pulled a knife and was busy trying to cut the knotted muddy rope around the box, while the leader of these men stepped closer to Cade and pressed again about its contents. "A treasure chest of gold. Is that what she said?" Drake asked—and Cade gave a silent nod.

"Halsey, get that box open!" Drake commanded before he stepped a little closer to Cade. "How much gold—"

"I got it!" Halsey said before Cade could answer, and the other two gunmen turned their attention to their companion with the box. And with the rope around it untied, the latch slid over and the lid popped open with a rusty hinge squeak.

"What's in there?" Drake asked his friend, and Cade watched him anxiously lick his lips. He also noticed that

Halsey was no longer paying attention to Joanna—who had slowly stepped back to where Red Sky's spear was by her foot.

"There's two bags of Yankee gold in here!" Halsey replied. "Just like she said."

"Well, I'll be damned," Drake said with a smile. "We're rich, boys!"

While the three men howled and laughed with each other, Cade felt like he had a good sense of their motives—and that they weren't exactly experts at this sort of thing. As all of them seemed completely preoccupied with the gold, it seemed like a good time to play up their ego and their greed.

"Why would you think that?" Cade asked. "And what are you doing here?"

"We're wanted men in Texas—"

"Shut up, Miguel," Drake said to the man guarding Cade, and then smiled after he corrected his friend. "We're in the horse trade business, but we've recently been accused of trading horses that don't belong to us. So we're headed to Mexico and just taking some rest with the Lord… and now we're taking this gold with us," he replied, and that triggered another round of laughter amongst the three.

Cade exchanged a quick glance with Red Sky and Joanna. Without saying a word, he sensed they both understood that they should follow his lead.

"No, but you could be rewarded. That gold doesn't belong to us, or you. It belongs to the man that hired us to retrieve it," he said to the leader to gauge his reaction, and the man did not disappoint.

"Say what now?" Drake asked.

"You heard me. We're here to retrieve three boxes of gold and some other treasures hidden here at the mission," Cade replied. "And I don't think he'd appreciate it if we didn't return with his money."

"There's two more boxes?" Drake asked, and sounded completely dumbfounded before he retrained his focus and pistol on Cade. "How do you know where they are?"

"Well, you certainly aren't professional thieves," Cade said with a chuckle. "You're not the only men on the run to hide out here. And yes, there's two more treasure boxes hidden here.

"I have the map here in my pocket," he continued, and gestured with his left hand to the inside of his coat—and the folded parchment with the riddle he had saved there. "The owner of that chest is like a father to me, and a very dangerous man. We were sent here to retrieve that first chest from the well, and then dig up the other two. But I'm sure he'd be willing to part with some of it, if you'll help us find them."

"Miguel, why don't you see what he's got in his pocket," Drake said to the man behind Cade. "And if it's not a map, I'm going to put a bullet between his eyes."

Cade glanced at Red Sky and then Joanna to let them know this was the time to make a move. She just smiled back and looked ready to fight. He knew she was situationally socialized and probably a better liar, but the three men had all but forgotten about her when the prospect of a map captured their attention.

"Now, real slow… I want you to reach into your pocket and hand over that map," Drake instructed.

As the man moved in closer, Cade carefully slid his left

hand into his pocket and pulled out the folded parchment. "Here it is," he said, presenting it for everyone to see—and then held it out for Miguel to take. But as Miguel went to clasp his fingers on the paper, Cade flicked his wrist to spring Scorpion's stinger from under his left sleeve, and it stuck the gunman in the middle of his palm with the toxin covered spike.

"What the hell?" Miguel said, and withdrew his hand. But it was too late, and Cade could tell the paralyzing toxin was already beginning to work.

"What's the matter?" Drake asked. But his friend didn't answer, and Cade quickly moved to his left to put Miguel between him and Drake—who had hesitated to pull the trigger.

"Get out of the way," Drake yelled at Miguel, but Cade had grasped the man to keep him upright as a human shield. While Drake was distracted with Cade, Red Sky pulled his tomahawk and ducked into a roll that put him in striking distance—then slashed Drake's wrist and the man's pistol fired harmlessly into the dirt.

Out of the corner of his eye, Cade saw Joanna put the toe of her boot under Red Sky's spear and flip it up into her hands. As Halsey turned to her in surprise, she spun around on one foot and struck him in the gut with the blunt end. When Halsey doubled over, she spun around again and swept the man's legs out from under him. And when he hit the ground with a thud, she twisted the spear in her hands and put the bladed tip at the man's throat.

Cade let Miguel fall to the ground and slipped the parchment back into his pocket. They had gained the upper hand, and he motioned to Joanna to get Halsey on his feet and bring him closer. Then he pulled his pistol and walked slowly to the man who had dropped the torch to hold his bleeding wrist.

"I need you to listen," Cade said very intently, and made sure Drake was paying attention. "Your friend over there is temporarily paralyzed. Don't worry, it will wear off soon," he explained as he picked up the torch.

"You are being rewarded tonight, but not in the way you might have thought. Your reward is that you should consider yourselves lucky to have crossed paths with death and lived to talk about it. But now I need you, and you, to pick up your friend and sit together by this wall," he said as he pointed his pistol at Drake and Halsey and gestured to the third man on the ground.

"Joanna, let's use their rope to bind them," he said as she retrieved her pistol. But when she handed Red Sky his spear and bent down to pick up the rope, it was the first time he noticed the priest who had emerged from the small side door of the church.

The priest just stood there without saying a word, but Cade could feel the weight of his judgement just like the first time he had drawn blood on this holy ground. But the priest wasn't trying to stop them either, and when the three men were all sitting together as instructed—he motioned for Red Sky and Joanna to tie them up.

As he holstered his pistol and walked over to the box, the light of the torch produced a soft glint on the coins visible from the one open bag. And even though they didn't fire a shot, there was a feeling that he had to try and make things right, so he reached into the bag and pulled eight coins from it.

"I'm sorry this has all happened the way it did. While I didn't ask to come here the first time, I apologize for hiding this gold in the well. I knew that either I or someone else would come for it eventually," he said as he walked over to the priest and offered him the coins. "Please take this. For your troubles."

The priest took the coins, but he looked at Cade with a curious expression on his face. "I do not want this," he said. "Gold is man's curse, and it has caused nothing but bloodshed and destruction in this holy place. It is worthless to me, and it doesn't change what happened here. But if you would like to confess your sins and ask for God's forgiveness, I will listen."

Cade could only nod and gracefully step back. The priest was a man of principle, and he could respect that. "Another time, padre," he said. "And if the gold has no value to you, then you can give it to these men," he continued and handed the torch to Joanna.

"How about you and Red Sky go fetch the horses. That gold is heavy, and let's fill up our canteens before we go," he said, and watched as his friends disappeared through the gate. Then he turned back to the priest and gestured to the three men who were bound and tied.

"I know it may be bold of me to ask, but could you please do me a favor," he said with a smile. "You can tend to that man's cut when we leave. But for their own good… please leave them tied up until morning."

CHAPTER 10

Landholders

The Sunday church bell rang, and a large flock of townsfolk filed into the street and made their way to the front of the Rocky Creek Landholders Company—where Jon Cobb was waiting for them.

He knew the best way to gather everyone to explain everything related to Mr. Whitmore's offer was to catch them on a Sunday afternoon, as it was the day most people in town gathered in one place at the same time. So, he had Hicks spread the word that he was hosting a special meeting after church today.

It was a windy day for early April, and the footsteps of people walking his way blew dust across the road like a trail of ghostly apparitions. He could see the families talking amongst themselves, even if he couldn't hear what they were saying as they gathered around. And once his audience had assembled,

Cobb cleared his throat to get everyone's attention and begin his carefully worded sermon.

"Hello everyone, and thank you for coming," Cobb said and acknowledged the crowd with raised hands. "I assume you all have some questions about what's been talked about lately. Specifically, the stories floating around about plans to build the railroad through Rocky Creek, and the man that has been working to make this all happen.

"First, let me say that Mr. Whitmore is both a friend of mine, and a very savvy businessman. And I can assure you that his efforts to bring prosperity to our valley will be to the benefit of everyone once there is money and commerce flowing through," he said, trying to appeal to their common interests.

As the crowd grumbled and sounded skeptical of his opening statements, one voice could be heard above all. It was Ron Dearing, the owner of forty acres north of town—and he was going to be a problem. "This is all fine and dandy for you, Cobb. You're going to benefit the most while also making money on the sale of our land," Dearing said in a sarcastic tone. "So how much is this Whitmore fella offering? Because it better be more than what you offered me."

"Well, you see now… that depends," Cobb answered swiftly, but stumbled in his effort to retake the conversation. "What we're working to ensure is that the railroad will be happy to build track through Rocky Creek. Because if we can't agree on terms, they will go somewhere else.

"To make this as easy as possible, Mr. Whitmore will make a generous offer based on your property and only what will be needed to lay track," he said and paused for effect with his best smile. He knew his words were insincere, but he also knew that these land deals were going to get done—one way or another.

"You call what you offered me fair?" Dearing asked with a laugh. He was a mature gentleman that was well established in Rocky Creek—and Cobb also knew he could rile up a crowd with one of the most respected voices in town. That influence was second only to Lucy Tucker, and he was surprised not to see her in the crowd.

"Wasn't it Whitmore who sent those men after Cade Wilson and shot up the town? Why would we want to do business with a man like that?" Daniel Johnson asked as he stood on the front stoop of his General Store, and loud enough that everyone could hear.

Cobb respected Lucy's brother as a businessman, but he hated the mere mention of Cade Wilson—so he took his question personally. "Yes, Mr. Whitmore sent those men," he said aloud for everyone to hear. "But he sent them to protect us from that deadly killer. And Mr. Whitmore's men will offer us that same protection when he does business with this town."

"When he owns this town, more like it," Dearing said, and immediately there was a wave of grumbling amongst the crowd. "I don't know about the rest of you, but I didn't survive the war and the move west just to be bought out by some carpetbagger. I built my house with my own two hands; on the land I've owned the past ten years. And if I do decide to sell it, I'll do my own deal with the railroad company and make more than double your offer."

Cobb pulled a handkerchief from his pocket and wiped

the sweat from his brow. He felt the crowd beginning to turn on him, and he needed to talk fast. "Now see, that's exactly why we need to make this deal with Mr. Whitmore. He knows these railroad people, and he knows how to make it easy for them to do business with a town like Rocky Creek.

"Because otherwise, they will just build around us, and then nobody benefits," he said to deliver his best argument outside of the truth. He was intent on swaying the majority any way possible and doing whatever he could to avoid bloodshed.

"We should all see this as a great opportunity!" Cobb proclaimed from his pulpit to try and sell them one last time. "The railroad will bring new people to Rocky Creek. New businesses… and new products and goods. There's a way we can all benefit from this!

"Just wait and see. I believe Mr. Whitmore will be making his way to town sometime soon, and we will be happy to schedule a meeting to discuss his offer with each and every one of you individually," he said, and took a deep breath while the townsfolk began to grumble and whisper again.

"This conversation isn't over. And I suppose we'll just see about this Whitmore fella when he gets here," Dearing said, and Cobb sensed he was speaking for at least half the crowd that was still mumbling as it began to disperse.

"I'm afraid so," Cobb whispered to himself.

...

Chasing the Sun

As the weary travelers followed their tracks on the return trip, Cade felt a little more anxious and uneasy about being out in the open.

The weight of the gold was more than just the contents of the two bulging saddle bags—it was the burden of riches that seemed to attract its own attention. Leaving those horse thieves behind at the Mission de la Rosa probably wasn't the best idea, but it felt like the right thing to do. Hopefully, they would be smart enough not to follow, and the three of them could be back in Rocky Creek before anyone was the wiser.

"I think the horses could use some rest," Joanna called out from over his shoulder. "I know mine can."

Cade knew she was right. They traveled a few miles in the dark after they retrieved the gold and had barely stopped for a few hours of sleep before riding again at first light. When they pushed past their camp site from the previous night, he convinced them to press on to the spot they rested earlier in the day because it had water for the horses and maybe something to hunt for food.

"We're almost there," he said, and looked back to Red Sky. When his friend gave a nod, he waved them on. "The wash on the other side of this ridge will be a good place to camp," he continued. But as he squinted into the setting sun to try and recognize the landscape, the bigger surprise was what waited for them.

Someone was staked out under the small cluster of trees near the only pool of water for miles. It was a lone rider sitting on a tree stump next to a small fire, and he was cooking something over the flame.

Cade raised his hand as all three stopped their horses—and then lowered it on the butt of his pistol. He knew the rider could see them, and there was no turning back now. The horses needed water, and they all needed the rest and something to eat. "Follow me, slowly," he said quietly, and saw Red Sky ready his tomahawk out of the corner of his eye.

"Hello there," Cade called out as they approached the glow of the fire in the fading light. "We'd like to water our horses. Do you mind?"

The man said nothing, but he stood slowly and rested his right hand on the butt of his pistol. He was a strong looking fella, with broad shoulders and tanned skin. And by the bulge under the left side of his brown coat, Cade guessed he wore a shoulder holster under the star in a circle badge on his chest.

"I don't mind at all," he said. "In fact, I found this spot by following you."

"Pardon me, but I don't think we've met," Cade said as his eyebrows twitched. He didn't like the feeling of being followed.

"No. I don't believe we have. But I've been following you since El Rey," he said—and Cade remembered the lone rider who watched them ride around the pass-through town.

"I'm guessing you're a Texas Ranger by the star on your

chest. But why are you following us?" Cade asked suspiciously with his right hand resting near his pistol.

"Tobias Moore… pleased to meet you," he replied with a tip of his hat. "And no, I'm not tracking you. I just happened to be heading in the same direction since El Rey, and I figured that I might benefit from one of your camp spots if I followed your trail," he said with a chuckle and a gesture at their surroundings. "Besides, there's something about the three of you that interests me, so why don't we sit and talk for a bit?"

Cade eased down on his pistol and glanced at Red Sky and Joanna. They seemed equally assured by the Ranger's statement, and that he was willing to share the watering hole. He dismounted slowly at first, and then his friends followed one at a time as if they'd learned their lesson about approaching strangers.

After he walked his horse to the water, he casually removed the gold-filled saddlebags along with his saddle and blanket. Then he approached the Ranger from the opposite side of the fire. "Cade Wilson, pleased to meet you," he said with a tip of his cap, and continued with the introductions. "This is Red Sky, and this is Joanna. We're on our way—"

"Back the way you'd just come from?" Tobias asked with a sarcastic tone. "If you don't mind me saying, that doesn't make a lot of sense unless you're going back for a reason. And something else y'all might want to know… you stand out like a bull in a herd of sheep. Not many people looking like you out there on the trail. Not many at all." Tobias said as he sat back down.

"So, I'm thinking y'all were trying to get somewhere in

a hurry and avoid being seen. I suspect that's why you didn't pass through El Rey, and that's because the people there would recognize you. Sound about right?" he asked, but sounded as if he'd already arrived at his conclusion. "And believe me, they all had some tall tales to tell about you, Cade Wilson."

Cade looked Tobias in the eye for any sense of trouble, but he couldn't get a read on the Ranger. Still, he decided to play it cool for now.

"I hear the same thing, everywhere I go," he replied. Then he carefully laid the gold-filled saddlebags on the ground and covered them with his saddle and blanket. "There are a lot of tall tales and stories about me, but you can't believe everything you hear. And I swear that I did not spill any blood in El Rey."

"Not you. But someone that looks like you," Tobias said and pointed at Joanna. "That someone was after you sometime last year, and he was wearing a crimson red coat with a sword strapped across his back."

Joanna moved in next to Cade and dropped her saddle and blanket by the fire. Then she removed her hat and smiled. "I can assure you, it wasn't me," she said.

"I see that. But to be fair, I said someone that looks like you," Tobias explained and turned to Cade. "The man who was after you also killed a young woman you spent the evening with," he continued

"Scarlett is dead?" Cade asked, having no reason to believe the Ranger was lying. The guilt of her death washed over him and for a moment he felt every scar he still had from his fight with Falcon, and this anguish was followed by another familiar feeling of being haunted by a curse. When everyone unlucky enough to cross paths with him is either dead or in danger, it was hard not to.

"She was a better woman than what she got in life, and she didn't deserve to die," he said solemnly. And knowing Falcon, he could only imagine the worst of what his former samurai brother might have done.

"I've heard the man you knew as Falcon is dead, and that you killed him. Is that true?" Tobias asked through the smoke of the fire, but Cade still had to shake off the memories of his fight to the death and one night at the Dixie Hotel & Saloon before he could answer.

"Yes. He's dead," he replied. "And knowing that he killed Scarlett, I feel even less remorse for his death."

"But I'd heard you were dead, too," Tobias said to Cade. "Because you're right. The stories about you seem hard to believe, but here you are… and traveling with a runaway girl and Comanche, just like I've been told.

"I've also heard stories about a man named Whitmore. This man and his father have been pushing settlers off their land in Texas, and now here in the New Mexico Territory," he added. "Is there any truth to this?"

Cade took a drink from his canteen and nodded. The water from the church and the warm glow of the flame seemed to invite his confession, so he told Tobias about Whitmore, the fort, and how he was forced to fight Falcon and Scorpion in Rocky Creek—but skipped the details about the gold. He would have gotten to how he met Red Sky and Joanna on the way to Denver, but that was a lot to say in one night.

"How about you?" Cade asked. "I'm sure we'd all welcome

a little something to eat and let you entertain us for a bit," he added, and gestured to the prairie chicken over the fire and the pot of beans in the coals.

Tobias obliged and turned out to be a gracious trail host, willing to share his fire and his food. And as they ate, they listened to the Ranger explain why he was on his way back from Santa Fe.

He was on the trail of a suspected assassin headed west to California, as part of a murder investigation in Texas that might have been politically motivated. But that man was killed before he could be questioned, and that's when Tobias first heard about some of the other strange happenings in the territory.

"I didn't believe the stories about the samurai cowboys until tonight," Tobias confessed. "And I'm sure there's a lot more than you're able to share, but that's not what interests me at the moment. Have you ever heard of a man named Bradley Aldrich?"

"No. Should I?" Cade replied.

Tobias picked up a stick and poked the fire. The burst of embers from the coals danced in the cool night air, and Cade sensed he wasn't the only one waiting to hear what the Ranger had to say next.

"From what I've pieced together, Mr. Aldrich is a shrewd businessman from California. He's been making deals with Mexican landholders and former Spaniards, and he and Mr. Whitmore Sr. have been business acquaintances for some time," Tobias said as he continued to poke the fire. "Aldrich and Whitmore have wanted this railroad business wrapped up as quickly as possible, and all so they can open a supply chain of manufactured goods heading west… and trains full of raw materials returning east. And their plan all along was to own or control as much of this land as they can."

Cade suddenly felt that he'd been a fool all this time. "If what you say is true, then my former Benefactor and everything that's happening right now is just part of a bigger plan to own everything from Texas to California?"

"I'm afraid so," Tobias replied. "Your Benefactor, Joseph Whitmore II, is just a player in the game. His father likely tasked him with controlling everything east of Santa Fe, and Aldrich would control everything over the mountains and on to California.

"Again, this is all speculation. But if what you've told me about your Benefactor and his father is also true, then maybe there is something we can do about it," Tobias said, and then snapped his stick in half and tossed it in the fire. "Now, how do we prove it?"

Cade shook his head. He suddenly remembered every mission for his Benefactor and how they always followed orders from the colonel—and now it all made sense why they didn't leave any witnesses.

"Maybe you could meet with Sheriff Barnes and Judge Roberts in Rocky Creek," he said, thinking of the two people that might be able to lend some credibility. "They can verify some of the stories, and that my Benefactor built a private army of shadow riders. Believe me, the sheriff knows first-hand how Whitmore uses these former soldiers to control the New Mexico Territory."

"Interesting thought," Tobias said, and Cade studied the Ranger as he leaned back and took a long look at the fire. "So how far is it to Rocky Creek?"

•••

Second Thoughts

Something about the man in black continued to trouble Cobb as he puttered around his office. He also didn't appreciate how Ron Dearing and Daniel Johnson stirred up the landholders of Rocky Creek at his town meeting while he tried to talk sense to everyone—because if they won't sell, who knows what will happen when Whitmore comes to town with a man like that.

"Hicks!" he called out and took a drink of his whiskey. Sunset was his favorite time of day, and he loved to watch the sky change colors from his office window. It symbolized closure, and that what was his at the end of each day would still be his tomorrow. But tonight, it was also a time for reflection, and feeling agitated because the thoughts that nagged at him would not go away.

"What is it, boss?" Hicks asked as he entered the room, and Cobb decided that it was time to put everything on the table.

"I know that you spoke with Sheriff Barnes and Daniel Johnson. I also know that you have concerns about Mr. Whitmore," he said.

Hicks raised his hands in surrender, or defense, and it really didn't matter to Cobb. "I'm sorry, boss. But I was just—"

"Never mind that. I'm not angry with you," Cobb said, and looked his foreman in the eye. "You've always proven yourself loyal. And even if I don't appreciate what you did, I know your intentions were true.

"That said, I'm starting to have a bad feeling about what's coming our way. If today was any indication of what might happen, I'm afraid that the townsfolk won't accept Mr. Whitmore's offer," he continued. "And if they won't sell their land, I really don't know what he's capable of to get what he wants."

"What should we do?" Hicks asked, and Cobb could hear the concern in his voice.

"We'll send our own messenger. Dylan can do it. He's young and strong, and I imagine it will be a few days' ride to Whitmore's fort," Cobb said as he mused through his options. "We'll send Dylan with a note and have him tell Mr. Whitmore what he should expect when he gets here. Hopefully, he'll reconsider how we negotiate with some of them."

"I don't know, boss. Do you really think that's a good idea?" Hicks asked. "Dylan is awfully young and our hardest worker. I wouldn't want anything to happen to him. Are you sure we can't just send Whitmore another telegraph?"

Cobb shook his head. He could tell that Hicks was being a little over-protective and didn't necessarily understand how the world works. To stay on the good side of men like Whitmore, you needed to show strength and communicate clearly. "No. We've already sent the telegraph, and there has been no reply.

"What we need Whitmore to appreciate is that we'll be

here to help manage things when all the deals get done, and that we'll be the ones to help him get rid of Cade Wilson… once and for all."

CHAPTER 11

Show of Force

Whitmore looked out at the expanse of his property and smiled. He loved the view from his front porch in the early morning, and to watch the fiery gold horizon slowly advance against the fading violet in the sky. The dawn symbolized progress and his grand vision for what lay beyond the sea of grassland and rolling hills.

It was the morning his calvary was scheduled to leave and advance on Rocky Creek. The smell of chimney smoke mixed with the earth being disturbed by over thirty horses prancing in anticipation—and he couldn't help but think of everything he'd accomplished despite some unfortunate setbacks. He also watched with pride as his loyal army of shadow riders gathered on horseback and readied themselves for the journey ahead.

The sound of the front door opened behind him, and Whitmore knew the footsteps that followed belonged to the bounty hunter, his bodyguard, and the military commander of his shadow riders.

"The men are ready, sir. And the supply wagons, along with some travel guard, have over a day's head start on us. Should I have your horse brought up?" the colonel asked, and Whitmore touched two right fingers to his temple with an informal salute.

"Look around, gentlemen," Whitmore said and turned to address all three of them. "Today represents everything we've built, while tomorrow holds everything we have yet to become.

"And out there," he continued as he pointed to the western horizon. "There is a quiet little town that's worth more than it knows, and it's the lynchpin of the vision my father shared with me. This town is an important part of the legacy I'll create, and the fortune I'll inherit.

"There's also one person who could threaten it all. But that's not going to happen, because I have you… and a full calvary of shadow riders to make sure he doesn't," he said with a hand gesture to his private army.

Then he held his hat and took a moment to run his fingers along the edge to smooth out the form, but he wasn't ready to put it on just yet. "Nobody should suspect when we're coming to town, and we'll likely catch everyone by surprise," he said confidently. "I prefer it that way. And when we arrive at Rocky Creek, I want everyone to take notice and feel well incentivized to sell."

"I can't imagine anyone in town not agreeing to your terms. And Cade Wilson will eventually have to come out of hiding. Especially when we revisit the Johnson Ranch,"

Swift said, and Whitmore smiled as the bounty hunter had continued to be right about these things. "But don't worry, I'll be there to take care of him."

"I hope you're right, but I'm not taking any chances," Whitmore replied. "That man has cheated death in ways you can't imagine, just as he was trained to do. But not this time, and I'd have Viper killed a hundred times if I could."

"Been dead once myself. But the devil kicked me out at the gates of hell," Swift replied. "And he sent me back so I could get my revenge."

Whitmore nodded and turned to the colonel. "I don't want things to go sideways, but if they do… we'll have to be mindful of any sheriff or witnesses trying to be a hero," he said with a pause. "And if we need 'wild fire' to cleanse Rocky Creek, we'll just rebuild on the ashes.

"Now, please get my horse. It's time," he said to the colonel and adorned his hat. Then he turned to address his samurai bodyguard, and Toshi acknowledged him with a solemn and empty expression.

"What happened in Colorado has been discussed, and forgiven," he said with a heavy breath. "But let's understand each other, because we've organized the bulk of my men to make my intentions equally clear to anyone that would try and stand in my way.

"Expanding this frontier is my destiny… and you will not fail me again."

•••

Return to the Ranch

After days of hard riding, the familiar sight of the welcoming landscape was enough to inspire Cade to press on. The four riders had followed their tracks all the way back to Rocky Creek, and they only stopped when they needed to rest the horses.

The mid-day sun was warm as they crossed the prairie and found themselves on the road leading north into town. An hour later, Cade could see the arched sign for the Johnson Ranch in the distance. He was hungry and exhausted, and he figured everyone else was, too. But it was worth it to be back, and he was grateful that his companions and the Texas Ranger were also inclined to reach their destination as quickly as possible.

As they approached the sign and the turn toward the ranch, Cade brought everyone to a halt. His horse sounded equally tired, and it was time to get some rest. But first he needed to direct the Ranger to town.

"Just stay on this road for another mile," he said to Tobias, and pointed to the buildings on the horizon. "You'll see the jail and the courthouse plain enough, and you can tell Sheriff Barnes about our conversation. I'm sure he'll be happy to share his version of the story, and let you know when Judge Roberts will be back in town. And please get yourself a warm meal and a room at the hotel on me," he continued, and pulled the last gold coin from his coat pocket.

Tobias took the coin and examined it as if completing

the final piece of this puzzle. "Much obliged," he replied. "I'll be just fine, and I assume I can find you here before I leave."

"I reck'n so," Cade replied, and then watched for a moment as the Ranger continued down the road.

"I'm so hungry. I hope there's something to eat," Joanna said, and Cade realized that while they had returned to the ranch, they were likely unexpected.

"Let's find out," he said, and motioned for Red Sky and Joanna to follow his lead. As they made their way down the trail, the dog announced their arrival and the Bohannon brothers were the first to see them coming.

"Would you look at that, Mick. Because if I didn't see it for myself, I wouldn't believe it," Finn said with a chuckle. "But here he is. The legend of Rocky Creek has returned."

Mick laughed and tipped back his hat. "Welcome back, Mr. Wilson. It's good to see you again, and hopefully you've returned with what you were looking for?"

Cade smiled and gave a nod. Given that he had lost sense of what day it was or how long he was gone, it just felt good to be home. "*Home*," he thought to himself, and it occurred to him that more than ever, it felt like this is where he belonged.

"Boy, do we have some stories to tell you," Joanna said as she dismounted. "And if I never have to ride south again, I'll be all the happier for it."

"C'mon Red Sky, let's get our horses some food and water," Cade said as he dismounted, and Lucy and Pa emerged from the house.

Lucy didn't say a word, but the smile on her face was bright enough to break through any clouds of fatigue—and

Cade could almost smell the scent of her hair from where he stood.

"Don't worry yourselves. I'll take care of the horses," Mick said, and Cade sensed that his friend was freeing him up to be welcomed back by the Johnson family.

"You must be starved. We've got some biscuits leftover from breakfast, why don't you rest a bit and I'll cook up some bacon," Pa said and went back inside the house.

Cade smiled and took a moment to appreciate the gathering of people that seemed just as happy to see him return as he was to be here. It was a good feeling to have friends and family again, and to be somewhere where his heart was at peace.

"Let me get something first," he said as he pulled the gold-filled saddle bags of gold and slung them over his shoulder. "Because my horse has been bearing this burden long enough."

"Is that what I think it is?" Finn asked.

"Indeed it is, my friend," Cade replied. "Your payday has come."

• • •

The Church Bell

Sheriff Barnes walked into the General Store for some cigars, and he caught Daniel Johnson in his usual spot, having some afternoon coffee.

"What can I do for you, sheriff?" Daniel asked, and Barnes thought he was joking. He'd been coming here for the past two years about this same time of day, and he was usually looking for the same thing every time. But he smiled at the pleasantry, and could appreciate that Daniel was always helping a customer or sitting in front of his window—and the store owner treated each time he came in like it was a new day.

"A handful of cigars, if you please. There's a Texas Ranger in town, and he's getting settled in at the hotel. I thought it would be nice to have some cigars and a little whiskey," Barnes replied, and Daniel smiled. But as the store owner got up to open the wood cabinet, his attention was distracted by a young rider who came racing into town and tied up his horse across the road.

He recognized the young man by sight, but not by name. The rider was one of Cobb's men, and from the looks of him, he was bringing some urgent news to his boss the way he entered the Rocky Creek Landholders Company.

A few moments later, Barnes was still exchanging pleasantries with Daniel and curiously watched as Cobb, Hicks, and the young man emerge from the building and the two of them went off in different directions. Hicks started walking towards the sheriff's office while the young man hurried up the street towards the church. And then a moment later, the sound of the church bell echoed through the town—and it continued to ring, which was an alarm that something was wrong.

Barnes stepped out of the General Store and onto the front stoop, and the sound of the church bell was just that much louder. Daniel joined him outside, as they were both invested in knowing what all the commotion was about.

"What's going on, Cobb? Is there a fire?" Daniel asked, but Cobb did not answer.

Barnes appreciated the question and suspected Cobb might be waiting until everyone had gathered in the street to explain himself. But whatever it was, Barnes sensed it was anything but good news.

Soon enough, everyone in town had gathered and looked north to the church as the school children filed out. The crowd on the street was full of familiar faces, but there were a few new ones, too. And from the south, Hicks made his way back to the crossroads with Tobias following behind.

When the church bell had stopped, the young rider made his way back to where everyone was gathering and stood next to Cobb.

"Folks, there's something you need to know," Cobb said as he raised his hands to bring attention to himself. "Let's not be too alarmed, but let me tell you that—"

"There's an army of men heading this way!" the young man blurted out. "I saw them about a day ago and high-tailed it back. At least thirty men on horses, and I'm guessing they'll be here by mid-day tomorrow."

Barnes could tell that Cobb didn't appreciate the young man stealing his thunder, but it was too late now.

"Is this Whitmore, the man you've been telling us about?" Barnes asked, and the gathered crowd began to grumble. "Because it sounds like that man is coming to take over the town."

"Let's not jump to conclusions," Cobb tried to explain.

"We have Dylan's word for what he saw, but I'm sure this isn't anything to worry about."

"Nothing to worry about?" Daniel said aloud for all to hear. "The last time someone came to town because of Whitmore, over a dozen men were killed, the sheriff and my family was almost tortured to death, and I had a piece of my ear shot off.

"I think you know more than you're telling, and we should definitely be worried," Daniel continued as Eli walked up beside the two of them.

"That was because of your friend, Mr. Wilson. If we had just turned him over, none of that would have happened," Cobb replied to try and calm the crowd, but it was clear to Barnes that what Daniel said was true—and it was time to prepare for the worst.

"We can't trust that to be true," Daniel quipped back. "And the fact that you and Mr. Whitmore are in business together means we should trust you even less."

The gathered crowd grumbled even louder, and Barnes tapped Daniel on the arm. The store owner had made his point, but arguing with Cobb was not going to stop the men from coming or assuage the concerns of the townsfolk.

"What should we do?" Eli asked, and Daniel put his hand on his nephew's shoulder.

"Get back to the ranch, as fast as you can," he said to the boy. "Tell Pa and your mom the news and see if those two brothers who arrived with Cade can come meet with me at the store after supper tonight."

Barnes watched as Eli took off down the street and weaved

his way through the crowd. He was a smart boy from a good family, and the sheriff couldn't help but remember what had happened out at the Johnson property last year.

"I suppose there's much to discuss," Barnes said to Daniel. Then he exchanged a glance with the Ranger who was standing with the crowd—and with only a nod between the three of them, he sensed they all knew what needed to happen next.

•••

Call to Arms

It was the time of day that Cade was accustomed to afternoon tea. There were a number of things he appreciated about Moira and his stay with her, but only one reminded him of the rituals that were consistent with training—and that was the time of day everyone would stop to socialize.

He sat back in the cool shade and reflected on how far they had journeyed to the Mission de la Rosa and back just to be here on the Johnson's front porch, and how some tea would go well with all the conversations going on around him. And for a moment, he thought he heard a bell ringing off in the distance as everyone caught up on the events of the past week.

Mick and Finn told the story of their fight with Cobb at the Five Point Saloon. Like everything else they did together, they shared details like brothers, but Mick was definitely the funnier one of the two. Aside from having to spend time in jail with him afterwards, they were happy to hear that Cobb was the type of fella that had it coming.

Joanna detailed her experience in the well, and she got a few laughs at Cade's expense for having to climb down into it. She added the part about the three men who tried to steal the gold from them when she crawled out, and then she took Red Sky's spear and did a little demonstration of how she disarmed one of the horse thieves.

"Another curious thing happened on our way back. We met a Texas Ranger," Cade said as he removed his hat to cool his head and ran his fingers through his hair. "He's in town right now to meet with Sheriff Barnes and talk about my former Benefactor."

Rolly's ears perked up, and he barked in a way that sounded more like an announcement than a warning. Then the dog bolted from the porch and down the trail to meet Eli, who was running up the trail on his way home.

"Why is he home so early?" Lucy seemed to ask herself about her son's return, as Cade and everyone else turned to watch the boy approach. And he must have run the whole way from town, because he was completely out of breath when he arrived at the front porch.

"Cade, I'm so glad you're back," Eli managed to say while catching his breath. "One of Cobb's men rang the church bell to alarm everyone in town. There's more than thirty men heading this way. The man that works for Cobb said so, and I think he was telling the truth because he looked really scared.

"The man said the army of men will be here by tomor-row, and so uncle Daniel sent me to tell you right away," Eli continued and looked at the Bohannon brothers. "He says there will be a meeting tonight at the General Store after supper."

"What's the meeting about?" Lucy asked, but Eli only shrugged his shoulders and Cade could tell that's all he knew.

Cade took a deep breath before he stood up and waved for Eli to approach him. After he gave the boy a big hug, he put his hands on Eli's shoulders. "Thank you for getting here as fast as you could. I suspect your uncle is trying to prepare for what's coming."

Then he looked at Red Sky, Joanna, and the brothers to think hard and be considerate about what he would say next.

"I didn't expect that this would be the next move, or that it would come so soon. But it sounds like Whitmore is sending a whole lot of trouble this way. More trouble than any of you deserve," he said and slowly shook his head. "Because if this means what I think it does, Whitmore is heading towards Rocky Creek with his army of shadow riders. And that's a dangerous thing, because there's no limit to what he'll do to get what he wants.

"But this isn't your fight, and I'll understand if you won't be joining me at the meeting tonight," he said with a furrowed brow and a heavy conscience.

Red Sky was the first to stand. "Our fight isn't over yet, and I'm with you to the end," he said as Joanna moved in beside him. "And instead of us taking the fight to the great house, we can defend ourselves better here."

"Agreed. That man needs to be stopped," Joanna said confidently—and Cade took notice that something about her had changed since they left Moira's and retrieved the gold.

"We stand a much better chance of being prepared for him if he isn't expecting us."

"That's true," Cade said. "We have surprise on our side if he doesn't know we're here."

"But he probably does," Lucy said, and sounded a little embarrassed. "Cobb knows you're alive, because I told him the day Mick and Finn got into that fight. And Daniel knows that Hicks sent a message to Whitmore. I'm so sorry."

"It's okay. It's not your fault this is happening," Cade said and hoped she wouldn't despair over something beyond her control. "The man in black was probably sent here because Whitmore already suspected that. And now we know why he's bringing a full cavalry of shadow riders," he continued and turned to the brothers. "But he doesn't know about the two of you, and this is as good a time as any to clear out."

The brothers looked at each other and then Finn smiled as he spoke for both of them. "Appreciate you looking out for us. We've got a little money in our pockets because of you, and it makes sense to enjoy it before we're dead.

"But Moira would never let us live it down if we cut and run, and it sounds like you still need all the help you can get," Finn said with a tip of his hat. Then he gave the coins in his hand a little toss, and the sound of them clinking together made him smile. "Besides, if there's a chance to earn some more of these… then count us in, too."

...

Empty Chairs

Supper was pleasant, but the mood was solemn and the conversation light. As Lucy glanced around the room full of people, she could appreciate that everyone had fashioned something to sit on because they didn't have enough chairs. But it wasn't at all festive of Cade's return, and there were moments where the only sound was the ting of utensils on plates.

The tension surrounding the meeting tonight hung over the house like a cloud. The sense of dread that accompanied the unknown was something she still wasn't used to, even though the past year seemed like there were too many days like this.

"How true is this story? Are we really supposed to believe that an army of men will be here tomorrow?" Finn asked, and Lucy wished she could join in his skepticism. But she couldn't.

"Hard to say," she replied with a glance at her son. "But I believe what Eli heard in town today, and I've seen the Dylan boy around town. He seems pretty honest, and too good of a person to be working for Cobb."

Everyone looked at Lucy. The attention made her feel uncomfortable and desperate for someone to change the subject—and only Cade seemed to truly realize the danger heading their way.

"I want to thank you all for being here," Pa said with a big smile, and the awkward mood seemed to dissipate like smoke in the fireplace. Her father was always a gracious host, and that was something she admired about him.

"You're here out of the kindness in your heart, and I can't imagine what you're all thinking right about now," he continued. "But God is looking over us. And for the moment, I hope you've all enjoyed supper with us and whatever hospitality we can extend to you. Because we're also glad to see that Cade has such good people for friends, and we can't thank you enough."

"We all appreciate your hospitality," Cade replied, and those words were echoed by the others. "And speaking of the meeting tonight, we better get a move on before dark."

As everyone began to stand up and the sound of chair legs shifting under their weight filled the room, Lucy was quick to comment about the cleanup. "Yes, of course. My brother will be anxious to talk with you. We'll take care of your plates… you just take care of yourselves," she said, and then realized how foolish that must have sounded.

But nobody else seemed to mind or didn't catch what she said over the shuffle of footsteps on their way to the door—and Pa was there to escort everyone and bid them good evening.

"We'll be back in a few hours, and we'll try to turn in without disturbing you," Cade said as the last person to leave. "Unless you want to wait up for us," he added with a smile and adorned his hat.

Lucy smiled, but opted not to follow him out the door. She didn't want to watch Cade ride off, and she didn't want to think about the meeting.

As she looked around at all the dirty plates and empty

chairs, a thought crossed her mind that was also something she'd been trying to ignore—and that was the feeling that everyone might not be here tomorrow.

174

CHAPTER 12

Seven of Eight

Sheriff Barnes stood in front of the General Store in the fading light, and he looked up begrudgingly at Cobb's backlit silhouette in the window of his office across the road. He didn't expect the man responsible for this mess to join the meeting tonight, but he was equally frustrated to feel watched in silent judgement.

He had just spent the afternoon explaining the events of the past year to the Texas Ranger who stood next to him, and how he'd never witnessed anything like Cade Wilson or how he cut down all those men. And after he listened to Tobias tell the story about why he was here, the business connection between Cobb and Whitmore made sense. But neither of them really knew what to expect tomorrow when Whitmore would arrive with his private army.

"What exactly are you hopeful to accomplish tonight?" Tobias asked, and Barnes turned to answer as best he could.

"If what I believe is about to descend on our town tomorrow, I can only hope to be prepared for the worst," he replied as Daniel had stepped outside to join them.

"Yes, sheriff," Daniel replied. "And we should also hope for the best."

The sound of horses interrupted their conversation, and they all looked to the south to see five riders approaching. They were quite a sight, and a welcome one at that. As they slowed at the crossroads, Barnes smiled for the first time all day when he saw who was leading them.

"Well, I'll be damned," Barnes said while the riders pulled up in front of the store. "I never thought I'd be so happy to see you again, Mr. Wilson."

"Thanks, sheriff," Cade replied. "Good to see you, too. And I brought some friends with me, if you don't mind," he continued with a hand gesture to the four riders with him.

As Cade dismounted and introduced Red Sky and Joanna, Barnes chuckled a little when it came to the Bohannon brothers. "Oh, we've already met," the sheriff said, and motioned for everyone to step inside the store.

Daniel was at the door to greet everyone and usher them in. He also appeared equally surprised and happy to see Cade again. "I heard you were back, but I wish it was under better circumstances."

"What's heading this way is much bigger than all of us, trust me," Cade said. "I appreciate you calling this meeting tonight, and it smells like you've made a fresh pot of coffee."

"Indeed. I put some on thinking we'd need it," Daniel replied. "Sheriff, is there anyone else coming tonight?"

"I'm afraid not," Barnes replied. He had hoped some of the townsfolk would be willing to stand with them, but he also understood why they'd opt not to as the eight of them filed into the General Store.

"I asked Mr. Dearing to shepherd the townsfolk and keep them off the street tomorrow. I also let him and a few others access the armory we collected the last time you were in town," he said to Cade.

"Understood," Cade said with a nod and glanced around the room. "Tobias, I assume the sheriff has confirmed some of the stories I've told you, and that you've heard what is coming this way."

"I have, and I want to meet Whitmore and see this army for myself. But unless he's wanted or I need to help uphold the law, there's not much I can do outside of Texas," the Ranger replied.

"There are only seven of us against Whitmore's calvary of shadow riders," Cade said, and Barnes couldn't disagree with the pessimistic tone in his voice.

"What about me?" Daniel asked. "And what about a few of the folks around here that are willing to fight?"

"You've proven yourself sure enough, but you need to look after your family," Cade replied. "Besides, someone will need to be here to help organize this town, no matter what happens."

"Who are these shadow riders? I've been in a lot of fights, but I've never heard of such a thing… right Finn?" Mick asked, and his brother nodded.

"The shadow riders are mostly former Confederate soldiers

who now work for Mr. Whitmore. Some were friends of mine who brought me to the fort," Cade explained. "They're called shadow riders because even though their allegiance has changed, they still conduct themselves like uniformed soldiers and they would follow us everywhere we went. They're good in a fight, trust me. But they also follow orders, and so our objective is clear."

"What is our objective?" Joanna asked.

"To avoid a fight and any bloodshed at all costs," Barnes replied, and the sheriff looked around the room to make sure everyone agreed.

"So, how do you suppose we do that?" Finn quipped back.

"We capture the leader and force a stand down," Cade replied. "Whitmore is the head of the dragon, and his colonel commands the shadow riders. If we can capture Whitmore and take out the colonel… we can all have peace."

•••

The Best Defense

The rest of the meeting shifted to tactics after everyone agreed to the plan, and Cade knew that nothing had changed since Colorado. He still needed to capture Whitmore to gain his freedom, or this fight would never end.

He also knew that executing the plan would not be easy. If Whitmore was coming, then so were Toshi and the colonel—and it would take more than fireworks to distract the men under his command. But somehow the conversation going on around the room made him smile.

"I can understand that capturing Whitmore is the objective, but there's still the part about us being completely outnumbered," Mick said, and Cade couldn't argue with him.

"Our best defense is using the cover of the buildings and whatever obstacles we can create for ourselves. If we can confuse them and catch them in the crossfire, we will have the advantage" he replied. "But we also need to draw them in and hold 'em at the crossroads. It will be the closest we can get to Whitmore, because he will likely be behind the front line."

"Just like Rio Diablo!" Joanna said, and her outburst caught everyone a little by surprise. "The story you told us about Captain Diaz. You drew them in and they took out their leader," she added with a look around to everyone that didn't know the story.

"What happened at Rio Diablo?" Tobias asked, and Cade was reminded that he was a Texas Ranger.

"It's an old story from years ago, but she's right," Cade replied. "We were outnumbered, and we drew the calvary of former Mexican soldiers into the center of town. Then we surrounded them from the corners and cut off their exits. I was able to hide in a great position until my target, their captain, was close enough to attack. After I took out their leader, any rider still on a horse retreated."

"We call that an ambush," Barnes commented. "And how would we keep innocent people from getting caught in the crossfire?"

"Gather everyone in the church," Cade replied.

"The church will be our last stand, and we should have some men with rifles to defend it. I want to believe that Whitmore isn't coming here to destroy the town, but I wouldn't put it past him either. He's ordered us to do similar things to drive people off their land and burn any trace of them, and he calls it 'wildfire.' If there's no witnesses and everything they owned is burned to the ground, he can make up any story he likes. So be mindful if you hear those words.

"There's a reason he's bringing such a force to bear, and I know how badly he wants to control the land meant for the railroad. If he controls it now, he'll control it for years to come. I've also done some terrible things in all the years I regret being loyal to him, and I know that our freedom is tied to our defense of Rocky Creek."

"So, we corner Whitmore and these shadow riders, and then what?" Daniel asked, and Cade appreciated that he brought the meeting back to focus.

Cade could appreciate the question, as Daniel had some experience with shadow riders, and they would be up against trained soldiers. He tried to remember his previous survey of the town and how they might be able to defend themselves when his friend offered some advice.

"We attack from everywhere at once to confuse them," Red Sky said. "The army will need to defend an attack from the street, the corners, and the high ground."

"Nobody in this room is going to be the first to fire a shot. Do you hear me?" Barnes said, and Cade respected his position as the town's law man.

"If we have to wait until they shoot first, then how do we keep them from shooting at us?" Joanna asked.

"Nail bombs," Finn said matter-of-factly. "We reduce their visibility and create a distraction with some nail bombs."

"You're going to stop them with nails?" Cade asked with a sarcastic curiosity.

"One time we were out surveying and laying some track, and there happened to be a pile of railroad spikes near a crate of dynamite. A little brush fire broke out and got to that crate of dynamite… and let's just say that the result was surprising," Finn replied with a hand gesture and then dug his hand into the crate of hardware nails in front of him. "If we can find some gunpowder or couple sticks of dynamite, I might be able to do something similar with some dirt and these nails. And it could help take the fight out of some of them, too."

Cade looked to Daniel and then back at Finn. "Remind me to tell you about my experience with dynamite sometime," he said with a smile. "I'm sure Daniel can help you gather some supplies, and the owner of the mining and hardware store should have anything he doesn't.

"Now let's go over the plan once more and what we need to do tomorrow."

...

Joanna's Gambit

Joanna was the first to step out of the General Store, and she inhaled a deep breath of the cool night air. She felt pretty confident about her role tomorrow, even if the idea of defending a town against an army sounded like the furthest thing she could ever imagine doing.

She looked up at the illuminated office that was upstairs and across the road. There was nobody in the window, but she had heard plenty about Jon Cobb. And in this moment, she wondered if they should have given more thought to what he might do tomorrow.

"Hello, young lady," came a familiar voice from the shadows between the store and the saloon. A voice she remembered at the same time the Englishman stepped forward.

"I must say that you're looking much better than when we first met, and quite beautiful, too," Sinclair said with a tip of his hat.

Joanna instinctively put her hand on the butt of her pistol. He was too far for the sword, as she quickly thought through her options to defend herself. And with Cade and Red Sky just inside the store, she thought about how to warn them, too.

"Let's not play with guns," he said with the smooth, calm voice she remembered at the train station in Colorado. "If I wanted to shoot you, I could have done that already."

His words made sense, and she had to admit that he had the element of surprise. "So why are you here, bounty hunter?"

Sinclair smiled. "A woman that's quick and to the point. I like that," he replied. "And funny you should ask, because I've been paid to find you and bring you back alive to Mr. Victor Carmichael. It would seem the two of you have some unfinished business."

Seeing Sinclair and hearing the Carmichael name again was the last thing on her mind. It was also something she didn't need to be worried about tonight. And as he took a step closer, she let her fingers dance over the butt of her pistol.

"There's two ways this can go, and I should let you know that I only have to bring you back alive… he didn't say in what condition," he said with a smile. "And while I may shoot left-handed now, I'd bet my life I'm still faster than you. But I'd prefer not to," he continued and motioned with his right hand. "So, if you please, how about you slowly move your hand off that pistol."

Joanna was still thinking about going for the shot. If she was going to have a fighter's chance and warn her friends at the same time, this was it. But she also remembered that Sinclair was faster than Cade with a gun, so she reluctantly decided to back down for the moment and let her right hand fall away.

"There you go. Now we can be polite about this," Sinclair said, but he didn't sound as condescending about it. "Let's talk."

"What do we have to talk about?" Joanna asked.

"I'm no fool, Joanna Carter. I came here looking for you, and here you are," he replied.

"But I've also heard about what's coming this way, and

I'm guessing that's what the lot of you just met about," he continued. "You're all crazy if you think anyone is going to survive whatever fight Whitmore is bringing to town. And I should know, because I was with him back in Colorado and I know what he's willing to do to if Cade Wilson gets in his way.

"But I'm not here for him because that bounty has been pulled. As far as I'm concerned, you're best off coming quietly with me and avoiding any unnecessary trouble tonight—"

"Are you suggesting that I come with you right now without a fight, or die tomorrow in a fight I can't win?" Joanna said, and laughed in his face.

"Something like that," Sinclair replied. "While I do have some unfinished business with Whitmore myself, and as much as I'd like to get my stuff back… I also know when to pick my battles."

Joanna sensed that the bounty hunter had played his hand, so she decided to see how far she could push this conversation—and maybe even stall long enough for Cade and Red Sky to come out.

"I'll make you a deal, Sinclair," she said, just as the idea popped into her head. "There's no way I'm leaving my friends, and there's no way my friends would let me leave with you. But if I survive tomorrow, I will gladly come with you. And when you take me back to Victor Carmichael, I will finish my business with him, too."

There was a sound of shuffling footsteps from inside the store, and Joanna hoped that her friends were finally about to make their way outside.

"What do you say? Do we have a deal?" she asked.

"We have a deal, Joanna Carter. I'll see you tomorrow," Sinclair replied, and he slowly backed into the shadows.

•••

No Regrets

Lucy sat on top of her bedsheets and watched the shadows from the flickering candle dance across the ceiling of her room. Pa and Eli had both turned in for the evening, and the house was quiet as she waited impatiently for Cade and his friends to return.

She anxiously brushed her hair and couldn't stop thinking about how she felt the day she heard Cade was dead. That the news came from Cobb made her resent him even more. But the pain in her heart was that she had let him ride off without confessing her true feelings for him, or to herself.

Now he had returned, and so did the danger that surrounded him—but not entirely because of him. Either way, whatever might happen tomorrow, it wasn't hard to imagine the worst. And though she hadn't been with a man since her husband James had passed away years ago, she felt that it was time to feel love and be loved again. Because the thought of losing Cade without expressing her love would be a regret she couldn't bear for the rest of her life.

Outside her window, the sound of horses made Lucy

stand up. She didn't know what time it was, but the meeting in town must have lasted well over an hour. Long enough for it to be dark outside and hard to see, and that's why she left some oil lamps burning; with one on the table of the front porch window, one in the kitchen; and a third one hanging from a post at the entrance to the barn.

She listened as they came around the house to tie up their horses—and while Rolly let out a low growl, she was happy he didn't raise a fuss. Their voices and the conversation between them were quiet and indistinguishable, but there was a brief outburst of laughter and the loudest of the voices sounded like Mick. But whatever amused them was quickly shushed, as they were now between the house and the barn.

The time had come, and Lucy left her bed and wrapped a shawl around her shoulders. As she made her way to the back door in the kitchen, she opened it and stepped outside just in time to see all five of them about to enter the barn.

"Cade, can I speak with you, please," she said quietly, but loud enough in the stillness of the night that all could hear.

She saw Finn smile at Cade, and Mick tipped his hat to her. Red Sky said nothing, but Joanna offered a kind "good night" before she took the lamp inside the barn.

Cade ran his hand along his horse's neck and whispered something in his ear before he turned to walk toward her.

"Good evening, Lucy," he said softly. "I didn't expect you'd still be awake."

"I couldn't sleep. And besides, I was hoping you might tell me a little about what you talked about in town," she said and then stepped back into the kitchen. "Would you like to come inside?"

Cade didn't answer but gave a nod as he climbed the stairs to follow her into the house. When he closed the door behind him, Lucy put a finger to her lips and rolled her eyes toward her father's room and the upstairs loft to signal that those two were already asleep.

"I need to turn down the lamps. It will just be a moment," she whispered, and then proceeded to walk across the room to the front door. After she retrieved the lamp from the front porch window, she put it next to the one in the kitchen and turned them both down.

Without the lamps, the only light that remained was that of the moon shining through the kitchen window, and the candle still burning in her room. "Follow me," she said, and walked toward her bedroom door.

Cade didn't immediately follow, and instead took off his hat and began undoing his gun belt. Once he removed the weapons from around his waist, he set them in the spot he always placed them during meals and then removed the swords strapped across his back. After he finished putting everything down, he walked slowly toward her room as quietly as possible.

Lucy stood in the doorway, silhouetted by the candlelight inside. But as he came in closer, she pulled the ribbon from her hair and let it fall. Then she removed the shawl from her shoulders to reveal the sheerness of her nightgown underneath.

"I have a kettle of warm water by the bed, and I thought you might like a shave," she said seductively and tossed the shawl on her bed.

"Lucy, I—" he began to say, but she quietly shushed him and shook her head.

Then she took him by the hand, guided him into her bedroom, and closed the door.

CHAPTER 13

The Dawn

The rooster crowed to greet the dawn, and it woke Red Sky from a terrible dream. It was a familiar night terror, and each time he was unable to escape the images or the cries of his people.

It was a memory that played time and again through his head and tore at his heart like coyotes fighting each other for scraps. The image of the morning sun still low in the sky as smoke filled the air from the smoldering fires. All the men who had left for the hunt had returned to see their camp destroyed. Women and children mourned the dead as the men approached, and he would make his way to where his wife and son should have been waiting for him. But not on this day. And each time, he would wake from this dream when he saw his wife's body clutching their dead son, and the sight of them covered in blood scarred him forever.

He sat up and took a deep breath before the rooster

crowed again. The sun had not yet broken the horizon, but the call of the new day had come. As he stood and rolled up his blanket, he whispered to the spirits of his ancestors and it helped him move on from the horrifying images in his mind. But each day, these distractions were only temporary, and he expected this dream would continue until he joined his family in the spirit world.

As Red Sky stepped out in the cool morning air, he saw Cade doing his warrior dance in a small clearing to the east. He liked to watch the way his warrior friend trained with his swords, and how deliberate he was with his movements. This also seemed familiar to him, as he remembered the fight up north and how his friend was prepared to face death once more.

"Are the voices of your ancestors with you today?" Cade asked without looking at him, which surprised Red Sky. His friend was moving with his eyes closed, yet he knew who was watching.

"Yes. The voices of my ancestors are with me. They are with us both," Red Sky replied. "I sense that death will also be with us today, ready to take those whose time has come."

"Indeed, my friend," Cade said, and slid both swords into their scabbards. "Death comes for us all, eventually. And if we survive today, maybe we'll finally get a chance to face the demons of our past."

"Yes. I am ready," Red Sky replied, as the first spot of sunlight peeked over the horizon.

...

Preparing for Battle

Breakfast was a feast, and Cade was pleasantly surprised at the generous spread of food that Pa had prepared for him and the others.

The smells and sounds of this house were something he could never imagine growing tired of, nor the looks he exchanged with Lucy as they ate. There was a light in her eyes he had never really seen before, and he felt loved and very much at peace with himself. Whatever else might happen today, it was a perfect morning.

But that feeling wouldn't last, and today was no different. Cade knew that perfect was just a moment in time, just like the last bite of his gravy covered biscuits—and chased down with the last sip of coffee. Pa really outdid himself, but now it was time to prepare for Whitmore's arrival.

"We should be getting into town soon. There is much to do," he said to his friends, who also seemed to appreciate this fine meal and nodded in agreement.

"Can I help?" Eli asked. "My mom said there wouldn't be any school today."

"Yes, you can," Cade replied. "You can help by staying here and protecting the ranch. Can you do that for me?" he said and ran his fingers through the boy's tussled hair.

"I'm not scared," Eli replied. "In the barn. Don't you remember how I helped you? I can fight."

Cade shook his head. "I do remember, but my answer is the same."

He knew that wasn't what the young man wanted to hear, but it was the best thing for him. There was going to be some dangerous business in town today, and it would be best if all the women and children were safely away from it. And from the look that Lucy gave him, he knew she wanted her son out of harm's way, too.

"Well then, let's get a move on," Finn said. "The sheriff will be expecting us to meet up with him first thing this morning, and I need Mick to help me gather supplies."

As everyone excused themselves from the table, Lucy reminded them not to worry about cleanup and ushered them out of the kitchen. "Go on now… who knows how much time you have."

"She's right," Pa said as he walked to the door with everyone else. "You need to be gettin' into town, but let's be proper about it before you leave."

Cade and Lucy were the last to exit the kitchen and down the back steps toward the barn. Pa and Eli were already outside with the other four, and the elder Johnson asked everyone to stand in a circle and join hands.

"Let us pray," Pa said, and Cade could feel the soft touch of Lucy's fingertips in one hand, and the boyish grip of Eli's in the other. "Oh Lord, please look over our family and friends today. Give them courage in times of trouble, and strength in times of need. Protect them from evil and deliver them from harm. Amen."

"Amen," Joanna said, and Cade looked up to see her and Red Sky nod at each other before everyone released hands.

"Thank you for breakfast," Cade added, and the others echoed his sentiment. "Let's hope we have time to prepare for what's heading our way."

Then he turned to Lucy, but didn't have the words for what he wanted to say. He'd thought about last night for so long that he almost felt robbed of its joy this morning. But the other thing that made it so beautiful was that he didn't remember what he dreamt, and he wasn't up all night thinking about today. She made all of that go away for one evening, and their night together was something he would never forget.

Before he could utter a word, she lifted her finger to his lips. "Come back to me," was all she said.

•••

The Map

As the five riders arrived in town, Cade was happy to see Tobias and Sheriff Barnes waiting for them in front of the jail. Everything about the plan they hatched last night was dependent on teamwork, and now they would have to split up to get it done as quickly as possible.

Three of them pulled up in front of the jail, but the Bohannon brothers continued on. "We're going to meet up with Daniel," Finn said. "He'll take us over to the mining company for anything else we need, and then we'll meet back up when we're done."

"I reck'n so," Cade replied with a nod. "The hotel will be our gathering place. And feel free to be generous with those coins."

Finn tapped the pocket of his coat and gave a nod before he carried on with his brother. Cade made sure the brothers had plenty of gold to purchase whatever they needed. Hopefully, the sheriff would have the weapons and everything else.

"Alright now, I think we have our spots mapped out this morning. We've got a good place for Joanna to hide, some crates for cover, and plenty of reloads," Barnes said, and Cade appreciated that he was straight to the point.

"How many pistols and rifles do you have in the armory, sheriff?" Cade asked.

"We've got five pistols, six rifles, and two shotguns from the last time Whitmore's men came to town," Barnes replied. "But remember now, we're trying to prevent any bloodshed today."

"Agreed. We'll plant the guns in the spots where we'll need them, and not where children will find them," Cade said, and picked up a stick to draw in the dirt. "So, I think we should have two pistols at the ready here, and here," he said over the outline of the town and drew a little X to pinpoint each spot. "Because reloading in a fight takes too much time.

"It's probably best that we clear the streets now and get everyone in town to stay inside or head up to the church. We don't need any church bells to let Whitmore know we're expecting him," he said and stood to take the saddlebags of gold from the back of his horse. "Now let's keep the contents of these bags safely in the jail for the time being."

"Follow me," Barnes said and waved for Cade to enter the jailhouse to deposit the gold.

Cade smiled as he passed Tobias, as he was grateful to have him on their side. "Thank you again for being here. We'll need every gun we can get today," he said.

"I'm not here to be part of your feud, but I will help keep the peace," Tobias replied.

"That's all I can ask," Cade said with a tip of his hat. "But if there is one more thing, can you please help us fill some store crates with rocks?"

•••

Three Scouts

"What's Rolly barking at now?" Lucy asked as the dog was raising some kind of alarm on the front porch. Pa and Eli had just finished cleaning up breakfast dishes, and she was carrying a sack of grain to feed the chickens. It wasn't odd for the dog to be barking, but it was the way he carried on made her curious.

"Mom, come quick! Riders are coming," Eli called out from the kitchen window.

Lucy dropped the sack of grain and ran to the kitchen door. Once inside, she joined her father at the front window with her son in tow. Right as rain, there were three men that looked like shadow riders making their way to the ranch. They were also fanned out and coming in slow, as if they were being intentional about it.

"I'm going to see what the hell they want," Pa said, and went for his rifle in the corner. But Lucy was quick to recommend an alternate course of action.

"Get your rifle and follow me. We know why they're here, and we can better defend ourselves in the barn," she said. "Eli, get the pistol in the drawer and call Rolly out to the barn with us.

"Now!" she snapped, as her father and son seemed to still be thinking about what she'd said—but then quickly did exactly as they were told.

On their way out to the barn, they closed up the house behind them and hurried to the barn without being seen. And while Eli called Rolly to follow him, Lucy helped her father get inside just when she expected the riders were in front of the house.

"Take that spot in the corner of the bunkhouse," she told her father, and pointed to the one place that had a missing board. "You should be able to get a good look from there," she continued, and then turned to her son. "Give me the pistol."

Eli handed it over, but Lucy could sense some reluctance. "Everything is going to be okay," she said with a smile and knelt down to kiss him on the forehead. "Trust me."

"What can I do to help without a gun?" Eli asked.

She reached behind her and pulled a pitchfork from a pile of hay. "I want you to hide behind the big door. And if you have to use this… make it count."

Eli took the pitchfork and shrugged, but Lucy didn't care

if his feelings were hurt. There was something more important at stake here. "Keep Rolly with you, too. And try to keep him quiet," she said as she watched her son and father get into place.

When she sensed the two of them were where they needed to be, Lucy tucked the Colt in the apron springs behind her. Then she smoothed out the front of her apron with both hands, grabbed the only empty store crate near her feet, and did her best to act like nothing was out of the ordinary as she heard the first of the three shadow riders come around the north side of the house.

The rider pulled his horse to a stop at the sight of her and whistled to his friends. "Back here," he said. And within a moment, the other two riders come around the south side of the house.

"Excuse me. This is private property. Why are you here and what do you want?" Lucy asked as calmly as possible.

"Well hello, little lady," the first rider said with a tip of his cap. "We're here looking for a friend of ours. Maybe you've heard of him?"

"Heard of who?" Lucy asked and did her best to reveal nothing. "Now state your business and move along."

"We're looking for Cade Wilson," one of the other riders spoke up. "He wouldn't be hiding out here, would he?"

"Mister, I don't know who you are… but if you haven't heard, Cade Wilson is dead," she said defiantly and determined to stand her ground. "Now I've got work to do, so why don't you head on back the way you came."

"That's not very hospitable. And what's a fine woman like yourself doing out here all by your lonesome? I figure there's no way you live out here all by your lonesome," the first rider said, and Lucy didn't like the tone of his voice or the look in his eye. "But if you are all alone out here, we'd be happy to keep you company until someone comes back," he said and dismounted his horse.

"Settle down, Hodge," said the oldest looking rider with gray in his beard. "We're only here to scout the property and report back to the colonel."

"In good time," Hodge replied. "We've got at least an hour or so, and a gal this pretty shouldn't have to do all this hard work on her own."

This wasn't going as planned, and Lucy slowly stepped back into the barn. "I don't need your company. Now please, just go!"

"How about you scream as loud as you want. If there is someone out here with you, maybe he will come out of hiding to help," Hodge said, and Lucy feared the dangerous nature of a man that would even say such a thing.

She took another step back into the barn, past the big door where Eli was hidden. But she never took her eyes off the shadow rider walking toward her—and after a few quick steps, he stood in front of her and put his hands on the crate she held between them.

"Now let's get rid of this," Hodge said as he wrestled the crate from her hands. But as he tossed the crate aside, Lucy reached behind her back and pulled the pistol from her apron strings.

"How about you get back on your horse and get the hell

out of here!" she said as she cocked back the hammer and took aim.

"Well now… she's beautiful, and deadly," he said with a chuckle and slowly brought his hands in front of him and took another step forward. "But I don't think a pretty gal like you is really going to shoot—"

The pistol exploded with a bang and it surprised the shadow rider. At first, Hodge looked confused and took a step back with his hands on his gut. "The bitch shot me," he said as he hunched over, and Lucy assumed the bullet must have got him in the stomach. But he wasn't dead, and he steadied himself as he pulled his pistol.

Before she could cock back the hammer to shoot again, Rolly barked and charged out from behind the barn door to lock his jaws on the rider's arm. As the man screamed in pain, Rolly tossed his head from side to side with the man's arm in mouth—and when his pistol went off, the shot fired harmlessly into the ground.

That's when one of the other two riders fired at Lucy, as she heard the shot and the bullet splinter the wood behind her. She quickly pointed her pistol in their direction and fired back—but she missed. And before she could take aim again, she heard the shot from her father's rifle.

As the oldest looking rider fell from his horse, the third rider pulled his pistol and fired a round in Pa's direction. The bullet must have passed through the dry wood and hit him, as Lucy never heard her father howl in pain like that.

"Dad!" she screamed, worried that her father had just been shot. But Hodge was still standing in front of her and desperately trying to fight off Rolly's attack. She was afraid that he might be able to get off another shot when Eli came charging out from behind the door.

"Leave my mom alone!" Eli said as he drove the pitchfork deep in the back of the shadow rider—and Hodge's face became tangled between fear and pain as if he was about to cry out, but no sound escaped his mouth as he fell face first to the ground.

Then she heard her father fire a second shot at the last shadow rider, but his horse had become startled and the bullet missed. Still, the shot proved to be too much for the last man alive—and he got off one more return shot in Pa's direction before he pulled his reins and took off in the direction he came.

Lucy stood in shock for a moment, and she tried to take in everything that just happened as the pitchfork stood tall in the dead man's back. Eli looked just as surprised as she felt, and then she remembered her father.

"Pa!" she said and ran over to where her father was sitting on the ground with his back against the wall. "Are you shot?"

Her father looked back at her with grim eyes and a hand on his right hip. "I'm afraid so. That bastard got me. Damn unlucky shot, too," he said while wincing in pain. "But the bullet passed through. I'm okay… I'm okay," he repeated.

"No, you're not. C'mon now, let's get you in the house," she said, and tucked the Colt back in her apron strings. "Eli, get over here. Get his rifle and help me stand him up."

As they helped Pa to his feet, they had only taken a few steps before her father spoke up. "We need to get into town and warn the others. Did you hear what they said? Those men were scouts, and they were supposed to report back to the colonel. They also said the others were only an hour away."

"We need to get you to Doc Miller. And yes, we'll warn the others, too," Lucy said while helping her father walk.

"I can go," Eli said. "I will tell them."

"No. I need you to help me!" Lucy said, but then felt bad for scolding him. "First, we need to get your grandfather to a place he can sit down. Then we're all going into town to see Doc Miller, because who knows if more of those riders will come back. That's why we're going to stick together, and nobody is going to be left here alone. Do you understand?"

"Yes, mom," Eli replied, and they walked Pa to the steps leading into the kitchen and sat him down.

"Now go get the wagon and be quick about it," she said to Eli, and watched him run off while she removed the pistol and untied her apron.

As she turned her attention to her father, it was hard to tell how severe the wound was with all the blood-stained clothes, but part of her didn't want to know or think about it before they could get to Doc Miller. Instead, she rolled her apron up to tie it around his waist and cover the wound. "Does it hurt?" she asked.

"Of course, it hurts, but only when I think about it. And I'm certainly better off than those fellas," he replied with a chuckle, and Lucy was suddenly reminded of the two dead men who came to the house looking for Cade.

"Eli killed that man," she said and looked sadly at the shadow rider with the pitchfork in his back. "Did that really happen?"

"Yes, and he did it to save you," Pa replied.

"We'll talk about it later," Lucy said and tightened the apron around her father's wound. As Eli brought the horse and wagon around, she decided it was best to focus on getting her father into town.

"We need to get you up and into the back," she said. "Are you able to lift yourself into the wagon?"

"With a little help," Pa replied. "But grab whatever else you need, because we're not coming back. More of those men are coming, and now they'll be coming for all of us."

...

Gunshots

Cade was helping Finn and Mick place their nail bombs at the east inroad to town when he heard the faint sound of gunshots.

"Did you hear that?" he asked, and the two brothers nodded. But as he stopped to listen for more, nothing followed—and it was hard to tell which direction they came from.

"Do you think those came from the Johnson Ranch?" Mick asked, and Cade dropped the spool of lead wire at the mention of it.

"Go on," Finn said. "We can manage. Go see if those shots came from the ranch."

Cade heard what Finn said, but didn't acknowledge him as he ran to his horse and jumped in the saddle. As he rode off on the south road, he also didn't bother to look back or see if anyone was coming with him.

In minutes, he was almost at the arched sign when he saw Lucy and Eli in their wagon. They were headed north in a hurry, and that assuaged his immediate concerns. But as he pulled on his reins and came up beside them, he got his first look at Pa in the back with a bloody bandage around his hip.

"What happened?" Cade asked, as he remembered hearing multiple shots.

"Three shadow riders came looking for you. They were scouts," Lucy replied without stopping the wagon. "We got two of them, and the third rode off. The one that shot Pa in the hip."

Cade didn't try to understand the details, except one, because it was enough to know they had been attacked at the ranch. "Did they say anything else?"

"They said something about reporting back to the colonel," Eli replied.

"We need to get Pa to Doc Miller's. He's lost a lot of blood, and we're not going back to the house," Lucy said with a crack of the reins.

"One of them said they had about an hour or so before the others get here," Pa said as he grimaced in pain.

Cade winced and gave a nod. The old man was tough, but they needed to get him to the doctor as quickly as possible.

He also knew that Pa was right. The colonel wouldn't have sent scouts if they weren't close enough to attack. And for him, and the man bleeding in the back of the wagon, time was not on their side.

CHAPTER 14

Scout Report

Joseph Whitmore II loved a good ride across the open plain because it gave him time away from the fort to think. But to lead an army of men and have supplies in position along the way also took planning and steady perseverance. Fortunate enough, that's why he leaned on the colonel when it came to organizing his shadow riders.

He could imagine that Rocky Creek was just beyond the horizon, and this town would be one of his crowning achievements. They had advanced beyond their supply wagons and would need to arrive there today, so he eagerly charged forward with blue-sky overhead—and the future seemed equally bright and full of possibility.

This mission was also the biggest endeavor he had ever launched, but the vision for having his own personal army was for this very reason. What started as a sanctuary for former soldiers and orphans after the Civil War had become a self-sustaining farm and the perfect fortification to expand his landholdings.

His fort had also become a very structured militant training ground, and he was most proud of his samurai cowboys until they met a tragic end. Over the years, he estimated that close to one hundred soldiers had come and gone as shadow riders. Some would stay for a year or so, and others moved on to towns in Texas or near the Mexico border to help protect his interests and the transportation of goods.

But at the moment, his interest was drawn in by the lone shadow rider who approached at full gallop—and he raised his hand for the colonel and the entire calvary to pull up on their reins.

"One of our scouts is back," Whitmore said to the colonel. "But why only one?" he asked as all horses came to an abrupt halt.

"What's your report? Where's Martin and Hodge?" the colonel asked.

"Martin and Hodge are dead," the scout reported. "There was a shooter in the barn at the Johnson Ranch. The place we were told about," he continued, and pointed over Whitmore's shoulder at Bullseye.

"Was it Cade Wilson?" the colonel asked.

"I don't know. I couldn't see," the scout replied. "It all happened so fast. The gal shot Hodge, and then the shooter in the barn got Martin. But I got a shot off and it sounded like I may have wounded him," he said, and Whitmore believed his recount of events.

But Whitmore didn't think it was Cade in the barn,

because Viper would likely take any fight head on. Or would he?

"You say he might be injured?" Whitmore asked and began to speculate. "Maybe that's why he was hiding in the barn?"

"I don't know, sir. But I'm pretty sure I got a piece of him. The bullet went through the wood and I heard a man groan. Then he fired another shot at me, and I came back to warn you since I was the last one alive," the scout explained.

"Understood. Now fall back in line," the colonel said, and the scout did as he was ordered. "How would you like to proceed Mr. Whitmore?"

"Let's ride straight into town," Whitmore replied with a confident sneer. "If Viper is out at the Johnson Ranch, and wounded… then we can set up in town before we flush him out."

...

Whitmore's Army

"That one, the man in the military-looking coat with the brass buttons. He's the colonel," Cade told Red Sky, and handed him the spyglass. From their vantage point on top of the saloon, they had a good view of the army of riders heading their way—and Whitmore and the colonel were out in front.

"I see," Red Sky replied, and returned the spyglass. "He's the one who ordered my family killed?"

"Yes, and I'm still sorry for everything that happened that night," Cade offered with a pat on his friend's shoulder. "I wanted you to know who he was, because this is the best chance you're going to have to get your revenge."

"I will find him today, and see his blood on my knife," Red Sky said as he picked up his bow and knelt down out of sight beside a rifle and a shotgun.

"It's time for me to get into place, too. I'll see you on the other side," Cade said with a smile.

"*Haitse*," his friend replied, and they touched palms before Cade took the spyglass and walked quickly to where he could climb down from the roof. On the ground, Joanna was in the spot she would hide and wait to execute her part of the plan.

"You can hear them coming," she said as Cade stepped around some crates they had stacked for cover behind the saloon. "How many are there?"

"Plenty," he replied sarcastically, and hoped the joke might calm her nerves. "Try not to think about the numbers. Just wait here and let them pass. Red Sky will provide protection from above, and you just wait here for the right time to capture Whitmore."

"How will I know it's him?" she asked with a concerned tone and Red Sky's spear in her hand.

"Trust me… you'll know. He'll be the finest dressed man, and different from everyone else. He'll also be the one that does all the talking," he said with a chuckle. "You'll be fine. Remember your training. Your fear can be controlled, and we have the element of surprise on our side."

Joanna looked at him in a way she'd never had before,

and he felt the weight of friendship and being her teacher on his shoulders. She seemed anxious but confident, and ready to prove her worth—and he couldn't have been prouder of her in this moment. But she looked more worried about him.

"We'll both be fine," he said, and she smiled back. Then he grabbed her by the shoulders and pulled her in for a hug. It was the way he would hug his sister Sarah, and hopefully he would be able to see her again, too.

"Go," she said and pulled back from him. "They'll be here any minute. Besides, I have a guardian angel looking over me today."

Cade assumed that angel was Sinclair. She told him about last night and the deal they made outside the General Store. Although Cade was happy the bounty hunter wasn't here to start a fight, it seemed crazy to think he might protect her. But Sinclair did have an incentive to keep Joanna alive, and they could bargain with him tomorrow if they survived the day.

He made his way across the street and had mere moments to make it to the hotel without being seen. And along his way to the building on the corner, he passed Sheriff Barnes standing at the crossroads of town.

"Let's hope we can keep the peace today," Cade said as he hurried past.

"Yes. Let's hope," Barnes replied while he levered a round into his rifle.

Tobias stood on the front porch of the hotel, and he gave the cylinder a spin after he checked the loads and holstered the pistol inside his coat.

"Is that your backup?" Cade asked.

"Something like that," Tobias replied with a smile. "Now get inside before someone sees you."

Cade stepped into the modestly furnished lobby of the hotel, and Tobias followed him in. He gave a nod to Mick, who was already inside and set up at a table near an open window with three rifles laid out at the ready.

"Is Finn in position, too?" Cade asked.

"See for yourself," Mick replied, and pointed out the window at Finn tucked behind the Johnson wagon they had parked across the road in front of the courthouse.

Cade waved and Finn signaled back with a thumbs up. It was the best spot for him to have some cover and control the demolition he set up on the east and south roads.

"Looks like we're ready as we'll ever be," Cade said, and Mick nodded.

"Just remember our deal," Mick replied as he levered a rifle, and Cade had to laugh. At a time like this, the thought of surviving this fight and sharing the gold with his friends was a pleasant distraction from what was coming their way.

As the thunder of horses grew louder and closer, Cade looked out the window and took a slow deep breath. Whitmore and his army had arrived.

•••

Sheriff Barnes

"Whoa there!" Barnes said aloud with a raised hand to slow the riders. He stood in the middle of the street with his Winchester rifle in hand, but kept it pointed high and unthreatening. Still, the riders stopped in their tracks, and the sheriff was happy to keep them bottled up on the east road—and the first part of the plan worked.

"Are you Mr. Whitmore?" he asked the man who looked in charge, and he assumed it was the best dressed fella out in front.

"I am," Whitmore replied. "And you are?"

"Sheriff Barnes," he replied. "There's been some talk about you coming to town, and Mr. Cobb says that you're here to make a business deal with some of the folks who own land around here. Is that true?"

Whitmore looked a little uncomfortable being openly questioned, but he also seemed to respect the badge enough to answer. "Yes. I've come here to do some business. And I'm also looking for someone that might be hiding amongst you. Maybe you've heard of him?"

"Let's not mince words. If you're referring to Cade Wilson, then yes. I've heard of him," Barnes replied. "Is that why you've brought so many men with you?"

Whitmore tipped back his hat and swatted away some flies attracted to the smell of sweat and horses. "Look sheriff,

I don't mean to be impolite… but I didn't ride all this way to quibble with you. I'm here to make a land acquisition and bring prosperity to this quaint little town," he said with a quick look around.

"I'm also here to remove a thorn in my side. The man you know as Cade Wilson once worked for me by another name," Whitmore continued. "But then he stole from me and killed some of my best men, and I'll be more than happy to exact my own justice.

"So, if you're looking to keep the peace, then I would ask that you kindly step aside," he added in a threatening tone. "Because it won't do either of us any good if you don't."

Barnes didn't like being told what to do, and he already didn't like Whitmore or trust his intentions. "That's not—"

"Welcome to Rocky Creek! It's good to see you again, Mr. Whitmore," Jon Cobb called out from over the sheriff's shoulder, and Barnes turned to see him and Hicks coming his way, and Dylan and Kershaw who stopped just outside his landholdings business.

"You'll have to forgive the sheriff," Cobb continued with a big smile as he walked quickly across the road with Hicks trailing behind. "He doesn't fully appreciate our business, and he's got folks in town worried that you're here to take over. But I've assured everyone that there won't be any trouble as long as they're willing to sell."

"Hello, Cobb. It's certainly been a while, and I appreciate the way you've handled things so far," Whitmore said with a tip of his hat.

Barnes glared at Cobb and started to regret not asking him to stay out of this until he had a chance to settle things down. But instead, Cobb was a few feet away and acting like he ran the town—and Barnes had a feeling in his gut that he was about to ruin everything.

"You see, sheriff. This is all a little bigger than you," Cobb said with a smug look on his face. "Mr. Whitmore and I have plans for this town, and a shared problem.

"We also know that Cade Wilson is in town right now," he continued as he pointed to the hotel. "In fact, he's right over there—"

"Stop right there, Cobb. There's no part of what you're doing that will help matters," Barnes said with a piercing glare for this man to shut his mouth. But Cobb didn't seem interested in abiding by him or the law, and the damage was already done.

"Did you say Cade Wilson is inside the hotel?" Whitmore asked, as he pointed at the same building on the corner.

"Yes, sir. That's what I'm saying, and I'm turning him over to you as promised," Cobb replied. "Hopefully, we can talk about any reward later. But for now, I would assume you and your men might want to take care of some other business first."

Barnes wasn't naturally prone to violence, but he wanted to punch Cobb in the mouth. While the two men responsible for this very moment continued to exchange their pleasantries, one of them just provoked the fight he was trying to prevent. As he already feared the worst was about to happen, he heard the door open and turned to see Cade step out of the hotel.

...

The Challenge

Cade walked a steady pace to where the sheriff was standing with Cobb and Hicks at the crossroads, but he never took his eyes off Whitmore. Whatever might happen next, the order would come from him or the man to his right. But the colonel didn't look like he was making any sudden moves, and neither were the type of man to flinch.

He didn't mind or care that Cobb and Hicks slowly backed away as he approached the sheriff. Cowards are good at starting fights, and first to run when trouble starts.

"Well, my plan might have worked. Hopefully, yours will do better," Barnes whispered to Cade as he turned to follow Cobb and Hicks in getting out of the way.

Cade slow blinked his eyes to give the sheriff a moment to clear out, and then he took a deep breath to focus on the fight in front of him. He could sense the tension and travel fatigue of the shadow riders, even though he wasn't looking at any of their faces. They would wait for the next order to come from the man they followed here, along with Toshi and the man in black behind him. And as much as Cade wished this day could have been different, he could finally tell Mr. Whitmore his story—and hope to resolve what was between them without more bloodshed.

"I've been waiting for this moment for a long time," Cade said looking directly at Whitmore. "Because all I've wanted is a chance to explain what happened that night. After all these years, and all I've done for you… I believe I deserve that chance."

"I'm glad you're here because we have unfinished business, but your story doesn't interest me. You stopped being under my protection when you stole from me," Whitmore said with a scowl.

"And you stopped being my Benefactor when you sent Falcon and Scorpion to kill me, and then tried to blow me up on a train," Cade replied sarcastically. "But that seems so long ago now, and all I want is to put whatever is between us, behind us."

"Behind us?" Whitmore quipped. "There's more at stake here than whatever you could possibly imagine. If you're asking me to just turn my back on what you did and what you've done, you're asking too much.

"You turned on me. Stole from me. And you killed your brothers," Whitmore said matter-of-factly, and Cade could only stand there accused. "You've also threatened my family business and everything I've worked to build over the past ten years.

"After all I've done for you… you were supposed to be loyal to me," Whitmore said loud enough for the whole town to hear.

"I'm not betraying you now. But I don't want to kill for you anymore," Cade said defiantly. "The time I've spent away from the fort has changed my perspective on many things. I was honor bound to defend you, but not to spill innocent blood. My loyalty still belongs to the Way of the Samurai, and not to a bloodthirsty man who is corrupted by greed.

"I also know what you've been trying to do all these years, and why you built a private army to do it," he said with a gesture to all the shadow riders. "But how you're doing it, and how I've helped you do it, is wrong."

"Don't tell me my business," Whitmore said and scoffed at Cade. "The New Mexico Territory is a wild horse that needs to be tamed, and the path to California will go right through here. This is my vision, and I'm going to make it happen. But I also need to protect my interests by any means necessary. There are bandits and thieves everywhere," he said with a sneer.

"But who's protecting the innocent from people like you?" Cade asked, and for the first time, he saw Whitmore as less of a father figure—and more like a desperate man who tried to use ego to overcome his fears.

"Enough of this. Your opinions don't concern me. But if you really want to put everything behind us, you can start by returning my gold!" Whitmore demanded, and Cade sensed this was the time to put his part of the plan into action.

"What's left of your gold is safe enough for now. And if you want it back, you'll have to fight me for it," Cade said, and slowly pulled his left sword from its scabbard and put his right hand on his holstered pistol.

"I challenge you to a duel."

...

Winner Take All

Whitmore felt like he should have seen this coming. When only one scout returned, he should have known that Cade might be waiting for him—and he may not be alone.

"You're challenging me to a duel?" he asked, as he weighed his options and glanced around to see if he had ridden into a trap. He could see Bullseye coming up on the other side of the colonel, and he felt emboldened by the number of guns he brought with him. "Why should I entertain such nonsense when I can have you shot where you stand?"

"Because I'm not the only one with a gun pointed at me," Cade replied with a smile.

Whitmore was suspicious of this claim but nodded, as he had no reason to doubt it.

"There's no need to turn this town into a shooting gallery," Cade continued. "Instead, I hoped we could settle this the way I was trained… like honorable warriors."

"You're already dead to me, so I need you to help me understand something," Whitmore said sarcastically. "If I agree to this duel, then what happens after I have you killed?"

"If you win, someone here knows the location of your gold and will retrieve it for you. And with all that gold, you can use it to buy the land from everyone you said would get a fair offer," Cade replied.

"I would already expect that," Whitmore replied. "So, what if you win?"

"Then you and your men have to leave the people of this town alone. Just turn around the way you came and let them be. They don't need you to short sell them to make deals with the railroad," Cade replied.

"But I will trade the gold for my freedom, and the freedom of my sister, Sarah," he added. "That's all I want, and you'll never hear from me again."

"Toshi, come forward," Whitmore commanded, and motioned with his hand for his bodyguard to join him at the front. He wasn't fond of this deal or being challenged in front of his men. But he also didn't intend to play fair, and now he knew Cade had an emotional connection to his sister back at the fort.

"Sarah's a fine young woman. I've thought about marrying her myself," Whitmore said and rubbed his fingers under the bottom of his chin as he mused. "Or maybe I'll let her entertain my men when we return to the fort and celebrate your death.

"Either way, it sounds like all the spoils belong to the victor. And I'll accept your challenge on two conditions. One… I don't want anyone taking shots at me, so call off the Comanche I've heard about and whoever else you have hiding out there," Whitmore said with another look around at open windows and possible hiding places. "And two… you have to fight Toshi."

"I accept," Cade replied, and didn't look surprised by the conditions. Again, Whitmore felt like he should have anticipated this. But it didn't really matter, because he was playing this game to win no matter what—and he smiled as his samurai bodyguard rode up on his left.

"What about me?" Swift asked. "We had a deal. I would hunt Cade Wilson down for you, and all I asked in return was the opportunity to kill him."

"What about you?" Whitmore snapped back, but quietly, in hopes not everyone could hear. "Do you really think you're the only one that thirsts for revenge? Besides, you'll get your chance. I promise that you'll get to put a bullet in Cade Wilson. Be patient."

"Toshi, are you ready to prove your loyalty to me?" he asked the man to his left. As he studied the face of his samurai for any hint of betrayal—there was none. Only the same solemn look of servitude he'd come to expect from his bodyguard over the years.

"*Hai*," Toshi said with a nod, and dismounted his horse. And while his samurai bodyguard walked toward the crossroads, Whitmore caught the glimpse of a familiar face.

"Well, well… what a surprise to see you again, Sinclair," Whitmore said curiously as the bounty hunter emerged from the saloon on the corner. "Did you join the other side?"

"Not at all," Sinclair replied. "I'm here on business, but nothing to do with you or Mr. Wilson over there since you pulled the bounty. But I do enjoy a good fight."

"Fair enough," Whitmore replied. "But I'd appreciate if you just stay over there and keep out of this."

"Where did you get that whip?" Swift asked Sinclair, surprising Whitmore with his outburst. He was not accustomed to men in his employment that did not respect their position.

"Oh, this," Sinclair replied, and tickled the bullwhip that adorned his right hip with his fingertips. "I picked this up in Colorado. Took it from the man who broke my arm and shot my foot. I've become quite handy with it, but it doesn't make up for my lost saddlebags."

"Marshall Blackburn was my partner, Englishman," Swift replied. "I'll be coming for—"

"Silence! Let's settle one grudge at a time, if you please," Whitmore said to the bounty hunter, and he didn't appreciate the look he got in return. But Swift needed to be put in his place, and the colonel was here to keep his shadow riders under control.

"Now, where were we?" Whitmore asked, and turned his attention back to the crossroads, where his samurai was ready to fight for him.

"We're at the same place we've always been," Cade replied. "Where you're too much of a coward to fight your own battles, and all too willing to have others die for what you want."

CHAPTER 15

The Ronin

Cade tried to calm his mind and did his best to reset his senses, but there was no chance he could close his eyes for even a moment as Toshi emerged from a crowd of men on horses ready to shoot him down.

The warm mid-day sun baked the smell of Whitmore's army into the air, and it was an unpleasant and unwanted distraction. As he tried to focus on the sound of Toshi's footsteps, it was too difficult to distinguish them from everything else going on around him.

He resigned himself to rely on his sight and, from the corner of his eye, he had seen Sinclair step out of the saloon. But what he gathered from the contentious conversation between Whitmore and the two bounty hunters, Sinclair seemed content to stand and watch.

The colonel quietly directed some men to fan out, and Cade assumed that some shadow riders might soon try to flank the town from the south or north roads. It was a move he assumed the colonel would make, and his friends had planned for that.

When Toshi was about twenty feet in front of him, Cade could also see Whitmore ease back on his horse while two shadow riders surrounded him. It was disappointing that his last words with the man who helped raise him were angry and unfulfilling.

If the relationship with Whitmore was based on loyalty, it was loyalty to him and it wasn't mutual. Because here they were when they could have made peace. Instead, Cade would have to fight Toshi to the death. They were warriors of the forgotten way, and the Way of the Samurai is found in death. Freedom would have its price, and Whitmore would have his pound of flesh.

"I honor you, Toshi," Cade said with a bow. "It troubles my heart that we must fight each other over a man like Whitmore, but I respect that you must serve your master."

"I honor you," Toshi replied as he pulled one of his swords. "You are a cunning warrior, and a survivor. But you are a ronin now, and so it must be.

"Only one of us will remain. It is how a samurai should face his death," Toshi continued as he drew his second sword. "Are you ready?"

Cade drew his right sword and took a defensive stance. He planned to save his viper strike for the right moment when Toshi was the aggressor, but that also meant he would need to survive Toshi's first attack and then some.

That strike came quickly as Toshi charged, at first with a

slash at Cade's right side as he ran by. But Cade easily defended it and the clash of their swords rang twice.

Then Toshi spun around and tried to slash at Cade's back, but he was quick to defend that, too. So quick that Cade was able to counter with a slash across Toshi's abdomen. It wasn't a deep cut, but it caused Toshi to retreat.

Cade took a step back to further separate himself from Toshi. His sensei was not the same man he fought on the train. Toshi should have defended that counter, or so he thought.

Sweat and dust began to burn Cade's eyes as he studied his opponent, and he was surprisingly focused on more than Toshi's movements. It was as if his sensei and everything around him was moving slower than he was accustomed to.

Toshi let out a low-pitched warrior's shout before charging again, this time with a right thrust to the face, followed by a slash from the left—and then another slash from the right as he continued to step forward. This attack was more fierce than the first, and the clash of their blades echoed through the town. But again, Cade was able to defend it while Toshi was able to duck under his counterattack as he ran by.

As both men squared off again, Cade's curiosity scratched out one last question for his teacher. "What was the ultimate lesson of the five rings?"

Toshi seemed surprised by the question, but he also appreciated it. "A man who conquers himself is ready to take on the world," he replied.

"When a man has conquered himself, does he see every-thing differently?" Cade asked. As Toshi nodded, Cade could tell he was about to attack again—so he forestalled his opponent by calmly attacking first.

His aggressive charge at Toshi was to his advantage, as Toshi was shorter in stature. But Cade was determined to attack Toshi at the corners, and he slashed with his left so he could strike at Toshi's shoulder with his right.

The attack scored a cut across Toshi's left shoulder armor. But Toshi was low enough to counter with a slash across Cade's abdomen.

Toshi's counter strike could have been deadly without Cade's chest armor. Something he thought his sensei might remember, but that didn't matter. It was the perfect set up for his new fighting strategy.

After he passed by Toshi, he turned around and crouched down on one knee. To be even more convincing, Cade hunched over as if his opponent had scored a painful blow to his gut. The sound of cheers rose from the ranks of the shadow riders, and he thought that helped sell his vulnerability.

But Toshi was not a man to be influenced by the jeers of others, and he appeared to calmly take his normal stance and plan his next attack.

Cade steadied himself for his viper strike. He leaned a little forward and held his swords out at the ready. All of his weight was on his left leg, with his right knee slightly tucked under him and his foot positioned to push off. His right leg was the stronger of the two, and he had practiced being able to jump forward from this position about five to six feet. That would be far enough to close the distance when his opponent attacked. He would use this element of surprise to attack Toshi when he charged—but the timing of his pounce would have to be perfect if this was going to work.

Toshi did not waste time, and his low pitch shout was quickly followed by the shuffle of his feet as he charged. When Cade saw that Toshi was ready to rear back for a strike, he jumped forward with a powerful right slash that surprised his sensei—and it had to be defended. This left Toshi open to Cade's left sword as the thrust pierced his chest.

A dull hush fell over the shadow riders as the two samurai and everyone watching knew the battle had turned. The speed of Cade's strike was so quick that he was able to let go of his sword and step back to watch as Toshi staggered and coughed blood from his mouth.

But as the warrior remained standing with the handle of a sword sticking out of his chest, Cade could feel his own heart breaking. The respect he had for his teacher swelled inside him, and his thoughts and feelings began to stir conflict in his soul. He had just defeated Toshi, the deadliest man he knew—and by his teacher's death, he was free. But he just killed another man that shouldn't have had to die.

"Take the shot," was all Cade heard before the sound of a pistol caught him by surprise. He fell back on one knee when the slug hit his chest armor, but what stung more than being shot was feeling betrayed when Whitmore didn't honor the way.

• • •

Double-cross

Cobb was surprised to see Cade win the fight with Whitmore's bodyguard. The man he loathed had looked defeated before he somehow turned the tables. But that wasn't as incredible as what Cobb just saw when Cade took a gunshot to the chest without falling over dead.

What he witnessed would be a story of legend. But it also suggested that Hicks was right, and Whitmore was not to be trusted. The duel to the death should have ended with Cade's victory over the bodyguard—and the contest was governed by some sort of code between them. But it was Whitmore who ordered the shot, as he would not accept defeat.

"He's wearing chest armor. Shoot him again!" Whitmore said to the man in black.

Cobb winced at the mention of shooting Cade again, even though he'd often wished for the man's death a dozen times or more. But while he was at least thirty feet away from Cade, he started to feel unsafe just being out in the open.

The man in black took careful aim, but Whitmore's bodyguard stepped in the way just as he took the shot.

"Toshi, no!" Cade cried out and tried to catch the warrior as he fell to the ground. The act of sacrifice seemed to make everyone gasp in surprise, followed by a brief hush, and Cobb turned to Whitmore to see what he'd do next.

"Stop right there!" Sheriff Barnes called out to the man

in black, and this time with his rifle pointed in that direction. "There was a deal… and everyone heard it. Cade won. Now I suggest you holster your pistol, or I will have to get involved as the law."

Cobb sensed that Barnes distracted Whitmore and his men for a moment, but it wouldn't last. Out of the corner of his eye, he saw the Texas Ranger step out of the hotel. The man had just arrived in town yesterday, and now he looked ready to intervene with a pistol in each hand. As everyone on the street was suddenly locked in a standoff, he heard a familiar voice cry out.

"Eli, get back here!" Lucy called out to her son as the boy ran to Cade's side. Cobb couldn't tell if the boy's actions were courageous or crazy, but he was amazed to see the boy stop and stand in front of the two samurai and shield them with his body.

Lucy ran out after her son and grabbed him by the arm. "Please don't shoot. He's just a boy," she pleaded to Whitmore as she tried to pull Eli away. But while everyone was momentarily distracted, Cade dragged the bodyguard's body back toward the hotel.

The man in black raised his pistol. "If that's your boy, and you don't want to get shot… then you better get out of the way. Because I would track that man back to the fiery gates hell if I had to, and I will have my revenge."

Cobb had no reason to doubt the man in black would shoot. He also knew that Lucy would never love him, but that did not stop him from loving her.

"No! Enough of this," Cobb said as he put both of his

hands in the air and hurried to where Lucy and Eli stood to protect Cade. "Whatever has happened here can be resolved without further bloodshed," he continued, and joined the group of defenders as they shuffled toward the hotel.

"Have it your way," the man in black said as he took aim—and Cobb suspected that he may have overestimated his influence as he looked down the barrel of a pistol.

"Lower your gun, or I'll shoot your boss," Hicks said aloud, with his pistol pointed at Whitmore. Cobb couldn't have been happier to see his foreman come to his rescue, but he feared for both of their lives when half a dozen of Whitmore's shadow riders on the front line pulled their pistols and pointed them at Hicks.

"We need him alive, Bullseye. He has to co-sign all the deeds," Whitmore said, and Cobb didn't like the tone in Whitmore's voice or what was being implied. But he was relieved when the man in black lowered his pistol.

"Understood. So how do you want me to handle this?" the man in black asked.

Cobb looked at Whitmore and tried to guess what he might say, but he felt like a fool. He realized that he really didn't know this man, even as much as he wanted to believe Whitmore was a man of business—and not someone willing to kill for his ambitions.

"Who is that man threatening me, and why is he still alive?" Whitmore asked the military-looking man at his side.

The colonel nodded. "Nobody threatens Mr. Whitmore," he said aloud, and a single shot rang out.

"Hicks!" Cobb cried out as his foreman took a bullet

in the gut. But his man was strong enough to maintain his balance and pull the trigger—and the bullet caught Whitmore in the chest, knocking him off his horse.

The retribution was swift, and Cobb could only watch as Hicks was gunned down where he stood by the front line of shadow riders. At least six more shots riddled his body before he fell back and collapsed in the dust.

Cobb remained with Lucy and Eli as they continued to protect Cade in front of the hotel. But his foreman and best friend was just murdered in front of him, and he froze as fear and anguish left him dumbfounded in a blurry minded haze. Then he saw Whitmore rise from the ground and dust himself off.

Whitmore was still behind his men when Cobb saw him rise from the ground and dust himself off. "Colonel… it's time for 'wildfire'," he said. "No witnesses!"

Cobb didn't see who shot Sheriff Barnes. But he would never forget the sight of the sheriff falling to one knee, and the eruption of explosives and gunfire that followed.

•••

Honor in Death

Toshi was still alive as Cade dragged him to the front step of the hotel. And he was so focused on helping Toshi that he was vaguely aware of the voices around him, and that Lucy, Eli and Cobb stood between him and the army of shadow riders.

The samurai warrior coughed up blood and was struggling to breathe as Cade laid him down and propped up his head. He could feel that the fight in his sensei's body was fleeting and his soul wanted to be released. He wanted to ease Toshi's pain, but could not remove the sword from his chest without killing him. "Toshi, I—"

"No. Listen. My time is short," Toshi said, and he wheezed as he spoke.

"You are one of my finest students. The Way is a path, and the wise man knows that life and death are forever in balance on the path," he continued. "I respect your decision to choose life, but your fight is not over."

Cade's eyes began to tear up as he couldn't choke back his emotions. He did his best to loosen Toshi's armor to help him breathe. He appreciated what his sensei had just sacrificed for him—and he hated Whitmore all the more for it. Now there was so little time, but he didn't know what to say. "Why did you take that bullet for me?" he asked.

Toshi offered a rare smile but didn't answer. His blood-stained teeth did little to distract from the look of calm and happiness on his face. "My journey in death is just beginning… but your journey in life continues," he said with a cough. Then Toshi reached out with his hand and seemed focused on something distant in the sky. "I long to see my wife and son again. I am ready to be at peace," he said before his body tensed up for a moment, and then released.

Cade rested on his knees and watched Toshi's face become frozen and still. He could also feel the last breath leaving his sensei's body, even as the explosive sound of dynamite and gunshots surrounded him.

He couldn't help but embrace the man that taught him the Way of the Samurai, and so much more than he could remember in the moment. Then he laid Toshi's body softly onto the ground and gently closed the eyes of his teacher and former master.

"Goodbye, Toshi… and thank you," Cade whispered. "You trained me well, and I am ready to face death for the life I choose." Then he pulled his sword from Toshi's chest with his left hand, and his holstered Colt with his right.

"Cobb. Get Lucy and Eli inside the hotel," he said as he stood up and took command of the situation—and the three of them nodded back. Then he noticed the sheriff on his knees in the dirt, and Tobias helping him stand as a billowing cloud of dust filled the street and engulfed Whitmore's shadow riders.

He could hear the men concealed in dust scream in pain, but it was too hard to see anything in the fog generated by Finn's nail bombs. But Cade crouched down and approached slowly as riders began to emerge from the cloud—and he stayed low as Mick fired a shot from the hotel window behind him and picked off the first one out.

Cade shot a rider that came straight at him and continued to advance as Mick and Finn covered his back from their positions. Although he couldn't see Red Sky, he knew his Comanche friend had the high ground and knew the plan to disorient the calvary and catch them in the crossfire—and it worked. The shadow riders who emerged from the dust looked confused and fired their pistols in every direction, which made it easy to pick them off one by one.

He could hear the colonel shouting orders, but the riders still in the chaos were just indistinguishable silhouettes. Then a steady breeze came in from the west and Cade spotted a figure that looked like the man in black as the cloud of dust began to swirl—and he charged.

•••

Ashes to Ashes

Joanna was still in her hiding spot when the nail bombs went off, and she heard how it caught Whitmore's army completely off guard as the cries of pain told a dozen stories.

Earlier in the day, she watched Finn cut a hole in the bottom of three half-barrels and place two sticks of dynamite in each one before covering the explosives with handfuls of nails and shoveled dirt.

Two of those buckets were placed about thirty feet apart on the east road into town, and they looked like flowerpots. The bombs were built to spray the nails like little bullets and create a cloud of dust that would reduce their visibility—and they worked perfectly.

The detonation of the nail bombs was also her signal to come out of hiding and capture Whitmore. She could hear so many voices yelling and screaming, but she couldn't distinguish anyone and was almost impossible to see. But it was time to attack, so she used the handkerchief Cade gave her to cover her nose and mouth and stepped out onto the street.

As the shadow riders seemed more interested in trying to orient themselves and ride out of the dust, she was able to navigate her way through them while she looked for the one man who was shot off his horse—and as the other horses and their riders continued to scatter around her, she suddenly noticed the one man who was standing about twenty feet in front of her.

She lowered the spear and advanced, but a shadow rider suddenly came in between her and Whitmore. He was the first to see her on the street, but before he could aim his pistol or say anything, an arrow from above struck his chest.

"Thank you, Red Sky," she whispered through her handkerchief and stepped quickly around the horse and its rider to come up behind Whitmore.

"Hey Whitmore, I've come for you," she said as she lunged forward and put the tip of Red Sky's spear on his neck.

Whitmore seemed surprised, and initially froze with his hands out. Then he tried to wipe the dust from his eyes and turned to face Joanna. "Falcon's dead… who are you?" Whitmore asked, and he sounded momentarily befuddled in the haze.

Joanna's face was covered, and her hat was drawn down to her eyes. He must have recognized Falcon's coat, but didn't know who she was—and that suited her just fine. She didn't need to be acquainted with Whitmore to do her part.

"You're coming with me to the saloon and stop all this madness," she said. But Whitmore didn't budge, and before she could repeat herself, another shadow rider came up on her left with his pistol drawn.

The rider had her dead to rights, and she braced for the worst as she closed her eyes. But the next sound she heard was the crack of a whip, and when she opened her eyes to look, she saw the rider shaking his hand as his pistol fell to the ground. And the gunshot that followed came from behind her as the shadow rider fell off his horse.

"Careful now. You better watch your back, or someone will put a bullet in it," Sinclair said as he approached with a pistol in his left hand, and Marshal Blackburn's whip in the other.

"Thanks," Joanna replied. The bounty hunter had saved her life, but the distraction of the rider was enough for Whitmore to slip away. She was disappointed, but decided to turn this situation to her advantage. "I need to catch Whitmore again, so you better keep up."

Sinclair pointed his pistol in her direction, which surprised her. But he wasn't looking at her, so she ducked out of the way as he fired at another rider coming up behind her. "Well, we can't stay here, so let's go."

Joanna lost track of Whitmore in all the confusion, and she didn't feel safe out in the open trying to look for him. Then another shadow rider crossed her path, but this one had a nail stuck in his eye and an arrow in his back. He was dead in the saddle and could be useful as she walked beside the horse for cover to look around. From what she could see through the haze, Whitmore was headed toward the entrance of the saloon.

The saloon was where she needed Whitmore to go, but

not without her. Then five or six shadow riders dismounted around him and set up a defensive parameter as they ushered him inside. This wasn't going as expected, and her part of the plan would need to change.

"C'mon Sinclair, we're not done yet. And I like having you around to keep me alive," she said to her new bodyguard.

...

The Second Wave

From inside the hotel, Lucy could see what was happening outside and was completely overwhelmed by it all. The quiet town of Rocky Creek had become a battlefield, and the sound of gunfire was deafening.

She watched Cade as he crouched low with his sword and pistol drawn—and then charged into the swirling dust as if he'd found the right moment or the right person to attack.

Mick fired his rifle at shadow riders coming out of the cloud, and he had a good vantage point from the hotel window. "Take that, you bastards!" he shouted, and levered round after round to fire again. And after he emptied one rifle, he discarded it and picked up another from the table beside him.

Finn was behind her family's wagon across the road and taking shots with his rifle—and the Texas Ranger was protecting Sheriff Barnes with a pistol in each hand. Between the four of them, they were shooting at every man on a horse and had the disoriented shadow riders caught in a crossfire.

The Ranger must have emptied his pistols, because he holstered them to help Barnes get to his feet and walk him toward the Bank and Loan on the corner next to Cobb's business. Then Cobb surprised Lucy when he went to the door of the hotel and shouted to his men across the street who were also shooting at the army of riders. "Kershaw… Dylan, help get the sheriff to the doc." But when Cobb's men went to help, the biggest one took two bullets to the chest.

There was so much happening around her that she couldn't process it all. Then she flinched when a bullet shattered one of the windows, and when she opened her eyes, she saw Eli's reflection in the broken glass. In this brief moment of clarity, she turned to scold her son.

"What were you thinking by running out there? You could have been killed," she said as she grabbed Eli by the shoulders and gave him a shake before she pulled him in for a hug.

"I'm sorry mom, but I just couldn't let Cade die like that," Eli replied, but Lucy didn't need to forgive him. He was a thoughtful and caring young man, and she admired his bravery. But it would've broken her heart if anything happened to him, and he almost got them both killed.

She held her son's head close to her heart as Cobb suddenly pointed out the shattered window. "Riders coming in from the south," he said.

Lucy could see what alarmed him. There were ten shadow riders coming in fast with pistols drawn—and they were shooting at Finn's position.

Finn dropped his rifle and looked like he was trying to

wire the detonator. But he must have gotten shot as his body jerked and fell forward on the plunger.

The third explosion went off just south of the jail, and it filled the air with more dust and nails. It also stopped the riders in their tracks, and Lucy saw three of them blasted from their horses before the cloud of dirt consumed them.

"Finn!" Mick cried out and started to fast lever fire in the direction of the oncoming riders. Then he dropped the second empty rifle and picked up the third as he made his way to the door.

"Don't go out there," Lucy said, and tried to get in his way. But Mick passed by her and Cobb without a word as he stepped out and levered his next round. He headed straight toward his brother and shot two shadow riders as he crossed the road—but now he was out in the open.

"Look out!" Lucy said, but it was too late. A wounded shadow rider at the crossroads had managed to stand up and shoot Mick in the back.

Michael Bohannon was a strong man, and the bullet didn't kill him. But it did knock him down to one knee before he appeared to catch himself. Then he levered his rifle once more, and he was able to turn and fire a round at the shadow rider who shot him—and when Mick and the shadow rider had shot each other, Lucy screamed in anguish as both men fell to the ground.

CHAPTER 16

Swords and Guns

As Cade charged into the fray, he remembered the fight at Rio Diablo. Toshi had boldly done the same thing and used confusion to his advantage.

He was hunting the man in black with a sword in his left hand and his Colt pistol in the right—and for any shadow rider unfortunate enough to get in his way, his aim and sense of purpose was true.

The first shadow rider to cross his path nearly shot him, but the bullet just grazed his left shoulder armor as Cade fired a round into the rider's chest. As a second rider staggered forward, Cade lunged quickly and ran his blade through the man's chest. Then he used the man as a human shield while he thumbed back the hammer of his Colt and shot a third rider off his horse.

He turned to see two more shadow riders on horseback coming straight at him, and one with a face that looked cut to shreds. But it wasn't time to be merciful. After his shield absorbed a bullet meant for him, he pulled his blade and charged as the dead man fell to the ground.

The advantage of pressing the fight was that it reduced his opponent's time to react, and Cade jumped up and spun in the air between the two riders. His sword slashed one across the neck, and the other rider turned and shot his own partner when Cade passed through them. As he landed on his feet, he took quick aim and shot the second rider in the back.

"Nifty trick. Now try this," came a voice from over his left shoulder.

Cade turned in the direction of the voice just as a bullet caught part of his left arm below the shoulder. It hurt like hell, but it could have been worse if he hadn't been warned.

It was the man in black—and before Cade could raise his pistol and shoot back, he felt two more rounds catch him in the chest and knock him to the ground.

"Bullseye," he heard the man say, and Cade felt like the weight of a horse was standing on his chest. For a moment, he just laid on the warm earth and looked up at the sky through the wafting haze of dust. Then he took a deep breath and tried to assess the damage. One of the bullets was stopped by his armor, but the other was not—and he could feel burning pain in the right side of his lower ribs as he tried to sit up.

So instead, Cade rolled over onto his left and went into a crouched defensive stance. He expected the worst, but as his opponent was gloating, he finally got a closer look at the man that shot him.

"That was a nasty move with those dirt bombs," the man

in black said, and he approached slowly while Cade stared down the barrel of his pistol.

"You do remember me, yes?" he said as he stopped about ten feet from Cade. "Bill Swift is my name. Or was my name before I was cleansed in fire. And now I'm going to kill you for what you did to Marshal Blackburn… the man that was my friend, and my partner."

Cade barely recognized the man as Marshal Blackburn's deputy. But the scar on the left side of his face must have been from the fire at the iron factory in Pueblo. Swift also had two nails sticking out of the right side of his face and just below his eye.

"This is the second time you've scarred my face," he said while he reached to pull the nails from his cheek. "And I don't know why you're so hard to kill, but I wanted you to know it was me," he paused and thumbed back the hammer of his pistol. "This is for Marshall—"

Cade was just as surprised as Swift when an arrow stuck the bounty hunter in the chest as he pulled the trigger. It was Red Sky, and the angel over his shoulder saved him once again.

The shot missed Cade, and he wasn't going to waste his opportunity as he popped to his feet and attacked quickly with a spinning slash at Swift's right hand. As the pistol fell to the ground, Cade pointed his Colt right between the eyes of the man who killed his sensei. "And this is for Toshi, you son of a bitch," he said as he pulled the trigger.

As the man in black fell to the ground, Cade was reminded that the battle for Rocky Creek was not over when the sound of a bullet whizzed by his head. He turned to see two shadow riders on horseback and a third walking toward him with a shotgun—and then he darted for cover while he sheathed his sword and fired a shot in their general direction.

Earlier today, they had stacked six store crates full of rocks along the side of the courthouse to create some defensive cover. Cade was glad they did as he dove over the crates, just as the shotgun and pistol fire ripped into them. When he landed on his side, the pain in his ribs rippled through his body. But it was better to be in pain and out of breath than dead—and behind the safety of the manmade cover, he was able to get to his knees, holster his Colt, and find the two loaded pistols he had stashed here just for this reason.

He didn't need to waste time reloading, but he did wait long enough for the riders to get closer before Cade popped up with a pistol in each hand. His first shot hit the rider with the shotgun just before he fired the second barrel. Then he thumbed back the hammer on both pistols and exchanged a volley of shots with the two riders on horseback.

Cade got one of them high in the chest, but he missed the second rider who had fired back at him. The bullet splintered one of the crates and sprayed bits of wood in his face just before he heard the third nail bomb go off. As the sound of the explosion riled the second rider's horse, Cade took careful aim and squeezed the trigger—and he didn't miss twice.

He figured the shadow riders had split up and there must have been an attack from the south if Finn detonated the third bomb. And he used the explosive distraction to shoot another rider who was staggering toward him before he had to duck behind his cover again.

From this position, Cade could see some horses wandering around without riders—and some shadow riders wandering about like the walking wounded. He also spotted Red Sky on the roof of the saloon, and the colonel in front of it, trying to organize his men. But Whitmore and Joanna were nowhere to be seen.

Another volley of shots forced him down behind the crates, and they came from some riders in the middle of the road and a few others who had taken a position inside the saloon from a broken window.

Cade popped up and fired back with a gun in each hand—and he managed to take out two more shadow riders before he emptied his pistols and was forced behind the cover again. He started to feel pinned down and trapped, and he didn't want to get stuck behind these crates. At best, he figured this was a good time to reload and plan his next move.

He knew it was going to be dangerous trying to cross the road now that the dust from the nail bombs had all but settled or blown away—and that's when he saw that Joanna and Sinclair had just entered the back of the saloon.

●●●

Widowmaker

Sinclair followed Joanna through the back door of the Five Point Saloon, but he couldn't understand why he was doing it. He was here on business and this wasn't his fight, and he'd been telling himself not to get involved. Yet there was something about this young lady that intrigued him, and she was quite attractive, too. And now he felt caught up in this battle if only to protect his prize.

"I've never met a girl like you before," Sinclair whispered as he and Joanna crept through the kitchen and into the back of the house. The smell of whiskey barrels and stale beer was something he'd become accustomed to, but not so much in the company of a young lady.

"I doubt you ever will. Now shush," she whispered back as they came quietly up behind the bar. She still had the spear in hand, but it wasn't cumbersome, and she kept it in front of her as they came up behind the bar.

As they peeked over the bar, Sinclair could see three shadow riders taking turns shooting out of a broken window—and it was most likely at Cade Wilson. Across the room, there were two others attending to Whitmore, who was sitting at a table with his shirt open. He recognized one of the riders from the train station in Colorado, and he tried to listen to what they were saying over the gunshots.

"Damn, Lester, the chest armor saved my life," Whitmore said. "I didn't think it would work, but it did. Arguably the best damn thing we ever invented."

"I remember that guy. Lester is his name," Sinclair said quietly, and he touched Joanna's shoulder to point out the man of interest. "I'm pretty sure he'd remember me, too. But those three at the window have their backs to us, and if you still want to capture Whitmore, it's best if we can get as close to him as possible without drawing their attention. Would you agree?" he asked, and she nodded.

"Good. Then I have an idea," he said and they ducked back behind the bar. As Sinclair told Joanna what he had in mind, the simplicity of the plan was that he could be the distraction she needed—and with a wink and a smile, he grabbed a bottle of whiskey and two glasses.

"How about a drink?" Sinclair asked while he stood and paraded around the bar with the whiskey and glasses in hand. "Because you look like you could use a drink," he continued as he walked toward Whitmore.

Lester drew his pistol, and he seemed to do it instinctively to protect his boss. But he didn't shoot, so Sinclair kept walking.

All three shadow riders at the window stopped to watch him cross the room, and the rider standing behind Lester put his hand on his pistol, but just looked on. Sinclair continued to act like he wasn't a threat and didn't pay them any mind, because there was only one man in the room that mattered.

"A drink?" he asked while he gave the whiskey bottle a little shake and held up the glasses. "Amongst old friends being reunited in the strangest of places. And since the last time we saw each other, I almost lost everything… including my saddlebags," he added as a sarcastic accusation.

"Is that why you're here? To settle a score?" Whitmore asked as he stood with a confused look on his face. "Because I'd say you should have killed Cade Wilson when you had a chance, and I should have you shot for being a failure."

Sinclair stopped about eight feet from Whitmore and

exhaled. "I think I've suffered my share since that day, and I'm here on a job for Victor Carmichael. Remember him?"

Whitmore grimaced at the sound of the name, but didn't reply, and Sinclair sensed that he touched a nerve. But as the tension from his surprise entrance seemed to settle, the three riders at the window resumed their hunt outside of it. He hoped that would happen, and he looked into Lester's eyes as he slowly finished counting to 30 in his head.

"How about you? If you still have my saddlebags, then you can have a drink on me," he said to Lester and casually tossed the bottle in the rider's direction and dropped the glasses. Although he wasn't as quick with his left hand, he was still quick enough. And as soon as Lester was distracted by the bottle flying toward him, it was all Sinclair needed to pull his pistol and put a bullet in Lester's forehead. Then he uncoiled Widowmaker with his right hand—and with an underhanded flick of his wrist, he wrapped it around Whitmore's throat in one strike.

Whitmore's eyes became as big as saucers while he grasped at his throat and dropped to his knees. The rider behind Whitmore was still trying to pull his pistol before Sinclair thumbed back the hammer of his Colt. "Don't do it," he warned.

To his right, he was able to see Joanna launch her attack at the same time. She charged the first rider with the spear before he saw her coming, and the thrust went into his chest and pushed him back into the other two behind him. Then she released the spear to pull her sword and lunged. The blade slashed across the second rider's neck, and she reared back sideways to kick him in the chest before a single drop of blood hit the floor.

The third shadow rider fired a shot into the ceiling when the second one fell into him—and as he pushed the man's body out of the way, she charged in close and spun quickly to run the blade into his chest.

It was one of the most magnificent displays of fighting skills he'd ever seen, and the rider behind Whitmore tried again to pull his gun—but he wasn't quick enough. "I told you not to do that," Sinclair said after he fired a bullet into the man's chest.

As the last of the shadow riders hit the floor, Sinclair turned his attention back to Whitmore. "Sorry, old man, but this is just business. And now that you've had a taste of how deadly this whip is, I'm going to ease it back and let you up," he said with a pause. "But please don't do anything foolish. Do you understand?"

Whitmore slammed his palm against the wooden floor three times, and Sinclair assumed that meant yes. "Slowly now," he said as he twisted Widowmaker counterclockwise and released the whip from Whitmore's neck.

After he took a big gasp of air, Whitmore looked up and sneered at Sinclair. "You son of a bitch. How dare you—"

"Quiet!" Joanna snapped as she walked over from across the room. She had wiped the blood from her sword and sheathed it before she pulled the spear from the dead man's chest, and Sinclair stepped back so she could step forward and address their captive.

"You and Victor Carmichael could learn when to shut

your mouth and listen," she continued, and then put the tip of the spear under his chin to lift his head. "We could kill you now if we wanted to, but you're more helpful alive. And now we're going to walk you outside so you can put an end to all this."

Sinclair sensed that Whitmore did not want to concede defeat, and the man was fuming at being told what to do. But he slowly got to his feet and the three of them walked to the entrance of the saloon as the sounds of fighting and gunshots continued outside.

Joanna still had the spear tip at Whitmore's throat, but Sinclair stopped them just before they walked out the door. "Are you sure about going out there? Because stopping this fight might be easier said than done."

•••

Blood for Blood

As the dust settled and everything from his vantage point began to clear, Red Sky could see that the army of shadow riders had been cut down and divided. His position had gone unnoticed in all the confusion and poor visibility, and he was able to effectively attack from the high ground. Their plan had worked.

He could also see that Cade was pinned down by shadow riders firing at him from inside and at the front of the saloon. It was hard to tell how many shadow riders were inside, but the man leading the men in front of the saloon was the one Cade identified as the colonel—and the man who ordered the death of his family.

From what he could hear, the colonel commanded his men to "guard Mr. Whitmore," and to press the attack on Cade's position. Three of the riders were still on horseback, while seven more were not. But if they advanced on Cade, he would likely be overcome by their numbers.

There was no sign of Joanna, or the sheriff. He could see one of the Irish brothers lying in the street, but not the other behind the wagon. He figured he might be the only one able to help Cade, but he was out of arrows, the rifle was empty, and the shotgun seemed useless.

As he thought about his options, he figured this might be his best opportunity to attack the colonel. It was a move that could likely end in death, but he would gladly join his family in the spirit world for this chance to kill that man. And an attack on their military leader might distract the shadow riders enough for Cade to fight his way out.

Red Sky moved carefully to the front of the building to get a closer look. He saw the colonel order his men from the rear, which created some separation between them—so he dropped his bow and pulled his tomahawk as he took a running jump.

He sailed through the air before he landed on the colonel, who hadn't seen him coming. The element of surprise didn't allow the colonel to get off a shot, and as the two men rolled on the ground, Red Sky came out on top and used his tomahawk to cut the colonel's pistol out of his hand.

The colonel was on his knees but turned quickly to one

side and used his left leg to sweep Red Sky's feet out from under him. Surprised by the agility of the colonel as he landed on his back, he was still able to roll over and get up on one knee as he pulled his knife.

Armed with his tomahawk in his left hand and his knife in the right, he squared off in an attack stance as the colonel rose to his feet and pulled his calvary sword.

"I heard Viper was riding with a Comanche. Now you can die together," the colonel said and took a quick swing with his sword. But Red Sky leaned away from the attack and then stepped back, just out of range.

"You killed my wife, and my son… and for their blood, I've come for yours," Red Sky replied as the two slowly circled each other. Out of the corner of his eye, he could see that his fight with the colonel had created the distraction he hoped it might, as some of the shadow riders had turned their attention to them. But he remained focused on the colonel and how he moved. It reminded him of Cade's warrior dance, and he tried to remember some of the fighting techniques he had learned from his samurai friend.

"Stay out of this. He's mine," the colonel said aloud to his men before he lunged forward and slashed again with his sword.

The colonel's next attack was an aggressive lunge at Red Sky's head, but he leaned to his left and let the blade pass. The backhand slash that followed came so fast that he barely had time to duck. But the failed attack left the colonel open, and Red Sky charged in.

He came over the top at the colonel with his

tomahawk—and when the colonel blocked that with his left arm, Red Sky ran his knife into his opponent's exposed gut and held it fast before he withdrew and pushed the colonel back.

The push created some space between them, and the colonel countered with a slash across Red Sky's chest. The exchange left both men cut and bleeding, but the Comanche warrior was ready to face death and he knew his opponent had been weakened. It was time to finish him.

As he let out a guttural scream, Red Sky charged again. But this time, when the colonel went high with a slashing counterattack, he tucked into a roll that got him in much closer. With a backhand swing of his tomahawk, he smashed the blunt blade into the side of the colonel's left knee—and as his opponent fell forward, he thrust up with his knife and stuck the colonel under the chin.

Red Sky remained on one knee as the colonel reared back, blinked only once, and then collapsed on the ground with the blade still stuck in his throat. As blood stained the earth around the fallen leader of the shadow riders, he whispered to his ancestors that the enemy of their tribe was dead—and he hoped the spirits of his wife and son could be at peace.

Then searing pain on the right side of his face came at the same time he heard the gunshot, but he never saw who shot him before everything faded to black.

CHAPTER 17

The Dead Man's Charge

Cade watched Joanna slay three shadow riders through the shattered saloon window and save his hide in the process. But he was still pinned down by at least ten shadow riders gathered in front of the saloon. The riders had set up a defensive parameter, and now a couple of them approached to press the attack while the others provided cover fire on his position.

Then all the shooting on his position seemed to stop. As he peeked around the crates, he could see Red Sky and the colonel fighting in front of the saloon—and the shadow riders gathered around their leader were momentarily confused.

He knew this was his best chance to make it across the road while the riders had split their attention between him and their loyalty to the colonel. As he took one last look to plot his course, what he witnessed broke his heart.

Cade saw Red Sky kill the colonel, but then a shadow rider shot his friend in the face immediately after. As Red Sky collapsed to the ground, the rage inside him burned so hot that he didn't care that he was outnumbered—and with his Colt in his right hand and shotgun pistol in his left, he charged.

He stood up from behind the crates and took his first aimed shot at the shadow rider who killed his friend. While he was too far away to be accurate, the bullet caught the rider in the hip and Cade advanced with hammers on both pistols thumbed back.

The closest shadow rider in range was to Cade's left, and that would be unlucky for him. He didn't seem ready for a straight-forward fight, or he might have been more deliberate with the shot he wasted before Cade fired a barrel into his chest.

His vision was vivid and clear as the blast sent the man back and blood exploded from the rider's chest. The movement of everything around him seemed to slow again, just like it had in his duel with Toshi. Was this the fifth ring? Had he experienced so many battles that he'd become numb to the chaos and the fire of a fight? He had never pondered a curious string of thoughts in the middle of a battle, but he continued to advance and took aim at the second rider to his left—and a bullet grazed Cade's right shoulder armor as the second barrel he fired caught the rider just below the neck.

He was in the thick of this fight and so deep in thought he barely noticed another bullet hit the upper left of his chest armor. But the force of the bullet did make him pause for a moment, and that's when he saw Tobias emerge from Doc Miller's office.

The Ranger had a pistol in each hand, and he fired at the cluster of shadow riders from the other side of the street.

Between the two of them, Cade and Tobias had the remaining members of Whitmore's army in a pinch—and with the colonel dead, the shadow riders seemed to figure that out on their own.

Tobias shot two of the shadow riders, and one of them was on horseback. But that rider managed to stay in the saddle and got his horse pointed south as he gave a holler. The other two riders still on their horses were quick to follow him out of town, and Cade wasn't going to waste a shot on the three riding off in retreat.

He was focused on the man who shot Red Sky, and that shadow rider was still shooting at him and standing there with a wounded hip. The others didn't matter or were too busy exchanging bullets with Tobias, and Cade took the time to stop walking, aim carefully, and shoot that man through the heart.

"Stop! Don't shoot," one of the remaining shadow riders shouted out as the man next to him hit the ground—and he dropped his pistol and put his hands up. The other shadow rider did the same, and Cade eased back the hammer of his Colt and holstered his shotgun pistol.

He exchanged a glance with Tobias and tried to process everything that had happened. The shooting had stopped, and he felt confident they had the upper hand just as Whitmore was tossed out of the saloon and fell to the ground. Joanna and Sinclair followed him out and stood over him in victory.

"Is it over?" Sinclair asked, but Cade didn't reply. They had won the battle of Rocky Creek, but at what cost? He didn't feel like celebrating, and he didn't think Daniel and the other townsfolk who began to emerge did either.

The breeze was thick with the scent of gunpowder, and

for a moment he stood at the crossroads as the battlefield had become deathly quiet. But the silence didn't last as groans from the wounded came from every direction.

•••

Dust to Dust

Cade's mouth was bone dry, and he was desperate for a drink of water. He also winced from the pain in his ribs as he tried to take a deep breath and collect himself. The spoils of the fight belonged to him and the people of Rocky Creek, but there was something more important on his mind.

"Red Sky," he whispered to himself, and Cade ran over to where his Comanche friend lay on the ground. The aftermath of the fight had begun to sink in, and he was so concerned that he ran past Whitmore and the two shadow riders who surrendered as if they weren't there.

He dropped to one knee near his friend to look him over. After he brushed the bloodstained hair from Red Sky's face, he felt a soft pulse. "He's still alive. Someone get Doc Miller!" Cade said aloud to anyone able to get help.

"You're going to be okay," he whispered into his friend's ear—and Cade clutched Red Sky's hand and remained with him until Daniel and the doctor arrived with a few other townsfolk. Together, they were able to roll him onto a wood plank to move him.

"We're going to need a lot of space... and plenty of

whiskey. Let's get the wounded to the saloon and set up there," Doc Miller said, and Cade watched as the townspeople carried the board toward the saloon with Red Sky on it.

"Cade, come here," he heard Lucy say, and he turned in the direction of her voice. She was crouched down in the middle of the street, and he could see the despair on her face as he made his way over to where she was crying with Finn and Eli over Mick's body.

At first, Cade knelt down beside them and had to accept that their friend was dead. Then they all joined hands in a prayer to honor Michael Bohannon. The man had sacrificed his life for a place he'd never known, and there was nothing they could do to bring him back. As he reached out to take the surviving brother's hand, he noticed the blood on Finn's neck and shoulder.

"You've been shot," he said, and Finn barely acknowledged what Cade had said. Finn had the look of a lost soul as tears streaked his dust covered face. "C'mon, let's get you over to doc and get you looked at," he continued, and reached out to help his friend get to his feet.

Lucy and Eli got on each side of Finn to help him walk to the saloon. Cade remembered that she had experience working in medical tents during the war. "I think doc is going to need your help," he said, but then felt a little foolish for stating the obvious as she nodded back.

As the four of them made their way to the saloon, it was the first time Cade acknowledged Whitmore. His former Benefactor and two shadow riders were being guarded by Tobias, with Joanna and Sinclair covering the Ranger's back.

Defeat was a look Cade had never seen in Whitmore before, and today, he didn't resemble the same man he used to know.

"Eli, go to the store and get anything we can use for bandages," Lucy told her son as she helped Finn step up toward the entrance—and Eli peeled off to do what he was told. As Lucy and Finn disappeared inside the saloon, Cade walked over to stand with Tobias.

"What now?" Cade asked the Ranger.

"Sheriff Barnes is going to live. But these men are under arrest for shooting a man of the law," Tobias replied.

"Under whose authority?" Whitmore asked.

"My authority. These men work for you, yes?" Tobias asked as he gestured to the shadow riders standing with Whitmore. "One of them shot Sheriff Barnes, and the rest are guilty of threatening the innocent people of this town."

"You say 'one of them' but you don't know who… and I don't see how you can hold me accountable for that," Whitmore replied. "And what about Cade Wilson?"

"What about me?" Cade said sarcastically. "I was prepared to settle this honorably, the samurai way. Then your bounty hunter and shadow riders started shooting at your command."

"Says you," Whitmore replied. "I know people in high places, and who do you think they will believe when they hear my side of the story? A known thief and a killer, or a respected businessman from Texas to California."

"They'll believe me," Tobias said with a defiant tone. "There's been plenty of stories swirling around about the way you and your father do business. And I know a few judges in Texas that would be very interested to hear what I have to say."

"They'll believe me, too," Cobb chimed in, as he stood over his dead foreman. "This was a peaceful town, and you're not the man I thought you were."

Cade could see that Cobb's words frustrated Whitmore, who began to look like a cornered animal. But before he could anticipate what would happen next, Eli had come out of the General Store with an arm full of bed linens and tried to pass by the prisoners.

Whitmore grabbed Eli by the shirt collar and pulled the boy in front of him. Then he reached down into his boot and pulled a knife that he put against the young man's throat.

"I'm not going to jail, and I'm not staying in this god-forsaken town," Whitmore said as he held Eli hostage and turned to his two shadow riders. "Pick up your guns and get our horses. We're getting out of here."

...

Loyalty and Legacy

At first, the two shadow riders looked dumbfounded by their boss's actions and his command. Whitmore hated to repeat himself, but he said it a little louder to make his point. "I said go get the horses. Now move!"

Whitmore clutched the boy's collar and held him close as Cade and the Ranger stood their ground. The people of this miserable town were all looking at him, but they didn't do anything but watch as his men shuffled off to do as he ordered.

The sting of this defeat seemed so surreal, and the shame he might have felt about what he was doing would have to wait its turn. He was so angry and desperate to not be taken prisoner that he would take this boy hostage if he had to. After traveling for days and utilizing all of his resources to get here, he never imagined he'd arrive in this dusty little town less than an hour ago and lose it all.

"Don't try anything, and don't shoot," Whitmore said to the Ranger and the only man with a pistol aimed at him. "I'm wearing the same chest armor that's managed to save Cade's miserable life more than once. And you wouldn't want a stray bullet to hit this boy."

The Ranger didn't flinch and didn't lower his pistol as Whitmore bent down behind his hostage and turned his attention to Cade.

"You did this," Whitmore said, and he seethed at Cade between his teeth and a tight-lipped snarl. "I can't believe that everything I've built over the past ten years… you've managed to destroy in a day."

"No, you did this," Cade replied, and took a step forward. "This is the fight you wanted. It's why you trained me and built your private army. You don't know any other way besides taking what you want and justifying it as progress. But you can't control everything and everyone through intimidation and violence, and today is just another painful lesson you still haven't learned."

"What do you know, samurai? You're just a trained killer. An orphan that arrived at my doorstep with nothing," Whitmore said condescendingly. "And look at you now, standing against me with the scar of disloyalty on your face. But if you had remained loyal, none of this would have happened."

"Is this what you call loyalty?" Cade asked and gestured to Toshi's body, and all the dead and wounded shadow riders lying around them. "How many people have to die for your ambition?"

"Save your sermon," Whitmore snapped back defensively. "Because it doesn't matter, and today doesn't change a thing.

"This is far from over, and I still have very powerful friends that have a vested interest in my plans for this territory," he continued. "This land will be my legacy. And another ten years from now, nobody will even remember your name.

"But I'm through talking," Whitmore said, and felt increasingly anxious as he pressed his blade against the boy's neck and looked around for his men. "And I don't want you getting any ideas about following me either, because I'm taking this boy with me."

"No, you're not," Cade said as he took another step forward.

•••

The Dead Heart

Cade briefly closed his eyes to reset his senses. It was difficult to take in his surroundings as more townsfolk began to come out of hiding. But he tried to focus on Whitmore, and him alone.

He listened for his breathing and his movements. A

cornered man could be desperate and unpredictable, but it wasn't like Whitmore to do his own dirty work—and threatening to kill the boy was a mistake.

"Eli, no!" Lucy cried as she emerged from the saloon, and Cade put his hand up to stop her in her tracks. Whatever she might do next, he knew it wouldn't help the situation and he needed her to stay out of it.

"Don't come any closer, young lady, unless you'd like to come along," Whitmore said.

"No. You're going to let the boy go," Cade said calmly and took another step forward.

"There's a riddle on a piece of parchment, and it's folded up here in my pocket. Your man in black left it for me," he said and took another step forward. "What would I trade for a life? That was the question."

"Stay away from me," Whitmore said, and Cade could hear the fear in his voice.

"In my time away from the fort, I've learned there's nothing more valuable than life," Cade said calmly, and took another step that put him within reach of Eli's hand. "I'm free of you now, and you are free of me. So now, the life I'm willing to trade for is yours."

"What the hell are you talking about? Are you trying to negotiate?" Whitmore asked.

"Yes, I am. The boy is innocent," Cade replied. "I'm willing to trade a life for a life. Let him go, and I won't kill you."

Whitmore said nothing as the standoff was suddenly interrupted by the sound of horses. "Drop your guns," he said. "You too, Ranger. Toss them on the ground."

Cade was reluctant to give in to this demand, but he hoped Whitmore might agree to his terms if he cooperated—so he slowly unbuckled his gun belt and let it drop to the ground. And behind him, he heard Tobias do the same.

As the shadow riders rounded the corner on horseback, Whitmore looked increasingly confident in his position. "Here's your horse, boss," one of the riders said as he led one by the reins.

"I accept your terms," Whitmore said, and he released his grip on the boy.

Cade extended his left hand and Eli grasped it. As he slowly pulled the boy away, he turned to Tobias and gave a nod that everything was going to be okay—but Whitmore must have thought otherwise.

"Look out!" Joanna said, and Cade turned just as Whitmore lunged with his knife.

Cade was able to grasp Whitmore's hand, but the blade still pierced his gut just below his chest armor—and he held it there to keep the knife from going any deeper or turning inside him.

Whitmore used his left hand to grab Cade's right shoulder and tried to pull him in to thrust the knife deeper. But Cade put his left hand on Whitmore's right shoulder to fend him off—and the two men grappled as they stepped into the center of the road.

"What are you going to do, Viper?" Whitmore asked. "You're too close for the sword, and I'll gut you like a pig if you let go of my hand."

Cade tried to keep Whitmore off of him until Lucy and

Eli were safely out of the way. When he saw the two of them with Tobias out of the corner of his eye, he was about to push away with his left hand and try to spin out of this dance when Whitmore leaned in to whisper in his ear.

"I'll be coming back to this nothing little town and finish what I started. But you won't be here to defend it… because I've decided to trade your life for mine," Whitmore said and tried to push the knife deeper. "And I couldn't watch another sunrise knowing you're still alive."

"So be it," Cade replied and looked Whitmore in the eye as he flexed his left wrist to extend Scorpion's stinger.

Instead of spinning away, he stuck Whitmore in the neck with the poisoned spike that was invented at the fort. Both men were still locked in each other's arms, but only Cade was still able to move. And as he pulled back and removed the blade from his gut, he could see the look of paralyzed horror on Whitmore's face.

"You should have chosen life," he said as he dropped the knife. The stinger and its toxin had taken effect, as Whitmore was still standing but unable to speak.

Cade's right hand was cut and bleeding as he grasped the handle of his sword, but it was time to end his feud with Whitmore the samurai way. In one fluid motion, he pulled his sword and slashed the blade across Whitmore's neck. Then Cade stumbled back and dropped to his knees, and Whitmore's head hit the ground as his body collapsed beside it.

The shadow riders had already pulled their pistols, and now they pointed them at Cade in an attempt to avenge their boss. But while Cade was in no position to defend himself, what he didn't expect was the chorus of levered rifles and cocked pistols that followed. As he looked around, he was surprised to see that the people of Rocky Creek had come to his defense—and the riders could see they were completely surrounded and outgunned as they reared their horses to the east and rode off.

Eli was the first to rush to Cade, who was still on his knees and holding his bleeding gut. Then Joanna came over to help him up, and Cade could hear some of the conversations going on as Lucy guided them to the entrance of the saloon. "Let's get him inside," she said.

"Is he going to be okay?" Joanna asked.

He didn't hear Lucy answer as they laid him on the floor, and instead she responded for Joanna to help. "Please see if there are any other wounded men we can help, and let's line them up outside."

As Cade looked up at the ceiling and the dusty rafters of the saloon, it wasn't where he imagined he'd be or how he thought this day would end. But it was the first time he felt a sense of relief in a long time. His feud with Whitmore was finally over, and even though he was exhausted and bleeding—his spirit felt free.

"Doctor, we need a hot iron and some stitches over here," Lucy said aloud, and she was busy trying to remove his coat as her face came into view.

"Thank you," she said, and he felt her gently brush her hand across his cheek before she kissed him. "You can rest now."

CHAPTER 18

New Beginnings

"That was some good coffee," Cade said as he handed the empty cup to Daniel in exchange for some folded inventory notes. "But I should get back to the ranch, and I'll give Lucy this list."

"Take care, and thanks… for everything," Daniel replied with more than his usual storekeeper smile. This was Cade's first trip to the store on his own, and he was doing what he could to help out while on the mend. Fortunately, Daniel was a good man and his coffee made this errand that much better.

As he stepped out of the General Store, Cade took a deep breath and looked around. Summer would be here soon, and the clear blue sky overhead was a welcoming sign of longer days to come. The weather was so nice that he enjoyed not wearing his battle coat, or his weapons, and felt great to have the weight of them and the chest armor lifted off his shoulders.

Still, he groaned a little and held his stomach as he climbed onto the wagon and gave the reins a snap.

In the days following the battle of Rocky Creek, he was still healing from his wounds as the town was still recovering from what happened. He couldn't eat real food or anything that might upset his stomach for days, but now he could finally start to enjoy things like coffee again. And while the town may have looked the same, he and everyone else had to accept that the battle for Rocky Creek had changed everything.

Pa Johnson was able to return to the ranch and Lucy continued to care for him there. His hip was severely damaged by a bullet, and he would need to remain in bed until he felt strong enough to walk again. Until then, Cade did his best to help Lucy and Eli with the cooking—but he still had a lot to learn about working in the kitchen.

Red Sky's head was bandaged around his forehead and covered the right side of his face. Cade's friend remained in good spirits, but a bullet had taken his right eye, and the scar across his chest would be a lasting reminder of his fight with the colonel.

Sheriff Barnes was also doing his best to recover. He took a bullet in his right arm and left leg, which was the same leg he'd been struck by Falcon's arrow less than a year ago. Doc Miller was able to stop the bleeding and extract the bullets, but Barnes had lost some of the feeling below his knee to his toes—and he would need a crutch to walk the rest of his life.

Mick died of his wounds that fateful day, but Finn survived. The bandage around his neck was temporary, but his left arm would be in a sling for a month or so. But the strangest thing was that Cobb offered him a job as his new foreman after Hicks and Kershaw were shot and killed, and Finn agreed to help out as he healed up.

Cobb wasn't shot or wounded in the fight, but Cade thought that he had changed the most. The loss of Hicks and the burial of all the men that died that day left a different kind of scar, and he seemed very rattled and remorseful about what had happened.

Tobias suffered a flesh wound to his left shoulder but was otherwise fine and proved himself to be tough as hell in a fight. When Judge Roberts arrived in town in the aftermath, he asked Tobias to stay on and provide protection of the law until Sheriff Barnes could resume his duties. There was also a lot of cosmetic damage done to the town, and Tobias supervised the six shadow riders who survived their wounds as they worked on the repairs.

The judge ordered the work to begin as soon as the men were able, as part of their penance. With justice already served to the man they worked for, it was easier for the judge to be lenient, and he chose to believe that they were good men acting on orders from Mr. Whitmore.

Roberts was also lenient towards Cade and amended his previous ruling. Given that he protected innocent lives and saved the town for a second time seemed worthy of redemption.

Cade also made a large financial contribution by paying every merchant in gold for the materials needed for repair. He didn't even think twice about it, because it seemed fitting and appropriate—and there was still plenty left over to share with those he promised to reward.

Overall, it was a pleasant ride back to the ranch to be alone with his thoughts—but peaceful moments never last. As he turned the wagon down the familiar trail to the house, the thought of having to leave again made his stomach turn.

•••

Farewells

The breeze through the trees made a peaceful, calming sound, and Cade appreciated the cool morning shade as he came out to pay his respects.

He was also grateful that the Johnson family agreed to lay Toshi and Mick to rest out here on the edge of their property. It was a perfect spot on the opposite side of the big tree where Pa's wife and Lucy's husband were buried. The day of the funerals was a sad one, but today he was here to say goodbye.

"I'll be leaving for the fort today. It's time for me to return to the place where it all started, and where we met," he said to Toshi's grave marker. "I am forever grateful for everything you taught me. The Way of the Samurai was your blade, and I was just a block of wood. You pushed me to be better, to be stronger, and how to fight. You carved me into the man I am today.

"Now I choose life. From now on, everything you taught me will only be used to protect the innocent and those I love from anyone that would try and do them harm," he continued. "I have your swords, and I will find an honorable place to display them. You were, and always will be, my teacher… and a friend."

As he stepped to the side, he also paused at Mick's grave. "God bless you too, Mick. Your generous spirit and sense of humor are so dearly missed. And for what you sacrificed to help me and the people of Rocky Creek, our memory of you will live on."

Cade closed his eyes and listened to the world around him. He wanted to experience what Red Sky had said about warriors who never die, and how their spirit surrounds you and whisper to you in times of need. Suddenly the bird songs were in harmony and a gentle breeze seemed to say that the two warrior spirits were with him.

"Are you coming back to the house?" Eli asked from across the field. "Everyone is waiting for you."

"Yes, of course," Cade replied with a smile, and followed Eli through the late spring wildflowers.

In front of the Johnson house, everyone had come outside to wait for him. The small gathering of people who just finished breakfast included Red Sky, Joanna, Finn, and Sinclair—and everyone was about to go their separate ways.

"It's time," Joanna said. "A deal is a deal, and Sinclair is going to take me back to Victor Carmichael. But I think Victor will be in for a big surprise when we meet again, thanks to you."

As she came in for a hug, Cade could feel the chest armor she wore underneath her crimson coat. "Yes, he'll be surprised all right. How does the armor fit?"

Joanna smiled as she pulled back and used her hands to adjust the armor under her coat. "It's heavy, and it's going to take some getting used to. But if it works for me like it did for you, I will gladly wear it."

Cade nodded and smiled back. "It's definitely one of a kind. One of two that I know of, and I have the other. Yours was fashioned for Falcon, who is a bit more your size."

"Thank you," she said, and then leaned in to kiss Cade on the cheek. "I'll never forget you, or what you did for me."

Then she turned and wiped away the tears from her eyes. After Cade watched her turn and climb on her horse, he motioned for Eli to bring three of the small leather coin bags he had put in a wooden box on the porch. As the young man handed them over, he extended one to Joanna.

"No, you've given me plenty already," she said and patted her saddlebags, but Cade pushed it into her hand.

"Take it and use the money as needed to settle your business. The rest is for when you get to California," he replied.

Then Cade tossed the second sack of gold to Sinclair, who sat on his horse behind Joanna. "What's this for?" he asked.

"That's for the favor we talked about the other night. Before you take her to Victor, help her find Remy Chandler," Cade replied, and the bounty hunter gave a nod.

"Are you sure you can trust him?" Cade asked Joanna, and her smile gave him the confident answer he was looking for.

"Yeah. I think he's sweet on me," she replied with a chuckle. "Which is kind of funny, because I hated him when we first met. But now I'm growing a little fond of him, too."

"We should get moving if we want to make it through the pass today," Sinclair said, and Cade knew he was right.

"You'll know where to find me. Now take care of yourself,"

Cade said and gave Joanna's horse a little pat to send them on their way.

"Goodbye everyone," she said, and Joanna waved as the two riders started down the trail to the road.

"And this is for you," he said as he tossed the third bag of coins to Finn. "It won't bring your brother back, but I think you've found work and a new family here. Rocky Creek is a great place to get a new start."

"Indeed," Finn replied with a smile. "My new boss still has some big plans for this town, but I'll keep him in line. We're going to be doing things a bit differently around here, starting with some improvements to the bunkhouse and a new wood stove."

"Good to hear. Please look after them until I get back," Cade said with a gesture to the Johnson family, and Finn tipped his cap in return.

"We're next, my friend," Cade said to Red Sky. His bandages had been removed—but the black leather patch over his right eye would always be there. "We still need to stop by the sheriff's office to see Tobias and pick up the shadow riders who are riding back with us."

As he walked over to the porch where Pa sat in his chair and Lucy and Eli waited for him, Cade knew he needed to make this farewell as quick as possible. It was already too painful to be leaving again, even though he had to see his sister Sarah again.

"I'll be back… I promise. This time, for good," he said. "I plan to bring my sister back with me. I think she'd like it here."

"Of course. We're all family now," Pa replied. "That includes you, too, Red Sky."

After the family thanked Red Sky and said their farewells, Eli was the first to come over and hug Cade. It reminded him of the first time he left, but that goodbye was filled with such uncertainty. This time felt different, and they both hoped it was not forever.

Then Lucy approached him with a smile and a look in her eye that almost made him laugh. "Don't you be late getting back," she said with an affectionate sarcasm in her voice and stepped in close. As he took her in his arms, the thought of being with her again would be the only thing on his mind. And when he kissed the fullness of her lips, he felt complete as a man.

"If I'm not going to be late, we'd better get going," he said as he pulled back, and the soft touch of her hand was the last thing he felt before he let her go.

"Our first stop is the jail," he said to Red Sky and climbed on his horse. "Tobias is probably wondering where we're at."

● ● ●

Return to the Fort

Cade didn't like riding with six shadow riders in tow, so there was more than one sense of urgency to get back to the fort. He didn't want this trip to last any longer than it needed to, and even though the riders seemed to accept their Benefactor was dead, he still didn't trust them.

The riders had their hands bound the first day on the trail, and again on the second. But by the morning of the third day, and because they didn't have any weapons, Cade decided to cut them loose as a gesture of goodwill he hoped wouldn't backfire. He also wanted some help with breakfast and caring for the horses—and it was a little exhausting for him and Red Sky to switch up watching them.

Their approach to the fort with the shadow riders unbound would also be a display of kindness to whomever might greet them at the gates. The riders wouldn't be presented as captives or prisoners, and instead, Cade hoped he would not be seen as the enemy when he brought them home in exchange for his sister.

By mid-afternoon, the fort was almost in sight and Cade lifted his hand to bring everyone to a stop. They had long passed the wash where he and Red Sky first met, and now arrived where his Comanche friend needed to let him go alone.

"This is where we part ways," Red Sky said, and Cade had sadly anticipated this moment all day. "I don't like leaving you alone, but this is as close as I'd like to get to the great house."

"I understand," Cade replied. "And I don't know how they will react when I get there, so it's probably best you get back to your tribe.

"The spear is yours, and I hope some of that gold can help you somehow," he continued, feeling good about splitting a large share of it all with Red Sky and Joanna. "There will be some news to share with your people when you return, and I hope your soul has found a little peace."

"*Haitse*," Red Sky said, and held up his palm with the familiar scar.

"*Haitse*," Cade replied, and held up his palm in return before his friend turned his horse and rode off.

"Gentlemen, let's get you back to the fort," he said, and the riders resumed their dusty march across the plain.

In less than an hour, Cade and the six shadow riders slowed their horses at the front gate of the fort. It seemed odd that there was nobody guarding it, and even stranger there was nobody to be seen anywhere. The place was eerily quiet as they advanced slowly up the trail to the front of the Whitmore house.

"Where is everyone?" one of the shadow riders asked, but Cade had no answer. He hadn't been here in so long that it all seemed different to him. But what he could remember was that there were always people around and coming out to greet them whenever a small party returned from a mission.

Then a single gunshot broke the silence, and a voice called out from an upstairs window. "Don't move!"

Cade sensed the gunshot was just to get their attention, which worked quite well. There were at least two men upstairs with a rifle on them, but there was no telling how many guns in total. Then a teenage boy emerged from the front door with a Winchester pointed in the general direction of the riders. "Don't worry Abel, I've got you covered," the voice called out again from the upstairs window.

"Drop your guns, mister," the teen said, now focused entirely on Cade.

Cade could appreciate that this young man was protecting the house, but he wasn't about to drop his guns. "Look, Abel… is that your name?" he asked, and the teen nodded.

"I don't mean you any harm," he said, and spoke calmly as he slowly raised his hands. "I'm just here to return these men to the fort and find my sister, Sarah Wilson. Is she here?"

"We recognize you, Viper. Or Cade Wilson. Whatever your name is," the voice said. "And we heard about what happened in Rocky Creek."

"Our Benefactor is dead, and he killed him," one of the shadow riders said while pointing at Cade. "Shoot him—"

"Let's not do anything foolish," Cade said, and gave the shadow rider a side eye glance. "If you do know who I am, then understand that I'll shoot this man myself if he says anything that ignorant again.

"But with all due respect, I didn't ride three days with this man to shoot him in front of you. That's not why I'm here," he continued. "Yes, what he said is true. Mr. Whitmore is dead, and so is the colonel. They attacked a town of innocent people, and it cost them their lives."

Cade could sense that the news wasn't entirely unexpected, as the teen didn't seem to flinch and the guns in the windows remained. He began to worry that the more this conversation dragged out, the greater the opportunity for things to go sideways and get dangerous.

"Abel, I need you to lower your gun. I'm only here for my sister. That's all, and we can be on our way," he said and hoped to appeal to the young man's inexperience. Cade could tell he was trying to be strong and act the part with a rifle in his hand. Still, this wasn't a fight Cade was looking for, and the last thing he wanted to do was shoot the young man.

"So how about you tell me who's in charge around here?" he asked.

"I am," said the man who emerged from the front door of the house with a pistol in his hand. As the man stood next to Abel, Cade tried to recognize him but did not. He was average height and build, with reddish hair and a beard. A pair of circular spectacles and his buttoned-up shirt gave him the appearance of an intelligent man.

"Even if we can trust you, Cade Wilson… how about these men you brought back with you?" the man asked.

Cade wasn't anticipating this question at all. If anyone's intentions were in question, he thought it would be his own. But he could tell by the man's mannerisms that he was being sincere.

"I can't speak for these men, but I assumed they wanted to return to the place they call home. Most people do," Cade replied.

"I'd expect. Just like the shadow riders who returned from Rocky Creek two weeks ago. They told stories to the others left here to guard the place, and they talked about being ambushed and that everyone was dead. Then, after a few more days without any news, we all assumed the worst. A few of them decided to stay and make a home here, but the rest decided to move on and looted everything they could take," the man said.

Cade shook his head as he looked around. "Are you all that's left?"

"Yes," the man replied. "A few of the riders and the women and children in the orphanage. Your sister is one of them.

"Abel, please ring the bell," the man said, and the young man did as he was asked. The bell outside the front door was rung every time Mr. Whitmore wanted to draw an assembly in front of the house—and this time was no exception.

The ringing of the bell triggered an outpouring of children and a few women from the building that served as the school and orphanage. As everyone came out, it added new life to the place that had otherwise appeared abandoned. Then there was the sight of a beautiful young woman he could barely recognize as his sister, and she passed through the children to make her way to the house.

It wasn't hard for Cade to imagine that what this man said was true. If the fort was absent of the mystique and authoritarian leadership their Benefactor represented, and the military leadership of the colonel, then the desperation of every man for himself could easily prevail and upset the stability of this work farm colony.

Cade dismounted his horse, and no longer paid any mind to Abel, the man on the porch, or the voice in the upstairs window. As Sarah approached, he just wanted to hug his sister again—and she offered a thin smile with teary eyes as she picked up speed and ran to him.

Catching her as she fell into his arms, he could only remember her as his little sister and the promise he made to their mother to protect her. But now she was a grown woman, and her natural beauty showed through.

"I can't believe you're alive," Sarah said. "There have been so many stories about you."

"I know. But there's another side to those stories, and I would love to tell them to you someday," he said as he set her down. "And that's why I came back for you. It's time for us to leave this place."

Sarah pulled back at those words, and Cade was surprised by the look on her face. He thought she'd be glad to see him, and happy to leave, given the story he'd just heard about the fort being ransacked by the surviving shadow riders. "What's the matter?" he asked.

"Is Colby with you? Is he alive?" she asked and looked over his shoulder at the small company of shadow riders with him.

"I don't think so," he replied, and glanced back at the six shadow riders he'd arrive with. But the six riders still on their horses all shook their heads.

The look in her eyes turned to anguish. He knew his sister well enough to know when she was troubled, and he sensed that the news he was about to deliver might be bad.

"These are all the men that survived the attack on Rocky Creek. I didn't know their names, and I don't know a man by that name," he said, and her eyes began to well up with tears.

"Who is Colby?" he asked, and Sarah tried to compose herself. But then she clenched up her fists and came at him sobbing as she beat on his chest. "Colby was my fiancé," she said as Cade tried to catch her wrists and stop her from hitting him.

"You killed him," she said, and the agony in her voice was palatable. But then she pulled back, and Cade tried to understand her through her sobs.

"We were supposed to be married in April, and we were going to move away from the fort," she explained. "But Whitmore ordered them all on one last mission. Colby said he would be back and that we would be moving west to start a family."

"I'm so sorry," Cade replied. "I didn't know—"

"Of course you didn't know. You were always gone. And when you left me here alone, I met Colby. He wasn't like the others, and he never looked at me the way most of the others did."

Cade was surprised to hear this news, and he felt guilty even though he was completely unaware. Everything she said was true, and he had no idea she was in love. He cursed himself as his past continued to haunt him in ways he never expected.

The last thing he wanted to do was break his sister's heart. Yet here they were, and he couldn't do anything to take it back. But he didn't want to discuss sensitive family matters in front of strangers either.

"Can we please go inside and talk about this?" he asked Sarah and then turned to the man standing on the porch. "I would like to speak with my sister in private, if that's okay?"

The man nodded and stepped to the side before he addressed the shadow riders. "Abel will escort you to the barracks house to retrieve your things. But you should know that anything else of value has likely been looted. And you're welcome to stay on if you like, because we could use the help.

But if you give us any trouble at all, we won't hesitate to show you out."

As Abel stepped down from the porch and motioned for the shadow riders to follow him, Cade walked alongside Sarah up the front stairs. As they entered the Whitmore house, they were followed by the man in charge. "I'll make us some tea," he said while holstering his pistol, and Cade was already starting to like him.

"This is Jeffry Osmond," Sarah said to make introductions in the parlor. "He has become our caretaker since the shadow riders cleared out. The ones that were already married took off with their wives and whatever else they felt was owed to them. Others just left because there was nobody to tell them not to, and they didn't want to help with the farm work."

"I'll get that tea," Jeffry said. "Why don't you two have a seat at the table."

Cade and Sarah took a chair opposite of each other, and her eyes welled up with tears again. The news was a shock to both of them, and he couldn't help but see the sad girl that was once his kid sister. But now she was a woman grieving the loss of the man she loved—and Cade tried to console her as best he could.

"I pleaded with our Benefactor not to press the fight, but he did anyway. That was his way, and it's why he had Toshi train the three of us to begin with. But I wanted the killing to stop, which is why I left. Because, unlike you, Whitmore never spoke of allowing me to marry and move away. All I wanted was to negotiate my freedom… our freedom. I felt it was time to move on from this place," he said, and hoped she would forgive him.

"This place?" she quipped. "You brought us here. We've lived here since we were children. This place has been our home. Why did you think I needed to be free of this place?

"I've been happy here since leaving Missouri, and Whitmore treated us fair," she said with a pause. "I wasn't one of his chosen women, or the women that visited the barracks after dark. The only bad thing that happened to me here was that you were always gone.

"But I was proud that you were chosen for the samurai training. There were rumors that you killed another boy, but I never believed them," she said, and Cade felt another wave of guilt wash over him. "You were treated as one of the best of us, and I figure that came at a price. A price so high that every man at the fort wanted to be the one to kill you."

"I promised Mom I would protect you, and I feared they might hurt you because of me," Cade said, and tried again to explain himself and change the subject. But from the look on her face, she still seemed unappreciative and troubled.

"When you didn't come back last summer, I was upset because I thought you had abandoned me here. When I heard you were dead, I cried for a day," she explained. "But I was always sweet on Colby, and he became my future. We were going to start a life together.

"That's over now," she said, and wiped the tears from her cheeks.

"Here you go," Jeffry said, and placed a wooden plank with the tea set on the table. If his interruption wasn't planned, it certainly seemed that way. "Please forgive the informality. I guess there's no value in taking a tea pot, but the silver serving tray is gone."

"Thanks, Jeffry. Can you please join us?" Sarah asked.

"Of course," Jeffry replied, and sat down in the end chair. Cade sensed that his presence was calming to Sarah, so he didn't fight it.

The tea was pleasant, and it reminded Cade of Moira's cabin. But he didn't know what to do next, fearing that whatever he might say would upset his sister again. So, he waited patiently for her to offer up what was on her mind.

"I'm going to stay here," she said bluntly. "Colby is dead, and I will need to accept that. But this is where I belong," she continued and paused to take a sip of tea. "I can't leave these children behind. And with the farm and all the growing mouths to feed, we need all the help we can get around here."

Cade was now the person in shock. He understood everything his sister just said, and he had thought about every scenario he thought he'd encounter on the way here—but he never imagined leaving the fort without Sarah.

"Are you sure that's what you want?" Cade asked.

"Yes. I'm staying here with the children," she replied. "We'll tell them the news, but it's not going to sit well with everyone to learn the man that killed Mr. Whitmore is sitting here having tea.

"And because of that, I think you better leave," she continued. "You're my brother, and I love you. But my heart is breaking just looking at you."

That was some hard news for Cade to hear, but he knew that it was probably best for him to accept his sister's wishes. He didn't want to deal with everyone at the fort turning on him, or her for what he'd done. And he felt that he'd fulfilled his promise to his mother to look after Sarah, but she was a grown woman now and doing a good thing to stay behind for the sake of the children.

"I understand, and I love you, too," Cade said and reached over the table to take his sister's hand. "What you're doing here makes sense. And this place could be a good home again," he added as he glanced around the room.

"I'll trust you to look after her," he said to Jeffry, and felt confident he would. "Some of those men who came back with me are handy with tools and might also be willing to stay. But I'll let you decide that."

Then he looked back at his sister and gripped her hand tight. He realized there was nothing left to say, and that all of his stories would either paint him in a bad light or bring up painful reminders of Mr. Whitmore's death. He also wouldn't have Red Sky to watch his back if he slept here tonight.

"Goodbye Sarah, for now," he said with a smile.

"Thanks for the tea," Cade added with a nod to Jeffry. "Hopefully, I might be able to visit if I come this way again. And I'd also like to fill up my canteens and stop by the dojo on my way out, if you don't mind," he continued and stood up to leave.

"Of course," Sarah said, and managed to smile a little.

Then she stood and came around to give him a hug and a kiss on the cheek. "In time, I would love to see you again."

Cade smiled and turned to leave after he stepped back and shook hands with Jeffry. "I'm still honor bound to protect my sister. If you ever need me, you can find me in Rocky Creek."

CHAPTER 19

Home

The trail back to Rocky Creek was all too familiar, and Cade wasn't about to waste any time as he followed the well-trodden path. When a couple of wagons and dozens of horses travel in an organized line to follow, it made navigation that much easier.

Traveling with a pack horse was the only thing that slowed him a bit, but after the quick turnaround at the fort, he was happy to have the water and some supplies. He was also glad that he didn't stay the night in the dojo, as it was filled with too many painful memories. But he was able to gather a few things that Toshi had left behind, and one of those items was the samurai helmet he wore when he arrived at the fort—and something that would preserve Toshi's memory at his final resting place.

Still, there was something different about this journey. As he chased the sun west, he had already spent two nights riding and made it pretty far by his calculations. This morning, he woke from a peaceful vision of the ranch and decided to skip breakfast. If he pressed hard on this third day, he figured he could be home before suppertime.

Home. That word seemed to have new meaning now, and it carried a sense of love and belonging that was much deeper than anything else he'd ever known. He wished his sister had come with him, but it felt good to know they could both find a new purpose in this world.

By late afternoon, he and his horses were tired, so he slowed for only the third time today and offered them up the last of their water and grain rations. "We're almost there," he said, stroking the sweat off the neck of his black horse. The one partner that had been with him through the years and for many miles. "Are you ready to go?" he asked softly into his horse's ear, and the snort and nod of his head said it all.

They pressed on for a couple hours and until he guessed they were almost there. As he slowed the horses, he took a moment to appreciate the welcome home return from a successful mission.

The ride through these late spring fields at sunset was one of the most beautiful things he'd ever seen. As the warm day began to give way to the cool glow of sunset, golden rays of light illuminated a million little flies while they danced on the shadows of grass and wildflowers. Birds were singing to each other, as if calling each other back for the evening. And the soft silence of the breeze invited him forward with a nostalgic scent of his surroundings that was like food for his soul.

As soon as he passed under the sign at the gate, he could hear Rolly barking in the distance. It was good to know he was a faithful guard dog. But the announcement got the attention of everyone, including the two welcome faces sitting on the front porch.

"There's a sight for sore eyes," Finn said as Cade reared up on his horse. "I'm better than you in the kitchen, but tired of cooking with one arm."

"Welcome home, son," Pa said, and the words seemed to melt away every mile to the fort and back.

Cade dismounted and pulled off his hat to wipe his brow. He was just about to ask for some water as Lucy and Eli bounded out of the house and down the stairs to tackle him. The hugs and laughter generated by the three of them could have gone on forever as far as he was concerned.

As Eli stepped back and Lucy moved in, she took his face in her hands—and the soft glow of the fading sunlight was in her eyes.

"You're late," she said, and her smile welcomed a kiss. The softness of her lips and the smell of her were something he wanted to experience today, and every day after that.

"For supper, that is, because we weren't expecting you tonight," she said with a chuckle and took him by the hand. "But I'm sure we can make up a plate. It's good to have you home."

Home. There was that word again, and he could feel everything that it meant surrounding him. It wasn't just a place. It was all the love and freedom to be here that came with it.

"But what happened? Where's your sister?" Eli asked, while they climbed the stairs and Finn offered to go tie up the horses.

"It's another long story," he said with a laugh and rubbed his hand through the boy's hair.

Lucy beckoned him inside with a loving look. "We've got plenty of time. Why don't you come inside and tell us all about it," she said, and Cade obliged.

...

The Dragon

Cheyenne hadn't changed much since the last time Joanna was here. A little busier perhaps, but it was still a town where good souls could find bad people—and bad trouble.

The trails and trains to get here were a long but pleasant experience, and Sinclair turned out to be a charming and resourceful companion. She may have grown up traveling across the country with the railroad, but he traveled the country on the railroad and knew how to get taken care of. It was definitely the first time she'd traveled in a parlor car, and she managed to hide her sword and wear a black cape over her crimson battle coat to travel as inconspicuously as possible.

The sweet smell of afternoon rain and the cool breeze behind it didn't feel like May weather, and she was glad to have the cape to keep her warm. But as they arrived at their destination, the two riders reared their horses in front of the Big Rock Saloon.

As Joanna dismounted, her new boots squished in the soft, wet earth. Above her, the summer thunderstorm clouds swirled above like it could rain again at any minute. "Are you sure this is the place?" she asked and questioned the look of the weathered sign.

"Yes, this is the place," Sinclair replied. "From what I've heard, the description of the man you're looking for runs a card game out of this saloon. The house probably doesn't mind if he gives them a cut, but the word is he's been hustling miners and hard-working men out of their money for some time.

"But remember," he continued. "Once we're done with this, we still need to go back to Denver and deal with Victor Carmichael. And I have to believe he's heard about what happened in Rocky Creek."

"Don't you worry… Victor is next on my list. Now let's see who's inside," she said and pulled the black cape over her shoulders as she stepped behind Sinclair. To give the appearance that she worked for him, they found it best during their travels to let him lead the way.

The muggy damp smell of cigar smoke and alcohol was very familiar, but the patrons of this northern frontier were not. A piano player was playing a lively tune, and the place was full of laughter and people having a good time. There were small groups of burly men at the bar or sitting around a table, and the women were paying attention to the men who paid for it. But as they made their way to the bar, the one man who caught her attention was dealing cards at the corner window table.

"There he is, on your left," she said quietly and tapped Sinclair on the shoulder. "That's Remy Chandler all right."

As the dealer tossed cards to the four other players, all

she could see was the man that shot her father and got away with it. His dark hair and mustache looked the same as it did when he walked out of the courtroom a free man. Now she couldn't believe he was just twenty feet away, laughing and smoking a cigar.

She also recognized the man sitting across from Remy as one of his friends from the trial. They knew each other then, and they were still playing poker together now. *Maybe that's how they cheat people like my father?*

She was so busy watching the card table that she bumped into Sinclair's back when he stopped. "We're at the bar, I'm afraid," he said over his shoulder.

"Afraid of what?" she whispered.

"Afraid they won't have any decent whiskey," he replied.

"Well, could you please watch my back while you get a drink?" she asked. "I need to say hello to an old acquaintance."

As she made her way across the room, she tried to study Remy's movements and mannerisms—and she imagined her father sitting at the card table with him. She wondered what had really happened that night, because only one side of the story was told. It was easier to believe that her father caught Remy cheating, and was falsely accused and shot instead.

Joanna stopped a few feet from the card table and nobody playing seemed to notice. She quietly watched the players finish their hand, and Remy showed his winning hand before he raked the pot. "Three jacks. Read 'em and weep," he said as the other players grumbled.

"You're one lucky man, Mr. Chandler," she said to Remy as he passed the cards to the man next to him.

"Thanks, little lady, but I don't believe I know you," he said with a slick grin—and she could feel him look her over while he stroked his mustache. "I'm not looking for any company at the moment, but why don't you go freshen yourself up and come back in a couple hours."

As Remy's friend across from him laughed at the off-handed remark, Joanna just stood her ground and removed her hat. Her hair was pulled back in a ponytail, and she paused to give the man she'd tracked all the way back to Cheyenne a better look.

"You really don't remember me, do you?" she asked.

"Why should I?" Remy replied with a chuckle. "You're quite pretty, I'll give you that. But like I said, go clean yourself up and maybe we can get reacquainted a little later."

The players at the table were getting ready to start their next hand, but Joanna had no intention of leaving. Instead, she untied her black cape and let it fall off her shoulders to reveal the crimson battle coat and black riding skirt she had bought along with her new boots. She was also well armed with the pistol holstered on her right hip and Spencer's knife on her left—and the Katana sword strapped to her back.

"You murdered my father after cheating him at cards a couple years ago, so maybe it's no surprise that you don't remember me from the courtroom where you lied about shooting him," she said plainly to get his attention, and then dropped her hat on top of her cape on the floor. "And I suspect that three of these fellas playing with you don't know that you're probably cheating them right now."

She could tell that Remy took offense to the accusation

and was no longer smiling. But at least two of the other play-ers looked at him suspiciously while Joanna continued to provoke a fight.

"Do the other men know that the man sitting across from you is a friend of yours?" she asked. "Because I recognize him, too. Maybe that's how you take advantage of people?"

"Look, whoever you are, you best be on your way. I don't take kindly to being accused of murder, lying, or cheating," he said with a stern look on his face. "That you're a lady is the only reason I don't shoot you right now."

Joanna just laughed and pressed on. "Remy Chandler… you are a cheat, a liar, and a murderer. If my being a woman is too much for you in front of your friends, maybe we could step outside?"

Remy looked at his friend while he leaned back slowly and slipped his hand under the table. And from the corner of her eye, Joanna could see his friend drop his hand to his holstered pistol.

"Or are you a coward, too?" she asked and the three other players pushed away from the table and cleared out of the way. She didn't care, because it was about to get messy—and Remy's flush cheeks and furrowed brow showed his embarrassment and humiliation.

"You want to play games with me young lady, so be it," Remy said and pushed back his chair. But as he stood from the table and pulled his pistol, it wasn't fast enough.

Over the past couple of weeks, Joanna had rehearsed this moment time and again in her head. The moment she would avenge her father's death would not be denied, as she reached over her left shoulder to grasp her sword with her right hand. And with the speed of a surprise strike that Cade had taught her, she pulled the sword from its scabbard and slashed the blade across Remy's throat in one swift motion.

The man across from Remy also tried to stand and pull his pistol, but Joanna was quick to shift her feet and slash the blade down across his wrist. The man screamed in pain as his hand fell to the floor, and the gun it was still holding went off and fired a bullet into the wall.

"I wanted you to know it was me, you son of a bitch," Joanna said as Remy's eyes grew wide and the color ran out of his face. He tried to point his pistol at her as blood poured out of his neck, but he just collapsed on the table and tipped it over as all the cards and money fell to the floor.

Joanna didn't see the man behind her until the crack of the whip made her spin around to see him and a gun fall to the floor. It looked like Sinclair had disarmed him and had his ivory handled Colt pointed in the man's face. "If you don't mind, I believe this is a private fight," he said. The fella had grown a beard, but he looked like Remy's other friend.

She nodded and gave Sinclair a little wink before she turned back to the man holding the bloody stump where his hand once was. He continued to howl as Joanna wiped the blood from her sword on his shirt. "You might want to get that looked at," she said sarcastically. "And choose your friends a little better next time."

"Who are you?" the man asked in a trembling voice, but she did not answer.

Joanna slid Scorpion's sword back in its scabbard before

she bent down to pick up her hat and cape. Then she motioned to Sinclair that it was time to leave, and they both walked toward the door before she paused to address everyone in the saloon.

"I am a warrior of the forgotten way, and the enemy of men who would prey on the innocent," she said aloud.

"I am the dragon."

References

- Musashi, Miyamoto. *The Book of Five Rings*. Bottom of the Hill Publishing, 2010.

- Tsunetomo, Yamamoto. *Hagakure: The Book of the Samurai*. Kodansha International, 1979.

Acknowledgments

A very special thank you to everyone who has supported this adventure and helped me share this story: Sherrie and Max Wagner, Janis Bosley, Judy Moore, Deborah Harmon, Chuck Garcia, Adele Crane, Bruce Kral, Casey and Rebecca Porter, Jayson and Tedd Gibson, Jim McCall, Chris Mohn, Andrew Hodges at *The Narrative Craft*, the team at *Paper Raven Books*, and all of my friends, fans, and readers.

The Author

Nate Wagner is an independent author with an overactive imagination and an affinity for westerns, science fiction, thrillers, and horror. And with future novels in the works, his dream is to publish novels in each of these genres.

Before he began writing fiction, Nate spent most of his career in marketing and advertising; writing and pitching creative content and campaigns. Nate is also a Navy veteran that has traveled the world and called many places home—but now he resides in Arizona with his wife and son.

Nate is the founder of Creative Refinery LLC and is passionate about developing ideas and characters for future stories. As a mentor, he enjoys helping other first time authors share their stories from conception to manuscript, to becoming self-published authors.

Follow Nate Wagner,
and learn more about the series:

thesamuraicowboys.com